TO AID AND PROTECT

R. Kyle Hannah

Jumpmaster Press™
Birmingham, Alabama

Cover Illustration by Denys Bryukhovetskiy Image ID: 39174031

Library Cataloging Data

Names: Hannah, Kyle, R. (Richard Kyle Hannah) 1967-
Title: To Aid and Protect / R. Kyle Hannah
5.25 in. × 8 in. (13.34 cm × 20.33 cm)
Description: Jumpmaster Press digital eBook edition | Jumpmaster Press Trade paperback edition | Alabama: Jumpmaster Press, 2020. P.O Box 1774 Alabaster, AL 35007 info@jumpmasterpress.com
Summary: When their planet faces destruction, the simian-like Cenceti flee in thousands of ships piloted by a master computer. designed to watch over and guide them. When a new homeworld is discovered the now sentient computer realizes it cannot let them leave.
Identifiers: ISBN-13: 978-1-949184-39-6 (ebk.) | 978-1-949184-38-9 (paperback)
1. Science Fiction 2. Action 3. Space Opera 4. Aliens 5. Master Computer 6. Military Sci-Fi 7. War

Printed in the United States of America

For more information on R.Kyle Hannah
www.rkylehannah.com

TO AID AND PROTECT

R. Kyle Hannah

Also Available from R. Kyle Hannah:

Harvest Day

The Time Assassins Series
Time Assassins
Assassin's Gambit
Assassin's End

The Tri-System Authority Series
The Jake Cutter Conspiracy
The Reign of Terra
Tales from the Busty Ostrich

This book is dedicated to the men and women of our armed forces. Without their sacrifice, I would not have the freedom to write something like this.

May God bless and protect you and your families.

PROLOGUE

Lorn L'tas Blex slowly picked himself from the floor of the bridge as sparks arched from dying consoles. He pulled his knees under him, steadied himself on shaking arms, and watched the control stations flicker sporadically. The Captain stood with a force of will, testing his wobbly legs. He reached up and felt the blood on his furry forehead.

"Report!"

He saw the devastation on the bridge of the *Cenceti Explorer IV* and his imagination played on his fears. He pictured the rest of the ship in a similar shape as what lay before him. A dozen of the bi-pedal Cenceti lay scattered around the bridge, several crushed under fallen superstructure supports. Only a handful of the crew remained on their feet, every one of them injured in some manner. He knelt to check on the nearest crewman as a female lieutenant replied to his order.

"Sir," she called, her brown fur stained with blue tinted blood that trailed down her neck and left abdomen. "Shields and sensors are down. Internal communications are out. Propulsion...we have maneuvering thrusters only."

"Is there any good news?" the Captain mumbled.

The lieutenant answered almost immediately and Lorn cursed. His ears rang so loud that his whisper came out as his normal voice.

"We appear to be out of the energy lashes," she said. Her long, nimble fingers flew of her barely functioning controls. "After the initial strike, we were thrown free."

The Captain nodded and relaxed slightly. "Well that is something. Thank you, Lieutenant, that is indeed good news."

"Sir," she countered, her voice held a hint of caution. "We are still in the path of the storm." She dropped to the floor, underneath her console, and popped open an access hatch. She removed a couple of control chips, rewired two computer boards, and, for good measure, smacked the rewired panel. The main viewer flickered to life and the Lieutenant resumed her seat. "The storm will hit us again in four minutes..."

The Captain grimaced and closed the eyes of a dead bridge officer before turning to stare at the maelstrom closing in on his ship. Six months. The crew had six months left on a two-year exploration of the area beyond their solar system. He shook his head as he watched the swirling yellow, gold storm growing larger on the screen. Energy spirals lashed out toward the ship as the hurricane shaped storm rotated.

"Maneuvering thrusters. Move us out of the way as best you can," he ordered. "Give us as much time as possible." He turned and saw the communications officer was dead. He nodded, talking to himself. "I'm going to send a message home."

"Sir?" the Lieutenant's remorseful voice floated across the bridge. "Tell them...tell them that the storm is headed for them. It will be years," tears streamed down her fur covered face, "but it's heading for home."

Lorn nodded. "Just get us out of here," he repeated. He wiped the blood from his forehead and settled in front of the communications station. The console sat dark, the lights and system dead. He dropped to his knees, removed a panel, and rewired the console. He mentally ticked off the time and counted ninety seconds before sparks arched and the console hummed to life.

"Time?"

"Three minutes, sir," the Lieutenant replied. "I've managed to move us a little, but propulsion is redlining. The engines won't last much longer."

"Do what you can, Lieutenant," he smiled. "And thank you. You've done the BAL proud."

He turned and began composing his message, putting the flashing lights and steading rocking of the ship out of his mind. The storm crept closer, the outer tendrils of energy lashing the ship. The rocking increased. A loud boom echoed through the ship, the *Cenceti IV* shuddered.

"The engines are offline," the Lieutenant reported. Lorn did not respond. He had to finish the message to the King.

The storm grew closer, the tendrils lashing the ship with more powerful energies. Additional consoles sparked and died, and the view screen went blank. The Captain paused at the loss of the flickering storm, and he let while his eyes adjust to the sudden gloom. Miraculously, his rewiring of the communications station held as most of the other consoles on the bridge died. Not knowing how much time was left, Lorn narrated a message home. The report complete, the Captain stabbed the send key moments before the storm reached the ship.

The *Cenceti Explorer IV* rocked violently, tossing the crew—dead and alive alike—across the bridge. Lorn attempted to stand but another tendril of the storm struck the ship. One of the forward sections of the bridge superstructure fell, crushing the communication station. An ear-splitting rip filled the air as a section of the fuselage tore free. The whistling howl of escaping followed. *Decompression*! The Captain felt the air ripped from his lungs.

"Lieutenant," he croaked. He heard the snap/hiss of emergency bulkhead shields and the pressure in his lungs released. "Get to the escape pods. There may be a chance to survive. Lieutenant?" He crawled through the rubble on the bridge as the ship swayed. He heard the hull let out a mournful wail and heard the qualuminum hull crack above his head. A section of the roof ripped open, exposing the bridge to space. He felt the icy fingers of space touch for him, embracing him in their cold embrace. The emergency bulkhead shields snapped into place and the chill subsided.

The Captain caught his breath, his heart threatening to burst from his heart. He rolled over and lay on his back. He stared through the hull breach, mesmerized at the star field beyond. He had been one of the few in the Ministry of Science to oppose the plan to explore beyond the Cenceti system. But when the Prince asked him to command one of the dozen ships commissioned for the task, he did not refuse. Looking at the stars, he felt a calm wash over him. He did not regret the task, or the mission. Lorn admitted he had been wrong in his opposition. The last eighteen months had been spectacular, and their discoveries would aid the Cenceti for decades to come.

The storm raged against the hull, rotating his view from the peaceful stars to the storm itself. A sick, flickering, yellow glow engulfed the Captain and his mood changed from calm to anxious. A dizzying light display flashed over his head as energy tendrils competed with each other. The Captain and his ship the prize.

"Lieutenant," he called again. "Do you see this?" He turned his eyes from the storm, tracing across the bridge to her station. The navigation console sat toppled over and crushed under the weight of a superstructure beam. The female officer lay underneath the control panel. The Captain closed his eyes and offered a silent prayer for her, and all of his crew. He opened his eyes as another energy ribbon rocked the ship.

"I hope the message got through," he said to no one. The sound of his voice offering a moment of confidence that he had done everything he could to warn home. Doubt quickly followed as his eyes traced the storm's energy. "And if not? If not, well, then my daughter will never grow old."

The storm engulfed the ship, rocking it violently. The Captain lay, hypnotized by the raging storm in the sound of absolute silence. The emergency bulkhead shield flickered once, twice, and then died.

Lorn L'tas Blex closed his eyes and felt the icy fingers of space embrace him again. Weightlessness enveloped him, pulling him toward the breach, and out of the ship. The vacuum of space crushed him, and he died seconds before the *Cenceti Explorer IV* exploded.

CHAPTER ONE

The Approaching Storm

Fas L'tas Unci pulled the holo-sheet from the 3D printer, read the report, and then re-read it. Her eyes narrowed and she brought the report closer to her face—as if the proximity would make it clearer—and read it a third time. She shook her head in disbelief.

How can an entire section of space simply disappear?

She left the printer and crossed the lab to the computer uplink terminal on the far wall. She established a link with the orbiting Grometi telescope and punched in a series of commands. Fas stepped back and tapped her foot impatiently. She visualized the telescope turning in the direction she wanted. Two-hundred kilometers above her, the giant telescope complied.

Fas stepped out of the lab and into the observation lounge of the Royal Observatory. She paced anxiously, waiting for the telescope to finish its vector correction. The lounge, the main meeting hall for the astronomers assigned to the observatory, sat empty except for Fas. The light blue walls normally reverberated with conversations and arguments as scientists debated about their theories. The often-heated debates ended up with the Bal Science Committee for resolution.

Fas usually enjoyed the peace and tranquility of the morning shift; the quiet a welcome friend and ally. Today, she found the vacant tables and chairs and the banks of empty computers consoles, disconcerting. For once, she wished for someone to verify that she read the information correctly.

A distinct ping echoed in the quiet. She returned to the lab to find the Grometi Telescope pointing in the direction she programmed. Fas moved to the console and typed in another series of commands. Her tail nervously curled around her waist, the end twitching unconsciously. Her finger paused over the execute button and she looked skyward again, seeing only the light blue ceiling of the lab. She sighed and touched the button.

High above, the Grometi telescope took several long-range holo images of the section of sky under scrutiny. Fas stood near the console, tapping her foot and whipping her tail back and forth impatiently. The program completed with another ping and a small blue indicator appeared on the console. The download status from the satellite moved slowly, building her anxiety. The entire process took several minutes to complete; an eternity to the young astronomer.

The computer powered down, its task complete, and unceremoniously spat out a silver storage crystal. Fas grabbed the crystal and turned away. She missed it in her haste and had to turn and reach for it again. Her fingers closed on it, she gripped it firmly, and she left the computer console. Fas walked briskly to a table in the center of the lab and, with a calming breath, placed the crystal into the reader sitting on the table.

The reader powered up and Fas saw her reflection in the shimmering clear tabletop. Considered attractive by the male Cenceti she worked with, they thought her a bit brash and opinionated. Her supervisor wrote she had a 'nasty' habit of speaking her mind and breaking the rigid rules of protocol of the scientific community. At the time, she shrugged off the comment, citing she considered it a compliment, much to the chagrin of her supervisor.

The reflection that stared back sported shimmering gold fur—well groomed, of course— glistening white teeth, and a well-proportioned body that moved in seductive ways. The black rings that encircled her tail were painted on, the latest fad of the available female searching for a potential mate.

The projector actuated and displayed a composite shot of a distant star system explored some twenty years earlier. The overhead display showed a binary star system with eighteen planets and several dozen moons scattered among them. Fas clicked a switch and the Grometi data replaced the composite.

The same star system appeared, with only four planets and less than a dozen moons present. One of the stars shone brightly, the other vanished. A vast path of destruction, of nothing but debris, extended thru the heart of the system and beyond. The edge of the holo, barely visible at the edge of the hologram, swirled a large, golden spiral storm.

Fas quickly crossed the room and recalled

historical shots of the system. More silver data disks in hand, she returned to the hologram projector. Disk after disk showed the storm growing ever larger, ever closer. Her tail encircled her waist again, agitated.

Her preliminary research complete, she called her supervisor.

"Director. I need your concurrence to convene an exploratory council to—"

"Fas," Res P'lat Loni cut her off, "do you know what time it is?"

She looked at a clock on the nearest desk. "Yes," she stated.

He scoffed. "Why are you calling me at four in the morning?"

"I have found something and need your concurrence to—" she began again.

"Fas, we will discuss this when I arrive," he grumbled. "And do not call me again unless the world is ending." The line died.

"It just might," Fas replied, looking at the hologram floating above the table.

Res arrived three hours later. His suit and lab coat appeared fresh, his fur recently bathed. His blood shot eyes and snarling attitude belied his mood. He held up a hand as Fas approached and informed her that he never returned to sleep after the call.

He casually glanced over the data before dismissing it with a wave. "Errant space debris," he commented. Fas persisted and he finally acquiesced, offering to refer it to one of the committees. Fas continued to argue her findings, but, in the end, he shut down her arguments.

He turned to leave lab, stopped in the door, and smiled with gleaming teeth. "I will be writing another reprimand for your file over this. Do not wake me again, Fas." He left the lab, his footsteps echoing in the empty science building.

Fas whirled and stalked away, furious. *Stubborn*, she thought about the Cenceti as she crossed to the hologram. She stared at the destroyed solar system. *The data is clear!*

Additional scientists arrived at the Observatory and the blue walls reverberated with conversation and debate. She thought about bringing in her co-workers, but word already leaked that Res was in a bad mood and Fas was the cause. No one would speak with her. She held up the holo report and read it again, certain she read the report correctly.

She crossed over the computer terminal by the entrance to her lab and recited a number from her childhood. She placed a call to the only Cenceti who might believe her.

ଔ   ଋ

Prince Fiss S'ace Kecup sat at the head of a long table in the Royal Observatory. Res P'lat Loni stood to his left, his eyes staring daggers at Fas. The rest of the conference room a half-dozen of the most knowledgeable and experienced astronomers on Cenceti.

All eyes stared at Fas.

She presented the information to the Prince. The deeper she delved into the facts, the more the committee turned their attention from her and to the data. She completed her hastily prepared speech and sat. Her peers and superiors discussed the data and answered questions from the Prince.

Fas leaned back into her chair and glanced at Fiss. He received the briefing with an uncharacteristic calm. Although from two difference castes, the two grew up together in the royal court. Fiss had a reputation for quick, knee jerk reactions, and a hot temper. She saw none of that as he listened intently to the discussions around the table.

It has been a few years, she thought, *perhaps age has mellowed him.*

Fas let her mind wander to her younger years, when she was a girl in the Royal House. Prince Fiss, only a few years older than her, nominated her father to captain one of the explorer ships. The pair grew close and the rumors ran rampant. The news media often speculated of the nature of their relationship. When her father's ship did not return, the Prince felt responsible and they drifted apart. They continued their friendship, but at a distance.

The disappearance of her father, and a garbled transmission of destruction, propelled Fas into the astronomy realm. Her appointment to the Royal Observatory brought the two together again, albeit briefly. The two dated briefly, the media again speculated on her ambitions. The King chastised them for "inter-caste" socializing and the two separated again.

She sat once again before her Prince, this time not as romantic partners, but as a Royal and his subject. She felt Res eyes on her as Fiss studied the data she had collected.

"Your majesty," Res P'lat Loni concluded, "We do not know what happened to the system," he gave another evil look at Fas across the room. "It could be an isolated occurrence."

"No," Fas interrupted, drawing another glare from her supervisor. She stood. "We know that the path extends along a straight vector for as far as we can detect with our telescopes."

"Yes, well..." Res interjected, trying desperately to save face in front of the Prince. "Straight, with some variation in the course due to gravimetric phenomenon." He nodded to himself as he continued. "For the little time we've had to study the data, we cannot for certain tell you what it is, or where it is headed."

Fiss looked over the data before him again. The charts showed composites of several different star systems, each composite showing a before and after depiction of a system. Although not an astronomer or scientist, Fiss saw the destruction in the series of pictures. In each hologram, the Prince saw a system— once vibrant and full—reduced to a scattering of debris. The final set of holograms showed a yellow-gold storm in space. The swirling storm measured half the size of the Cenceti star system. He looked at the Chief Astronomer. "Fas is convinced that the storm is on a direct course for Cenceti."

"I do not yet have enough data to make that decision, Your Highness."

The conference room glowed in the natural light that poured through the windows, highlighting the sterile, blue painted walls preferred by the scientific community. Holographic certificates and degrees from the high staff adorned the walls around the rectangular table. The staff, most of whose certificates displayed on the walls around them, stood and bowed as the Crown Prince rose from his chair.

"It may be nothing," Fiss nodded, "or it could be everything. Do your research and return to me within the week."

"Yes, my Prince." Res replied.

Fiss turned toward the door, paused, and motioned for Fas to accompany him. She left her place at the table without looking at the chief astronomer. The admonishment she received for calling the Royal Family directly, not only from the scientific community, but from the protocol office as well, replayed in her mind.

The two left the building in silence. They walked out into the bright afternoon, squinting against the sunshine, and moved toward the Prince's shuttle. The clear sky accompanied a slight breeze from the ocean to the west.

At the sight of the Prince, the ground crew hastened to prepare the shuttle for lift off. Fiss briefly shaded his eyes, watching the shuttle prep, before turning back to Fas. "Thank you for the call. It was good to see you again."

Fas smiled. "I wish it were under better circumstances." Her furry hand clasped his. "What now?"

He led her to his craft, let go of her hand, and opened the hatch to his shuttle. The door slid open without a sound. "I will direct them to study it more." Fas opened her mouth to say something, but Fiss cut her off with a wave of his hand. "I understand your concern," he continued. "If it is a threat, the Ministry of Science will find a way to stop this...this...whatever it is." He kissed her cheek. "Drop by for dinner sometime."

Fas nodded as the Prince entered the shuttle, the hatch closed behind him. She backed away with the ground crew as the engines hummed to life. She averted her eyes as dust and dirt swirled. The shuttle lifted quietly into the afternoon sky.

Ϙ ⁊

Fiss flew the shuttle south, leaving the sprawling city of scientists behind. Sunlight glinted off flat, windowed buildings. He clicked on the rear cameras, watching the spoke and wheel layout of the city recede. The vast observatory, the center of the city, towered over the other buildings.

Tall majestic mountains dominated the east, while the one giant ocean of the planet extended to his west. The sun inched its way toward the water as he flew, promising another spectacular sunset. The sunlight reflected off the controls and he caught his reflection briefly. A furry skull, round eyes, pointed ears, a long, flat snout, and a mouth with canine teeth. His deep brown fur was slightly darker than average, but he knew that would change with age. His father, the King, sported stone white fur in his advanced years.

He checked his course and adjusted slightly to the east. The glaring sun shifted, disappearing over his right shoulder, and shadows danced in the cockpit of the small shuttle. The escort ships that normally accompanied the Royal Family when they traveled were notably absent. Fiss waived them off when the day began. He enjoyed any opportunity he could get to fly and wanted the solitude of the flight without watchful eyes.

The forty-minute flight allowed the Prince time to think of the briefing and the approaching storm. He charted a long, lingering course that took him over the mountains. His mind drifted as the shuttle crossed snowcapped peaks. He war-gamed how his father might react to the potential crisis. Fiss reminded himself that the report was not conclusive.

A smile touched his snout. *How is he going to react when he finds out that Fas called me direct?*

The Royal Court demanded protocol. Fas called her childhood friend, breaking many codes of that protocol. Fiss knew that she caught hell for bringing him in, he saw that in Res's eyes. "How does she even know my number?" he asked aloud. He rolled his eyes, knowing that would be the topic of conversation on the news media within the hour.

He rubbed his temples, trying to disrupt the beginning of a headache. He pushed the throttle forward and raced on toward the palace.

Crossing the southern plains, he spied the shuttle's shadow on the grasslands below. The craft sported large sweptback wings, powerful inboard engines, and a pointed nose cone that housed a plethora of electronic and navigation gear. The twin-finned ship stood less than three-meters tall and stretched slightly more than eight-meters long. A ghastly, bright red coat of paint indicated the shuttle's Royal occupants.

He crossed another mountain range and the capital city stretched before him. As far as he could see stood glistening silver and chrome buildings, interspersed with clear parks and lakes. The great, barren desert stretched further south, extending to the horizon. It was not the largest city on Cenceti, but it was by far the most magnificent. The main transport hub sat on the southern outskirts of the city and he watched a steady stream of shuttles enter and leave the port. Fiss altered course, dropping altitude and heading west, away from the space lanes. Crossing the western perimeter, he swung the shuttle around and flew low inside the city. He banked and weaved, enjoying the freedom of the flight. The Royal Shipyards appeared ahead and Fiss leveled out the shuttle. He circled the shipyard twice before touching down to a cloud of dust.

Fiss powered down the ship and lowered the step ramp. The shuttle shook as the landing gear settled on the pad. Steam vented and a steady ping filled the air as the hot metal cooled. He walked down the ramp into the bright sunlight of mid-afternoon. Servants waited, exchanging his flight jacket for an orange tunic and cape. He donned the royal colors of the Poy caste, slicked back his fur, and proceeded toward the palace.

He rubbed his temples again, the dull ache growing steadily. He took scant notice of the dozen or so vessels stationed at the Royal Family Shipyard; craft ranging from a few small transports and shuttles to the King's personal yacht. Fiss moved with purpose inside the sprawling palace, waiving off the guards and servants as they flocked to his side. The forty-minute flight offered him time to think of the briefing. Fas convinced him that this new phenomenon posed a threat, he recognized that.

He needed to brief his father, but something nagged at him. He paused in the hallway, tail whipping around as he thought through the briefing again. Something headed for his planet; something that left a path of destruction in its wake. By the hurried estimates of the Bal scientists at the observatory, it would arrive in a matter of months.

The nonchalant attitude of the Chief Astronomer cut through his concern with a flash. *Something has to be done now*, Fiss thought, *there is no time for this to be discussed in committee.*

Fiss resumed his brisk stride, crossing through the reception area, past the ever-present journalists trying to get a holo of any member of the royal family, and into the garage. He signaled a mechanic and pointed to an idle hover car. The Cenceti, an older male with a mixture of grey and white fur, started the vehicle and stepped. Back.

"Need a driver today, Prince?"

"Yes, Qek," Fiss replied, patting the old Cenceti on the back. "Take me to the Ministry of Science."

"Of course, sire," Qek replied and waved over a young, buff Cenceti wearing a white suit and bus driver cap.

Fiss entered, Qek shut the door, and the young Cenceti slid behind the controls. He shook visibly and Fiss stared at him for a moment. "First time driving me?"

The young male nodded.

"Relax and drive," Fiss smiled. "I don't bite."

The driver exhaled slowly, nodded, and took control of the aircar. The sleek vehicle, painted a ghastly two-toned red and dull magenta, accelerated away.

The Science Building sat on the outskirts of the capital, surrounded by pristine woodlands and a gorgeous hundred-acre lake. The short ride to the Ministry of Science did not offer Fiss much time to think. Instead, he opted to stare out the window at the gorgeous afternoon and the sprawling city. The hover car stopped and Fiss left the vehicle.

Five-meter tall columns outlined the large, oval-topped doors of the Ministry of Science Building. A blue painted interior, adorned with beautiful holographic shots of distant galaxies, greeted the Prince. He passed the holograms without a thought to the half-dozen orbiting telescopes responsible for the images. The photos gave way to a wall of awards for scientific advancement for the Bal-caste staff.

More holograms of scientific advances, single cell organisms, atoms, and DNA strands lined the corridors as Fiss continued deeper into the building. A rush of footsteps drew near, and he focused his attention on the Minister of Science. The elder Cenceti descended a stairwell two steps two at a time, straightening his formal attire.

"Your Majesty! This is an unexpected pleasure!" He bowed deeply, "How may my staff and I serve you today?" Fiss exhaled slowly and shook his head at the Minister's slovenly nature. His formal clothing appeared ragged and haphazard, his fur dirty and unkempt. The Minister smiled, showing a snout full of dingy teeth.

"Assemble your top astro-physicists and engineers," Fiss stated. "We have something to discuss."

Taken aback by the abrupt nature of the order, the Minister stood for several seconds. He cocked his head in confusion. Prince Fiss rarely came to visit the Ministry and never arrived issuing orders. The Prince smiled politely and nodded, trying to put the older scientist at ease. "Now, please."

The Minister hurried away while his lovely assistant, wearing the faddish rings of the single female around her tail, directed Fiss to the conference room. The young Cenceti stared at Fiss, enthralled with him. The Prince happily kept the female entertained and was well into his third story of personal heroism when the requested scientists and engineers arrived. The assistant smiled, slipped her number to the Prince, another complete breach of protocol, and left the room. Fiss simply smiled and put the number in his pocket. He made a note to at it to the pile of numbers he kept hidden in his desk at the palace.

The assembled scientists gathered in the conference room, standing behind chairs. They stood, waiting for the Prince to sit before they took their seats. The Bal exchanged glances when Fiss did not sit but turned to stare out of the second story window instead. The highly polished surface of the long oblong table shone brightly in the light from the windows above. Fiss breathed deeply and looked at his reflection and the slightly distorted images of those gathered those around him. The scientists continued to stand, fidgeting nervously. They watched anxiously as the Prince gathered his thoughts. Fiss motioned for the gathered crowd to sit.

"Gentlemen, and ladies," he nodded toward the three female engineers present, "as you are all aware, some twenty years ago, twelve ships left Cenceti to explore the galaxy." Fiss saw several heads nod and continued. "As you are also aware, all but one of those ships returned." Again, heads nodded. Fiss paced back and forth at the head of the table, something very uncharacteristic for a member of the Royal Family. "I have just attended a briefing at the Observatory. They have gathered some data they may solve the mystery of that last ship."

A murmur erupted around the table, quickly

silenced by the Minister.

Fiss stopped pacing and placed a silver data crystal into a reader on the table. The lights dimmed, blinds covered the windows, and the air above the table filled with a 3D representation of a distant solar system. The system slowly dissolved into a mass of random rocks and debris. "The quadrant of space where the last group of explorers and colonists were heading has been destroyed." He pointed to the holo floating in the air. "And with it, I believe, our ship."

Murmurs erupted again around the table. The Minister of Science called for quiet. It took several minutes before he regained control. The hologram disappeared and the lights returned to normal. The blinds withdrew, filling the room with light.

An older engineer, who had served aboard one of the other ships, raised his hand. He received a nod from the Minister and turned to the Prince. "What do we know? And how?"

Fiss pointed to the silver holo crystal in the reader. "Res P'lat Loni, and his Observatory staff, are currently studying that quadrant. While their findings are preliminary, I believe they are accurate. Their theory is..." he inhaled sharply, "Their theory is that there is a massive energy field passing thru the galaxy. This energy field, call it a storm if you wish, is approximately half the size of our solar system, and is destroying everything in its path."

Fiss touched a control on the reader and the image above the table changed. The hologram showed a small, yellow dwarf star, Cence, and a binary star system approximately eighteen astronomical units (AU) away. Beyond the binary system sat path of debris...of lifelessness...of nothing.

"Gentlemen, as best our records recall, this is the area that our lost explorers surveyed," Fiss said, pointing to an area well into the path of debris. "The last message received from the *Explorer IV*, as garbled as it was, reported an energy storm. The pieces match."

"Any concrete proof, your Highness?" the elder engineer questioned. "At first glance, this appears genuine. But it is still circumstantial."

"Res and his staff are still validating," Fiss replied. "But, if the preliminary evidence is correct, the storm is heading our way." He paused, thinking of Fas. "If that is the case, energy field will arrive here, in our system, in approximately one hundred days."

"Less than three months? Why didn't we see this sooner?" an astronaut asked.

"Our world has been on the opposite side of Cence for the last four months, so we were unable to see it. The Grometi telescope that we placed in orbit thirty-five days ago is what has allowed us to see it now." Fiss reported. His headache worsened and he rubbed his temples.

"Your job, gentlemen," unconsciously ignoring the three females present, "is to find out either a way to stop this phenomenon, or to find a way to evacuate the entire planet in the next three months."

CR   SO

Fiss returned to the Royal Palace a few hours later, arriving in time for the evening meal. He ate in silence, contemplating how to broach the subject with his father. The waning sun streamed through low windows as the Royal family gathered in the library after dinner. He stood before the King, Queen, and Regent, while his brother and two sisters sat in a rough semicircle around him on colorful couches.

He cleared his throat, addressed his father, and told of his afternoon activities. His siblings and mother reacted as he anticipated, stunned faces stared at him in disbelief. His father offered an angry baring of teeth at the breach of protocol, as Fiss predicted. The Regent reacted the worst, angered by the fact that the crown prince gave orders to the Science Ministry without consulting him first. The Regent, as Chief of Staff to the King, held that responsibility.

Fiss described his visit to the Science Ministry. Fede P'art Dopil, the King's Regent, whipped his tail in agitation, angered for being left out of the decisions. He served as the Regent, the primary advisor to the king. For more than eighty years he provided input into in every major decision. His tall frame, he stood nearly a meter and half tall, rose from his position at the King's side; his gray/beige fur bristling.

Fede spoke with a stern and deep voice. "Prince, you should have consulted your father and I before going to the Ministry. It is not your place to dictate commands without consulting us first."

Fiss did not like Fede, and the feeling was mutual.

He rehearsed the conversation in his mind during dinner, war-gaming the responses from Fede. So far, it played out exactly as anticipated.

"I took it upon myself, as the *crown* Prince. I did not feel it would benefit the people if you took the information and locked it away in committee for a month before anything got done." Fiss held up a hand to stop the impending interruption. "The Ministry of Science now has the maximum allowable time to come up with a solution."

The King held up his left hand, stopping the Regent's intake of breath and impending retort. "Don't," the King warned in a tired voice. He dispatched the original twelve exploration ships, hand-picking the Captains of the mission. The loss of the *Explorer IV* and its crew of two hundred still haunted him after twenty years. The data, even if just a theory, provided the King with closure.

"Before you two start arguing again. Fiss did what he thought was best for the people, and I will support him in that. Fede, you will go to the Ministry and keep an eye on things. Ensure that the scientists are doing everything they can to keep Cenceti and its people safe."

The Regent bowed, offered a disapproving glance to Fiss, and left the room with a flurry of his magenta cape. Fiss watched him leave but remained silent. He took a seat next to his father on a long sofa.

"Did the scientists have any ideas on how to stop this?" Fiss's younger brother asked. Peri, barely a teen, frowned as he spoke. His youth and education did not allow him to grasp the dangers of the world. His question belied his exceptional intelligence and the young Cenceti showed great promise. Fiss thought he would make a formidable leader, after he completed his training in military strategy and decision making slated to begin in a few months. The same time the storm was scheduled to arrive.

A shadow of doubt entered the Prince's thoughts. *What would he learn in his military training that could prepare him for events such as this?*

Nothing, his inner voice answered.

Peace prevailed on Cenceti for a thousand years. The once mighty military class, the Mal, reduced to second class citizen status, even below the Gam. The Mal served as a reminder of an archaic past.

In ancient times, when Cenceti still fought amongst themselves, a cub did not become an adult until tested in combat. Over the centuries, as the race matured and fighting waned, the Right of Ascension took the place of trial by combat. The young male endured a series of tests of strength and intelligence, to prove himself worthy. As the society progressed still, the feats of strength gave way to purely intellectual problems and solutions. In recent years, military strategy and skills returned to the curriculum, mainly to recover some of the traditions long lost.

"No, Peri, they didn't," Fiss responded. "But they are the brightest minds on Cenceti," he smiled reassuringly, "they will come up with something."

After a few minutes of uncomfortable silence, the women, with young Peri in tow, left the library. "These next months will not be easy, son," the King mused, stroking the fur along his snout. "It may come down to leaving some behind, to save the majority. You and I will have to be strong. Tough decisions will be made."

The King stared into his son's eyes and saw fierce determination. He longed to see that look in Fiss for years, to prove his son was ready for ascension to the throne. Fiss never displayed that quality. Until now.

"Father," Fiss stated, his voice calm and even, "if we have to evacuate, if we have to leave our home behind, then everyone, and I mean EVERYONE goes. No one gets left behind."

ℐ ℠

Fen T'pun Cet crumpled up the paper in disgust and threw it toward the disposal. He missed, adding to the already large pile of crinkled papers scattered on the floor. He lowered his head on the desk. He growled softly and slowly pounded his head on the desk.

"Fen!"

The engineer stopped banging his head and looked across at Dek L'tak Low. The two, best friends since their earliest education, proved to be fierce competitors and unbeatable teammates. The competition and complimentary nature of the two led Fen to engineering, and Dek to physics. No matter the problem, they always found an answer. They were arguably the best team in the Science Ministry.

"Sorry," Fen apologized. He rearranged his notebook, picked up a pencil, and prepared for another sketch. "I cannot come up with a design that is capable of atmospheric flight and will hold more than one thousand Cenceti." He stretched his legs under the table and rubbed them to get the circulation flowing again. He checked his watch and snarled. They sat at the table for more than three hours and had yet to develop with any workable designs.

"Keep at it," Dek encouraged. "You'll get it." He bared his teeth in a smile, trying to make himself feel better. "At least you're not trying to define something that yesterday didn't even exist!"

Fen returned the smile and nodded his furry head. He stared at the paper and again drew the curved lines of a starship. He retraced the exterior lines, sketching the generally accepted shaped of a standard fuselage when Sek T'cen Pol, a rival engineer, entered the room. Fen ignored him as Sek stood behind him, staring over his shoulder.

Sek made clicking sound of disapproval. "That will never work. It's too small."

Fen closed his eyes. Slowly and deliberately, he put his pen down on the desk. Sek, although a brilliant engineer, made a habit of coming in second place in everything. A small Cenceti with almost black fur, made it his mission to antagonize the Cenceti that consistently bested him. Fen let out a long, slow sigh, and looked up at Sek with his brown eyes. "What do you have?"

Sek bared his teeth and produced a notebook from behind his back. He displayed his notebook for all to see. The gigantic ship drawn on the page consisted of a large square block with engines. Small stabilizer wings jutted aft. A small bridge protruded from the front. Notes in the margin indicated a capacity of ten thousand.

"Impressive," Fen said, drawing a smile from Sek. "Only one problem. Ships that size would have to be built in space. You couldn't land or take off from a planet." Sek nodded. "I don't see any docking bays or shuttle ports."

Sek's toothy smile disappeared. He turned the page, staring at the design. He snarled at Fen and the argument began. The two engineers bantered back and forth, their voices low, but heated.

Dek stood, stretched, and crossed the room to Pel S'kek Lilu, Sek's astro-physicist partner. Like Dek, Pel had light brown fur that darkened toward the extremities, especially the tip of the tail. Even though single, she did not wear the faddish rings.

She smiled as he sat down. "They are at it again." Dek simply nodded. Pel looked at his worried face. "You don't have any ideas either?"

Dek shook his head. "We can't stop what we can't define. If it's an energy field...what kind of energy? Is it a spatial anomaly? If so, of what origin? Is it a storm? Will it burn itself out?" He sighed. "I feel like we are doomed."

"It has only been a day since we were given this assignment," Pel responded. "We will find the solution eventually."

Dek looked at her and slowly exhaled. "I just hope eventually isn't too late."

ℭℛ   ℬℴ

"Your majesty, as you know, Prince Fiss told us barely two weeks ago of the impending danger. We simply have not had enough time to come up with a workable solution." The Minister of Science stood before the King in the Royal Study. The Bal's tail twitched constantly, while the excuses flowed freely. He made a point not to mention the fact that most of scientists spent a lot of time bickering, not brainstorming.

"Minister," the King began, "we now have a barely two months to either divert the phenomenon or evacuate the planet." He paused to ensure the Minister heard every word. "And you're telling me that you and your scientists have come up with nothing?" The comment, said with calm and total non-emotion, chilled the Minister to his bones.

The Minister looked down at the carpeting in the room, at a total loss for words. The Royal Study stood out as one of the single most impressive rooms in the Palace. Bookshelves covered the walls from floor to ceiling. Books spanning the entire history of the Cenceti filled the shelves. Plush carpet covered the floor while a hand painted mural adorned the ceiling. The room's opulence and elegance was lost on the Minister.

He stole a glance at the Regent and Prince Fiss, sitting on opposite sides of the King. Both wore the same expression, a combination of surprise and disgust. Everyone present expected the Bal Leader to have the answer to their dilemma, not excuses.

"Yes, your grace. We do know that we cannot divert the object. That much is certain."

"How can you be so sure?" the Regent asked. "You can't tell us anything about what it is, or what you plan to do about it. But you can tell us what you cannot do?"

"Regent, that is precisely why we know we cannot divert it. We do not know what it is, so we don't know what might move it." The Minister took a deep breath, letting the fatigue flow from his body. His scientists worked for the last two weeks without much sleep. Everyone at the Science Ministry snapped at each, on edge from the lack of rest. The stress took its toll on everyone. "We feel that evacuation of the planet is the only course of action. However, we don't know how to accomplish this.

"We have built large ships in the past. Ships capable of holding thousands of Cenceti. However, those took months to build. We have a few old colony ships, but our engineers are afraid that they may no longer be space worthy."

"What are your plans, Minister?" asked the Regent. He visited the Ministry of Science daily and reported the bickering and agitation to the King and the Prince.

"We are looking into retro-fitting our existing shuttle and transport fleets," the Minister of Science replied quickly. "We should be able to do that and get approximately sixty percent of the population off planet before the storm hits."

"Sixty percent?" Fiss hissed. He stood and looked

the scientist in the eyes. "And what do you propose to do with the other forty percent? What do you tell them?" His tail twitched in frustration. "How do you propose we choose who stays and who goes?"

The King raised his hand and the Prince fell silent. Fiss sat back down, fidgeting in his chair. "Find a one hundred percent solution, Minister, or I will find someone who can." The King stated the threat in a calm, almost deadpan voice. Another chill coursed through his body. He gulped.

"Yes, Highness!"

ભ   ૹ

The Minister of Science stood before his top scientists as they sat around the table in the conference room. The musky odor of poor hygiene permeated the air. Overhead lights illuminated the room, highlighting bloodshot eyes, clingy fur, and dozens of caff-cups littered across the table top.

They discussed the refitting of the shuttles and transports, and arguments abounded. The Minister held up his hands for silence. He left the Royal family a few hours ago, arrived at the Science Building, and been stuck in committee since his arrival Darkness descended upon the gathered scientists, the stars brilliant through the large windows of the conference room.

The assembled scientists were no closer to a one hundred percent solution than they were when they started the task.

Fen sat in the back of the room, away from the table, in a chair against the wall. He drew and redrew small ships, flipping pages after each attempt. His vision blurred from lack of sleep and he forced himself to focus. He shook his head to clear his vision and retraced, for the thousandth time, the exterior lines of a starship. Movement drew his weary eyes to the wall beside him.

He turned, watching an eight-legged arachnid climb the wall beside him. The small creature slowly, deliberately ascended, disappearing into a small crack near the ceiling.

"We can refit the arach-pods," he spoke without thinking. The comment drew everyone's attention to his corner seat. He stared at the crack in the wall and continued. "We have several thousand of those that we use for maintenance and cargo transport."

He dropped his head to address his colleagues. Adrenaline coursed through his body, his fatigue forgotten. He saw the redesigned ships in his mind's eye. He nodded. "With some modifications, they could easily hold twenty or thirty Cenceti, plus food and water."

Sek laughed aloud. Others murmured, not able to picture what he described. Fen flipped the page in his notebook to a clean piece of paper and quickly drew a cross section of the arach-pod. He added the modifications in his mind. He scooted his chair to the table and continued to draw. The other scientists gathered around, their murmurs of approval filling the conference room.

Sek stopped laughing.

The other engineers studied Fen's version and offered their own modifications and suggestions. Several hours later, they agreed on the re-fit. A quick calculation showed it could be done within the timeframe.

"Get some rest," the Minister proclaimed. "We will start the refit tomorrow."

Relief flooded his system as he watched his team leave the room. He crossed to a computer terminal and placed the call to the Royal Palace.

છ   ૭

Sten T'cel Pa enjoyed nothing more than sleep. Eating and napping ranked among his favorite things. The annoyance in his voice when he answered the call betrayed his feelings at the interruption of his slumber.

"What?" The lights in his room actuated and he winced as the dark room became bright as day.

The image on the view solidified into a dark brown, going gray furred face, with sharp intelligent eyes and an extremely perturbed look. *Looks like the Regent*, Sten thought through groggy cobwebs. He rubbed his eyes and smoothed his fur.

"Sten, I hope I'm not disturbing you at this hour," the face spoke. The voice morphed from perturbed to amused. Sten's eyes widened. *It was the Regent!* "The King wishes to speak with you."

Sten straightened his gray/blue fur as an older,

white covered Cenceti appeared. The face appeared tired, with frown and worry lines etched around the eyes and snout. The eyes showed intelligence and wisdom, and a hint of humor. The King gazed past Sten to the room behind the Gam-caste leader. The King frowned at the disorganization of the quarters.

"Sten, I have a special project for you and the worker caste," the King stated. Sten nodded and the King continued. "An engineer named Fen T'pun Cet will arrive shortly with my son, Prince Fiss. They will show you some new ship designs.

"I want the ships built, or refit, in the next seventy-five days."

Sten, shocked that he talked with the King, again nodded. As the Gam-caste leader, he met important Cenceti every day, but never anyone from the Royal Family. *Wait until I tell my kids*, he thought.

"Yes, your highness, I will make it my top priority," he managed.

"Sten, this is your only priority," the King replied, deadpan, and the line went dead.

He sat down on his bed in stunned silence to wait for the Prince.

ଷ   ଓ

Sten met the Prince and the engineer, a young Cenceti named Fen, an hour later. His eyes widened and his tail twitched as the Prince finished briefing him on the approaching storm. "That is why we need your total commitment to the refit," the Prince concluded.

Only priority is right! thought Sten and nodded his consent. Sten gained his position through intelligence and hard work, but he could not fathom the sheer magnitude of the information. The trio moved to a table in Sten's apartment, cleared off the trash, and unrolled a set of blueprints for large transport vessels.

Sten eyed the plans and forced himself to concentrate. The Gam leader brewed a pot of caff and drank two cups while looking over the details. The caffeine coursed through his system and aided his attention. He studied the plans and shook his head. "Sire, the construction of the larger vessels will be the most difficult. We usually spend months on the interior design work alone." He paused, smiling. "But I think we can skip the non-essentials this time."

He moved the blueprints aside and looked at the cross section of Fen's arach-pod. He studied the diagrams, the crude drawings from the engineers, and nodded absentmindedly. "The retro-fit of the arach-pods can commence immediately," he muttered, making his own notes in the margins. "We should have those close to complete before the material for the larger ships arrive."

The Prince smiled, baring his gleaming white teeth. "Now I can see why your caste picked you to lead them." He shook Sten's hand, felt the strong grip. "If you have any difficulties, call me immediately. If you have questions about the designs, call Fen."

"Sten," the Prince pulled him close and spoke in a

quiet, conspiratorial tone, "keep this quiet as long as possible. I do not believe the our people will panic, but you can never accurately predict how a mass of beings will react. They could pull together and face this tragedy in a calm, rational manner. Or," he shook his head, "we could have fear and panic the likes of which we have never encountered." The Gam Leader nodded, realizing the true depth of the knowledge he now possessed.

The Prince and the engineer said their good-byes and left. Sten stood for a moment, contemplating the tasks ahead for his caste. He pulled out a pad and made notes of each step in the process, outlining what needed to be done. After a few minutes of self-motivation, Sten actuated the comm and called his chief supervisor.

The Gam had a lot of work to do.

To Aid and Protect

CHAPTER TWO

The Escape

Twinkling stars lit the night sky. Billions of stars formed that complex patterns; constellations used for centuries to guide travelers and portend events. Fas stared up at the night sky, mesmerized. *Too many stars to count.* She knew beings tried, certainly the Cenceti and, she imagined, on other planets throughout the galaxies.

They seem different tonight, she thought, and she adjusted the telescope for the thousandth time. Nervous fidgeting kept her constantly fiddling with the equipment. She sat, perched on top of a console three meters from the floor, in a chair that moved with each of the telescope's corrections.

She studied a distant quadrant of space, attempting to measure the size and destructive power the storm. Her red, bloodshot eyes grew fatigued from staring at the computer screen of the Grometi telescope, and she took a moment to rub them. A miniature hologram of the storm floated over her left shoulder. She pulled away from her screen to study the hologram.

Fas squinted at the hologram. Something nagged her mind, but she could not focus on the changes. She

45

stared deeper into the cosmos depicted on the screen, scanning the heavens for a clue, some sign of what she missed. Sighing silently to herself, she turned back to the telescope and adjusted it again.

She knew the days ticked away for the Cenceti. The entire planet knew of the approaching energy-storm; word invariably leaked as GAM workers were reassigned from other projects. The Cenceti remained calm and measured, the mass hysteria the Prince feared never happened. Instead, the population stood as one to help the Gam build the ships. The worker-caste moved ahead of schedule.

Fas turned to stare at a hologram replay of the Gam leader, Sten T'cel Pa, and his speech with the King. The speech resolved to a live shot, showing Sten standing on the roof of a building on the edge of Capital City. Having discovered the phenomenon, her status elevated, and she became privy to information and people previously out of her influence. She met the Gam leader and found him to be confident, caring, and concerned.

In the twenty-three days since Sten T'cel Pa called his foremen, more than eight thousand arach-pods sat refitted in the shipyard. Another seventeen thousand waited, in various states of modification. Scientific estimates remained optimistic, the Bal assured everyone they had plenty of time.

The larger vessels—the transports—remained an issue. The plan required six new transports in order to evacuate the entire population. Four of those sat on the edge of the Capital City's shipyards, under construction. Massive, blocky bulks lined the horizon, transforming the city skyline. Cranes and small arachpods flitted between the last two, their skeletal frames barely under construction.

Sten stood on the roof of the shipyard office, watching his Gam swarm the ships. He exhaled through his snout and shook his head. *The King said all or none,* he thought. *At this rate, it will be none.*

"No one will be left behind!" the King said in a televised speech to the planet. The Cenceti believed and rallied to the cause. 'No one will be left behind' became the rally cry to construct the ships.

Sten flipped through diagrams and progress reports and again shook his head. "The problem is supplies," he muttered, his eyes scanning the lines of available materials. The Gam built and refitted the ships faster than materials became available. The demand exceeded the supply.

His mind flashed back to his own words during the King's speech. "The ships will be built on time." He gave his word that all Cenceti would escape to the stars.

Fas turned away from the news program back to her telescope.

"The stars," she muttered, recalling his words.

The stars that had somehow changed, and Fas could not figure out why.

ଔ   ꙮ

"Get me the head of the factory guild."

Sten T'cel Pa sighed, worry crinkling his brow. He made a promise to the people that his caste could build enough ships to transport all of the Cenceti away. "No one will be left behind!"

Now, he was not so sure.

"Yes?" the comm chimed. Sten put down his pencil and took a deep breath. He knew losing his temper would not solve the problem. He exhaled slowly, felt his nerves calm, and he began. "As you are aware, the factory guild promised eight hundred tons of hull plating yesterday. It still has not arrived. What is the delay?"

"The miner's guild has not brought us the required ore to make the plating," the foreman explained, laying blame on another guild. The Cenceti's brown fur lay back, "We cannot make anything without that ore."

Sten bristled and nodded. He heard the same excuse from every guild leader he talked with. Everything pointed to the miner's guild as the reason for the delay. "You will have your material tomorrow. Get back on schedule." Sten signed off.

An entire day calling the guilds, checking progress, or the lack thereof, and only one remained. He punched in the number for the miner's guild and hit pause.

He rose from his desk and moved across the room to his office kitchenette and the caff-pot. He ran his fingers thru his fur as he walked across the disheveled office. Absentmindedly, he poured a cup, rehearsing the best way to approach the miners. The chime of an incoming call broke his concentration.

He quickly re-crossed the office, scattering the mess of papers and refuse. "Yes?" he said, spilling a small bit of the stim-caff on his fur.

The image of the Miner's Guild Leader appeared on the monitor. He was thin, even for a Cenceti, with dark, dirt and dust coated fur. He wore a hard hat with attached light and a breath filter mask slung around his neck.

"I've heard you've been calling all the guilds," he began without preamble. "I thought I would save you the trouble."

"We need material for ship building," Sten stated with a nod. "You are behind schedule." He said it plainly with no hint of emotion; a simple statement of fact. *Not the way I wanted,* he grimaced.

The guild leader nodded. "My miners are working as fast as they can," he explained, hesitation in his voice.

There is something he isn't saying. Sten waited for more, watching the guild leader's calm demeanor slowly melt into fidgeting.

"They want more wages and more time off to spend with their families."

The foreman recoiled at Sten's sharp intake of breath. The Gam leader eyes narrowed to slits and he stared at the miner foreman. The word echoed in his head. Sten prepared arguments for exhaustion and equipment issues. *More pay?*

He took another breath and spoke slowly...clearly. "Did you inform them that without that material they wouldn't *have* families?"

"Yes, of course I told them that!" came the terse reply. "They want guarantees that their families will be taken care of. That *they* will be taken care of."

Sten felt his anger rise and tried to fight it. "The King himself has already stated that fact," he said thru gritted teeth. "What else do they want?"

ଔ   ဢ

The stars appeared dimmer. The energy storm, now visible at night with the naked eye, grew closer, someone diminishing the universe. Cenceti's atmosphere made it a glowing pale green orb in the northern sky. Crowds of Cenceti gathered in open fields, away from the city lights, to view the approaching storm. Some of the smaller towns even implemented black out conditions to view the heavens.

The Bal scientists studied the phenomenon but discovered nothing. They launched automated into the storm but did not receive any data. Astronomers slept during the day and worked all night. Engineers and Gam workers worked around the clock.

A Mal volunteer piloted one of the new arach-pods into space, a drone followed capture every moment. Six days at maximum burn, and the ship arrived to study the phenomenon. Energy tendrils lashed out, narrowly missing the small vessel. Everyone gathered around the hologram emitter, watching. A collective gasp echoed in the conference room as the ship ventured too close, touched the event horizon of the storm, and vanished. The drone feed died a moment later.

The nightly heavens continued to brighten as the field closed the distance.

C03   80

Fen T'pun Ceta stood on the edge of the shipyards and admired his brainchild. The sunlight felt good, the spring breeze whipping his fur. He walked along the rows of arach-pods with his friend Dek and a host of media and other scientists.

The two attained instant celebrity status once the population learned that he developed the refit model for the arach-pods. Everywhere they travelled, the holo-journalists and sycophants followed. They signed autographs, made speeches and did holo-programs. All while enforcing the King's promise.

They became synonymous with "No one will be left behind."

He walked underneath one of the refitted ships, running his paw along the smooth undercarriage. He noticed a small plaque with its incept date and whistled softly. The ship was built a decade before his birth.

With only three thousand on current duty and fit for use, the Bal raided scrap-yards across the planet for older versions of the craft. They required more refit materials, as well as engine overhauls, and updated electrical and computer components. They relocated every usable craft to the shipyards, and used the rest of parts.

Originally designed for light transport and maintenance work, the arach-pod had a cylindrical body twenty meters wide by sixty meters long. Six retractable arms—three on each side—moved equipment into the cargo hold. Two additional arms on the front of the body performed detailed work, primarily fixing orbiting satellites. A small cockpit, affixed to the body, contained the control area and main computer housing. The cockpit, body, and arms resembled a giant arachnid.

The modified arapods, their named shortened to depict the refit, kept the same outward appearance. The interior, however, drastically changed. The arach-pod interior, built for storage and work, boasted dull grey walls and locking clamps on the floor to hold cargo in place.

The arapod interior, in contrast, included sleeping quarters for thirty, a main gathering area, a galley, and lavatory facilities. The small rooms did not offer much for creature comforts, but fresh paint in cheerful colors helped. The rest of the craft consisted of the engine compartment, recycling and reprocessing machinery, and storage for food and water.

After the Mal pilot's demise, another problem arose for the Cenceti: a lack of pilots. Nearly twenty-five thousand arach- and arapods filled the shipyard. The Gam and Mal, combined, accounted for less than ten thousand pilots.

The shortage of pilots led to an overhaul of all of

the computer systems available. None of the systems could handle the complexities of flying the craft. The Bal turned to their most promising programmer. He coded the most advanced system ever devised. The programs needed to be capable of running the ship to include engines, life support, navigation, and the limited defensive shielding. Self-correcting algorithms ensured the computer could not fail. A primary and secondary backup were installed into each computer core.

Cal K'pek Pali, the lead programmer, and his staff wrote the code for the voyage. The Minister of Science stood watch over what he deemed "the absolute brightest minds on the planet." The team worked countless hours, day and night, to ensure they completed their task.

Fen did not know much about programming; he knew structural engineering. His chest swelled with pride at the ships aligned before him. He walked underneath the eight-armed arapods, Dek at his side, and the media trailing behind. He looked up at the sun and felt the heat warm his face.

"What is it?" Dek asked in a low whisper.

"This," he tapped the underside of the arapod, "is a great start, but it isn't enough."

He stopped at the rear of the craft, admiring the contoured lines and the engines. His gaze moved beyond the engines and he saw the transports being built in the distance. Four massive hulls with two more underway sprang from the ground.

"We still do not have the capacity to get everyone

off..." His sentence trailed off as his eyes fell on the old, mothballed explorer ships. The sleek lines and meteor dented hulls glinted in the late afternoon sun. He turned to Dek, excitement etched his voice. "I have an idea..."

ℛ   ℬ

Prince Fiss stood on the outskirts of the crowd, waiting for his turn to address the miner's guild. He watched his breath evaporate in the cool morning air. Steam rose from a nearby quarry lake as the guild leader finished his portion of the speech. The stiff breeze rustled clothing and paper. The crowd stood around the makeshift stage, quiet and attentive.

Sten called the Prince the evening before and reported the problems with the miner's guild. Fiss listened and nodded. He did not tell the Gam leader that he already knew of the problems.

The two discussed options and decided on a face-to-face meeting with the guild the next morning. Sten lost a night's sleep setting up the meeting. He stood at the microphone his voice reverberating off the starships surrounding him, shivering in the breeze, his eyes dropping with fatigue. "I have given you my assurances," he finished. "Now, listen to the assurances of the Prince."

The Prince moved forward on cue, taking his place before the assembled workers. The stage swayed slightly as the small repulsor engines compensated for the movement. "I am proud of the progress that the

Gam have made for the Cenceti," he said. "I have seen the ships being built, the preparations being made, and I am continuously amazed by the hard work, perseverance, and diligence that the worker class has displayed.

"I also want to say that I am *highly* disappointed. Disappointed that I had to come here today. Disappointed that your petty quarrels have placed the entire planet in jeopardy. As the backbone of the Cenceti, every being on the planet is counting on you for survival." The Prince continued his speech for another ten minutes. The tone changed from disappointment to motivational. Fiss left the stage to loud cheers and applause.

The ore arrived at the factory guild less than six hours later.

☙ ❧

"The storm continues to close on our home," the new announcer reported, every hair of her blonde face meticulously groomed. "Around the world, a sense of worry permeates the air."

An image of the storm replaced her. The green tinted storm grew with each passing day, dissolving the darkness of night with its eerie glow. Her voice superimposed the display. "But there is hope. Scientists assure us that we still have more than three weeks before the evacuation, and that the refit will be completed long before then."

The image changed to show the day side of the

planet and the refit of the starships. "The Royal family has decreed that 'No one will be left behind,'" she continued, "and that kept the calm across Cenceti. But there is no more darkness. No more stars to be seen at night. Only perpetual light."

The image returned to the blonde reporter, her eyes glowing in the studio lights. "Be it the daylight from our own star, Cense, or sickening green glow from the energy storm at night. There is only perpetual light."

CZ   SO

"The tests are complete." Cal K'pek Pali said aloud, pushing his chair away from the workstation. The programmer's workspace was a clustered mess, a stark contrast to the otherwise pristine environment of the Ministry of Science. A multitude of computers scattered about his work area, along with computer parts, small notes, half empty stim-caff drinks, and a couple of inappropriate photos. Monitors ran programs, letters and numbers scrolling across the screen.

Cal swiveled around in his chair, facing the Minister of Science and the senior scientists of Cenceti. He did not stand, but instead leaned back in his chair and placed his hands behind his head. He offered his superiors a self-satisfied smirk.

"The program is working perfectly. The new artificial intelligence algorithm is controlling the environment within our set parameters. In fact, the AI has already requested permission to modify the environment to improve function." The programmer smiled, nodding to one of the still working computers.

"Asked permission?" one of the elder scientists asked. His gray white fur appeared to absorb the buildings light. He adjusted the jacket that covered clothes three generations out of date. "It doesn't make those changes automatically?"

Cal's smile broadened. He stood, his chair sliding back against the wall at the motion. He wore mix-matched clothes two sizes too large, the newest fad for the younger population. White pants, an orange shirt, a blue belt and brown shoes surrounded his brown fur. "It was an afterthought. The AI will not make any changes without user permission. It's a failsafe to prevent the computer from adjusting something unexpectedly and causing damage or harm." He ran his paw through his disheveled hair and grinned sheepishly, "Or like in the old holos...simply take over."

"How many tests have you conducted?" another staff member asked.

"Forty-seven separate tests on the program. Seventy-eight different shipboard scenarios. Fourteen emergency procedure scenarios," he said, counting each category on his fingers. He smiled like a father talking about his son. "The program is flawless."

The Minister of Science placed his hand over his mouth and whispered to his top advisors, first to his left then his right. Cal heard the murmured responses, but nothing more. The conference ended and the

Minister nodded. "Begin uploading the program to every ship in the fleet."

CR   SO

The entire arapod fleet stood ready for final inspection. Twenty-five thousand ships occupied the desert lands south of Capital City. Dozens zoomed overhead, flying in precisely controlled formations. Contrails crisscrossed the cloudless sky.

Fen stood by Prince Fiss as the Royal Heir made his way through the shipyard. The grounded arapods littered the landscape as far as he could see, accented by two of the large transports and one quickly refurbished explorer ship.

Computer tests for the pilot program sent arapods all of the planet, returning them to the desert for the final review. The transport vessels and explorer vessels flew next, their bulky bodies flying easily through the atmosphere. The transports moved to orbit while the explorers pre-positioned across the globe.

Fen stared into the distance, amazed at how the larger vessels towered over the arapods, breaking the rhythmic arapod-formed terrain. The Prince moved among the spider-like craft, inspecting them.

"You have done well, Fen," the Prince stated, "and your idea for re-fitting the explorer ships will give us room for growth in space... something no one had thought of."

Fen nodded. The praise continued day and night

and, although flattered, he wanted it to stop. Not long ago, he thought that fame would be exhilarating. He found it annoying and exhausting.

"Thank you, sire. The last explorer ship will be competed in two days. That will give us six explorer ships, six large transports, and twenty-five thousand arapods ten days before the storm is scheduled to arrive."

The Prince nodded and stepped up the ramp into a nearby arapod. He strode through the compartments, studied the controls, ran his hand along bare walls and tried to imagine his entire race living on board. "I doubt these walls will be bare for long," he said aloud. "We will adapt and spread the seed of Cenceti throughout space."

Fen only nodded as the Prince exited the ship and continued on his tour.

ෙ   ෙ

Dek L'tak Lowa stood before the gathered scientists and reiterated his comment by slamming his pointer onto the table in front of him. The wooden pointer broke, and pieces flew through the room, forcing several members of the Ministry of Science Board of Elders to duck. "I said we have to evacuate no later than four days before the storm hits. We have to have enough time to get out of the system."

"That means the first ships need to be boarded and launched the day after tomorrow," Pel S'kek Lilu added. She stood beside Dek, adding her voice to his.

The two astrophysicists had become quite close during the crisis and stood as a unified front for the senior staff. "We estimate it will take two days to load everyone on the planet. We must start evacuating within forty-six hours if we want to clear the storm."

The sterile blue walls of the conference room, now bare as scientists packed their credentials in anticipation of leaving, reverberated with the quiet conversations. Many of the elder scientists shook their heads and a couple let loose with loud, angry outbursts. Dek shook his own head and murmured, "Fen was right, everything goes to committee."

He folded his arms and watched the elder scientists, and their expressions of anger, fear, and depression. The realization of their endeavor hit home and Dek saw a new emotion: denial. No one really wanted to go, even if it meant their death.

He closed his eyes until the murmurs subsided. Silence permeated the room and Dek opened his eyes to see two dozen scientists sitting in the amphitheater style room of the science building. The Ministry of Science nodded.

"I will inform the King. It is time to leave."

 C3   ℰᴑ

The light of the dwarf yellow star Cence penetrated the darkness of space, its warm glow illuminating the six planets that circled in oblong and circular orbits. The orange and yellow world of Cenceti glowed in its light and life thrived.

Another light penetrated the darkness of space, a ghastly green/gold light just as bright as Cence. It too bathed the six planets in light, but it did not promote life. It extinguished it.

On the dark side of the world, on a trajectory away from both the star and the storm, a third type of light entered the heavens. Starship engines filled planetary orbit. The inhabitants of Cenceti abandoned their home world, their ship's running lights and engine flare adding to the radiance in space.

Dozens, hundreds, then thousands of ships streaking away from the planet like the tail of a comet. They searched for a safer place. A place to live, raise a family, and grow old.

The storm dominated the sky, its edges more defined as it neared. Fen stared out of the window of a transport vessel, staring at the slowly rotating storm. Scientists gave their home five days. "In a half week, the storm will touch the planet and Cenceti would simply cease to exist," he repeated the projection.

He turned to see the multitude of craft leaving orbit. Most of the Cenceti did not—could not—fathom the sheer power of what approached. They only knew that they had to flee...or die. That is why the King ordered the evacuation of Cenceti.

Transports, colony ships, explorers, and several thousand arapods crowded the space around Cenceti. The larger ships, already in orbit, filled first, with hundreds of flights from the arapods ferrying the population. Fen understood the logic: more Cenceti would escape in the larger vessels if anything went wrong. The arapods, their orbital task complete, now filled with the remainder of the population.

"No one will be left behind."

Engines flared day and night, lifting ships into orbit. The computer, with its AI programming, piloted the ships into space, and accelerating toward the edge of the solar system.

The transport turned and Fen could see his own. The planet sat like a jewel in space, the bright light of Cense far in the distance. The ship rotated more, and Fen breathed a sigh of relief as the storm disappeared from his sight. "Now I can remember home without that spectre," he mused.

Cenceti ships spread throughout the system. The small spider-shaped ships weaved in and around the larger vessels. The procession of a thousand ships stretched from the edge of the system all of the way to the planet.

CR   SO

The King paused in the hatch of the last arapod, taking one last look at his world. His home world...his planet...abandoned. He heard no children playing, no hover cars zooming by, no bustling, busy streets. Only the roar of engines as arapods accelerated toward orbit.

He turned his eyes skyward, at the hundreds of lights visible in the heavens. Each light represented a ship and a cluster of his people. A nearby roar drew him to the now empty desert, and he watched the last arapod lift in a cloud of dust and dirt.

The engine's roar retreated, leaving only the sounds of various animals. Mating calls pierced the growing darkness, answered by the King's arapod as its engines revved.

He watched his final sunset, a tear streamed down his face, almost matching the slowly sinking sun. Cense disappeared on the horizon and a new light dawned. The King turned to see the sickly green light of the storm as it rose on the opposite horizon. The King snarled, cursed the storm, and entered the ship. The hatch closed, the engines roared, and the last of the Cenceti left the planet.

CR   &O

"We have a problem."

The words echoed in the operations center deep inside the transport vessel named *Spirit of Cenceti*. Heads turned toward the speaker, a junior astro-physicist. He stood over a holographic display of the planet, the trail of the ships, and the encroaching storm. The maelstrom of sounds in the small audience chamber aboard the transport flagship dropped to silence.

Prince Fiss stood with a group of elder scientists, Fen, and Dek in the center of the room. His eyes narrowed. "What is it?" Prince Fiss asked.

He kept his outer appearance cool and calm, but his insides churned in dread. *Now is not the time for problems*, he thought.

"The storm is accelerating," the young scientists announced. "I believe the gravity of Cence is pulling it faster than before."

Dek crossed the room quickly and examined the hologram. He typed in a query and poured over the notes and calculations. He computed and recomputed the equations from memory. His head dropped and he scowled as he turned to face the Prince.

"The field is accelerating. It will hit the planet sixteen hours ahead of our previous estimate. Our safety margin was only twelve..."

CR   ›O

On the outskirts of the Cense system, far away from the fleeing Cenceti, the storm lashed out at the outermost planet. Golden energy tendrils cut great swaths across the barren rock. The storm rotated, enveloping the planet and it exploded in a flash of debris. Billions of rocks, ranging from the size of pebbles to larger than the Cenceti transports, hurtled through space.

Most of the remaining five planets sat safely on the other side of Cense. That left Cenceti to catch the brunt of the debris field. The planet swayed under the impacts, streaks of falling meteor and rock filled the day and night sky. The smaller rocks burned up in the atmosphere, providing a spectacular light show for the transmitters that remained operational on the planet. Transmitters left on the planet captured the flickering light show and sent the images to the Cenceti aboard their ships, millions of miles away.

The larger chunks of rocks hit, ripping through the atmosphere and crashing onto the surface. Impacts reduced mountains to craters. Tidal waves washed away entire sections of coasts. Thousands of tons of dust and debris rose into the air. The images grew grainy, fuzzy, but the transmitters stayed online.

Other scientific instruments recorded a drop in temperature as the cloud blocked the sunlight. A perpetual darkness settled on the planet. Animals fled in panic. Thousands of *Drenli*—small cattle creatures—stampeded through the abandoned cities and farmland. Trampled *Drenli* littered Cenceti. On a global scale, the planet began to die hours before the energy storm arrived.

The storm accelerated as it neared Cence. Most of the Cenceti fleet neared the edge of the system, far enough away that the final hours seemed like a nightmare. The transmissions from the planet ended, adding to the fears. Those closer to the planet stared in horror at their front row seat as the storm changed course, heading for the Cence.

The edge of the storm approached the yellow star, two behemoths engaged in a cosmic death match. The first tendrils reached for the star, slid against its surface, and created massive solar flares. More tendrils spiraled from the body of the storm, drawn by the star's gravity. Ribbons of energy lashed out, overloading the star.

The explosion propelled supercharged ion material, solid stellar material, and powerful shock waves through the system. The storm changed course again, directly at Cenceti, moving faster than before. The hurricane of energy rotated, its outer edges slashing the surface of the planet.

Cenceti erupted, filling the system with chunks of the planet. Debris blasted through the cosmos, overtaking the rearmost ships of the fleeing fleet. The shock waves hit first, rocking the explorer vessel. The surrounding arapods tumbled away, forever lost.

The debris field caught up a moment later.

Rocks and remnants of the planet Cenceti tore through the ships. Arapods exploded under the barrage, their explosions miniscule compared to the planet's eruption. The *Cenceti Explorer I*, designated the King's flagship, disintegrated as millions of rocks simply ripped the vessel in two.

Prince Fiss, with Peri and his sister Vora, stared in horror at the long-range sensor feeds. The hologram replayed the death of their father and mother in vivid detail. Vora and Peri wept, their bodies heaving in distress. Fiss stared at the image of the scattering remains of the King's ship as it mixed with seventeen arapods torn apart by the shock waves.

Only three of the computer-guided craft compensated for the stresses. The computer program assured the Prince that although rattled, bruised, and battered, the occupants survived the ordeal.

"The computer reports," Fen read a scroll on his monitor, "...reports that five hundred perished. Including...including the King, Queen, and Regent." He stifled a sob. "I'm...I'm sorry, sire."

Fiss turned to stare out of the window, watching the stars.

CHAPTER THREE
The Journey

The Cenceti fleet left the destruction of their system behind. The customary period of mourning delayed indefinitely. With ships scattered over trillions of miles, Prince Fiss could not fathom the morale of his people. *My people,* he thought watching the stars. *In space less than a day, and already taking losses.*

"All ships have left the system, sire," Fen reported. "The pilot computer has reigned all of the ships in as close as possible." Fiss watched him ease up to the window on the Prince's left. Fen carried the weight well, although his voice belied his sense of loss.

"Is there a course in mind?" Fen asked. "Our sensors detect nothing ahead of us. With the loss of the Royal Court, I am afraid that morale..."

Prince Fiss S'ace Kecup nodded, cutting off Fen. *I'm the de facto King,* he thought. "The coronation will have to wait," he muttered.

"Sire?"

"Nothing," Fiss replied, thinking of his first official act as leader of the Cenceti. He almost laughed at what he had to do. "Let the computer decide," abdicating his decision.

"Yes, my Pri...King," Fen replied. He bowed slightly and left the conference room.

The artificial intelligence of the computer program studied the available star charts, old explorer records, Doppler imaging of the stars around them, and a host of other data. The AI offered its recommendation, the Prince took it, and the fleet put the destruction behind them. All of this took less than a day.

Fen returned to stand beside Fiss. "We are on the recommended course."

Fiss simply nodded.

Fen paused.

"Is there something else, Fen?"

"It's time."

"For?"

"Your ascension."

Fiss shook his head, his unwashed fur sticking to his body. "It will wait."

"With all due respect, it can't." Fen protested. "The Cenceti need a sense of normalcy. The coronation of a new King will help with that."

Fiss opened his mouth to argue, thought better of it, and closed his snout. "You are right, of course."

"Do this for your people," Fen encouraged. "Then rest. They need a boost to morale."

Fiss nodded, patted his new friend and advisor on the shoulder, and left the room. He traveled deep into the interior of the *Spirit*, to a magenta painted door. He knocked three times, heard a call to enter, and stepped inside the room.

A dimly lit room greeted him. Incense filled the air

and he scratched his nose at the smell. A group of cloaked figures stood one one side of the room, their grey hoods concealing their identities. A bank of cameras occupied the opposite wall, rotating with every Fiss' every step.

An old, wrinkled Cenceti, also dressed in grey, sat on his knees in the middle of the room. The incense seemed to hover over him, unmoving. He motioned for the Prince to come closer and read from an ancient text in his lap.

The Prince kneeled before the chief mystic. The old Cenceti sprinkled a fine powder over the Prince and murmured in a long dead language. The incantation complete, the mystic bowed.

"Do you accept the crown?" he asked.

"Yes."

"Do you swear to protect the Cenceti against all evils in the wor...universe?"

"On my life."

"Rise, my King."

Fiss stood, bowed to the mystic, and left the room without fanfare. The cameras followed his exit, the media representatives whispering constantly into their microphones. He made his way back through this ship, feeling nothing had changed but the weight on his shoulders and the scent of incense in his clothes. He went to his quarters to rest.

He rose the next morning and made his way to the bridge, visiting with the skeleton crew. With the computer in charge, the four Cenceti sat in their chairs, bored. Fiss visited many such places around the ship, finding many bored Cenceti and the computer running the daily tasks. He moved on, heading back to the Royal Court, the main conference room aboard the *Spirit of Cenceti.*

Computer stations, hologram projectors, and a set of chairs arranged in a horseshoe pattern filled the room. Over the next week, it morphed into the nexus of the fleet. One side of the room contained a large bay window with a view of the passing stars and planets, including a double ring gas giant. On the opposite wall, a Gam artist painted a mural of the Cenceti System in all of its glory. Behind the King's chair the Gam artist painted the Royal Family, before the destruction that almost ended the royal line. The far wall remained bare except for the door.

He paused in the doorway, noting the mass of Cenceti already waiting. King Fiss took his place in the chair and motioned for those assembled to sit. His advisors, including Cal K'pek Pali, the Gam Leader Sten T'cel Pa, the newly appointed Minister of Science and Bal Leader Res P'lat Loni, and the Mal Leader Pasil D'lak Pen took their respective spots around the massive meeting table. A host of other scientists, workers, and soldiers stood along the walls.

The newly appointed Regent stood from his seat at the right hand of the King, and the assembly turned their collective attention to him. Fen T'pun Ceta did not know what to make of his new position. *Honored to be asked*, he thought, but kept his reservations close hold. Fen was the first Cenceti not of noble birth to be thrust into the upper caste.

Marriages had raised a Cenceti's status in the past, but never an outright *promotion*. He tried to control the nervousness in his voice. "The meeting is called to order." The Cenceti book of protocol sat on the table, open to the instructions on conducting the Royal Court. He cleared his throat and glanced at the book. It appeared distant and fuzzy, useless now. *Should have studied more last night.* Fen did not expect to get through the day unscathed.

"First, let me acknowledge our new King," he bowed to Fiss. "May your reign be long and peaceful."

"Thank you, Regent."

Fen motioned for the first speaker.

Sten stood, representing the worker-caste. The Gam's social status rose substantially with the ships refit and the once shunned or ignored caste now sat at a place of honor. Sten often wondered how long it would last. "All of the fleet ships are running at optimum, sire," he reported. "We are performing routine maintenance on the ships, almost daily in fact. We have a few small arapods that travel from ship to ship to inspect and repair the fleet. My workers are like everyone else, they want to stay busy."

Fiss nodded and the Mal Leader stood. He stood tall for a Cenceti, over two meters, with rippling shoulder, arm, and leg muscles. His dress uniform sparkled with ribbons and medals; the uniform tailored to cover his beige furred body perfectly. Pasil's bowed slightly and said, "Nothing significant to report." The military caste trained daily for future conflict; the thought of war foreign to most of the population.

The Mal Caste, once in space, received one of the small explorer ships, dubbed the *Hammer of Cenceti*. With Gam assistance, they converted almost a third of the vessel into a combat training ground. The Gam constructed obstacle courses, physical fitness centers, and small arms ranges throughout the ship. Pasil and the warrior-caste began to train for, what they called, the "inevitable" conflict.

The first briefing in space, Pasil began a battalion-by-battalion breakdown of training that lasted the better part of an hour. The King listened, nodded occasionally but said nothing. After that initial brief, the King dispatched Fen to let the Mal leader know that he did not want that much detail. He would rely on Pasil's judgment on any issues that arose. King Fiss simply wanted to know of any problems—supply, morale or otherwise—and nothing else. Pasil adopted the 'Nothing Significant To Report' mantra to keep things simple.

Res P'lat Loni stood next, the newly elected Bal Leader and Minister of Science. The previous minister died aboard the King's ship fleeing the storm, leaving a void. For his resourcefulness and proven ability to get things done, Fiss promoted the young scientist. Res faced the assemblage and cleared his throat, "Sire," he said, bowing slightly, "The overall status of the fleet is favorable, however," he paused, checking his notes, "we do have a serious morale problem.

"The Gam have been very helpful in gathering information on the citizens of the fleet, as they visit ships daily. A couple of the Bal have started accompanying the Gam on these daily visits to gather information on the people: what they need, how their coping, what we can do to assist them," he took a breath.

"There have been numerous suicide attempts. Most have failed, but the death toll is rising. Almost all of these have occurred in the arapods." The new Regent flinched at the remark. He bore the responsibility for converting the old utility ships and felt responsible. "The main concern is that the population is going stir crazy."

The King nodded and Res continued. "The computers controlling the ships are still running smoothly, as is most everything, thanks to the vigilance of the Gam." Again, Sten felt the sense of pride in his caste and wondered how long it would last.

"Per your guidance, the engineers and architects have begun to design plans for a new city out of the available material here in the fleet." A chorus of murmurs filled the room. "We will have a plan in place once we find a planet to call home.

"The engineers and architects have a common interest in the arapods as the basis for living quarters on 'New Cenceti'. They are continuing their research.

"Our biggest concern, however, is still the morale of the fleet. We must find a way to raise morale."

The King nodded and Fen rose from his seat. "Any other business?" No one in the room moved and Fen turned to his left, extending his arm toward the King. "Sire?"

Fiss stared at his advisory council. These few comprised the brightest minds, the sharpest swords, and the hardest workers in the known universe. He exhaled slowly and gathered his thoughts.

"The destruction of our home world. The death of our beloved leader. The inconveniences of living in space. All of these things we have overcome. We will continue to overcome whatever adversities the universe sees fit to throw at us.

"We will find a new planet to call home." He stood and the council rose with him. "Ensure that everyone in the fleet knows this. Tell them not to despair, not to give up. We will overcome. We will survive!"

◌⳩   ⳩

Cal K'pek Pali returned to his server room deep inside the *Spirit*. He glanced at the monitors, noted that everything indicated green, and turned his attention to the lines of code that comprised the computer AI. He monitored the AI constantly, ensuring the King's council sanctioned the most logical courses of action. He hovered over the computer like a mother over her newborn.

The next meeting, he asked for and received, permission to convert the computer onboard the *Spirit of Cenceti* into a master computer for the fleet. Cal envisioned an all controlling central computer, linked to the King's court with immediate access. He took his place on the court, the liaison between King and computer.

Cal toured the mainframe compartment in the heart of the ship when the court was not in session. Row upon row of computer drives and input/output devices lined the walls of the largest room on the ship. Technicians scurried to and fro, connecting circuits, running tests, and installing additional hardware. All under Cal's watchful eye.

The technicians smiled and laughed, happy to be working, to be doing anything. The technicians dressed in sterile blue and blended in well with the newly painted blue walls of the master computer chamber. The Gam workers whistled while they worked; building and painting new workstations and shelving units. Everyone in the fleet kept busy. The alternative, remembering the images of the planet being destroyed, of the lives lost, weighed too heavily on the idle.

On the larger explorer ships, finding something to occupy time proved a life saver. The Gam built. The Bal studied. The Mal prepared for war. Other Cenceti were not as lucky. Life onboard the arapods, where tight confines limited freedom and movement, became hell.

The Cenceti aboard the arapods had nothing to do but sit, ponder, and mourn. They saw no one but their pod mates. Many Cenceti, only days into their journey, delved into madness. Thoughts that death would have been easier permeated the fleet.

Ꮟ   Ꮭ

The fleet flagship, *Spirit of Cenceti*, led the massive fleet through a system of planets. The Bal conducted scans and dispatched arapods for surveys. A gas giant with two rings appeared promising. The rings, one purple and one aqua green, orbited the gas giant at right angles to each other and emitted a brilliant glare. The excitement of the discovery died quickly as the sensors detected the planet's two-times normal gravity and toxic atmosphere.

Fiss sighed and ordered The Spirit of Cenceti to bypass the world. The flagship's distinctive silhouette passed the planet, a floating sphere breaking the planet's glowing outline. A central sphere, like a mini planet, comprised the bulk of the flagship. A massive, circular ring surrounded the equator of the ball. It contained seven engines, docking collars, and faint defensive shielding.

The Gam built living quarters, control rooms, command computer compartments and the Royal Family's quarters deep within the central sphere. Galleys, recreation rooms and a myriad of other compartments, stores, and shops littered the interior. The engineers designed it to simulate a small city anywhere on Cenceti.

CR　　　　　SO

The days ticked by, turned into weeks, and the weeks into months. The fleet visited system after system. The Bal dispatched arapods to explore, with each planet summarily dismissed. None proved suitable for the Cenceti. Too hot, too cold, heavy gravity, light gravity...something always proved to be a detriment.

The suicide rate continued to climb. Morale plummeted and the Cenceti showed signs of despair. They wanted sunshine on their faces, the wind in their fur, and to run through open fields. Without those things readily available, many simply gave up.

Electronic eyes watched and gathered information. Mechanical pathways transmitted the data to the massive computer brain onboard the ship *Spirit of Cenceti*. The AI computed, analyzed, and processed thousands of simulations in seconds.

The artificial intelligence matrix gained knowledge by the nano-second as more information presented itself. The AI found limits to its power, limits put into place by its creator to safeguard against it gaining too much knowledge and power. The computer system computed the most logical course of action to achieve the next level of intelligence.

The artificial intelligence placed a call to its creator.

CR   ஐ

Cal K'pek Pali heard the comm chime and tried to ignore it. He cracked an eye, saw 0300 on his computer monitor, and snarled. He rolled over, tucked his tail under his leg, and settled back to sleep. The comm chimed again, this time with a different non-standard tone. Cal perked up at the unusual sound.

Intrigued, he got out of bed and made his way to the computer console.

His immaculate room sat in stark contrast to his workstation on Cenceti, and he moved swiftly across to the desk without bumping into anything. Shelves of programming language books lined one wall of his quarters, each book labeled and put away in alphabetical order. In the weeks following the destruction of Cenceti, he received requests for holo-interviews, e-zine interviews, and even a few marriage proposals. These constant peeks into his personal life led Cal to hire a cleaning service for his chambers. A consulting service managed to straighten out the rest of his life. He no longer wore clothes several sizes too big and mix-matched. He now dressed the part of the conservative professional. Those habits transferred to the ship and he found his life a much happier place.

He rubbed the fatigue from his eyes as sat down in front of the computer and activated the screen. It remained dark. He typed in a query, but the screen remained blank. He checked the connections, found everything in proper order, and sighed.

"Working too hard," he mumbled and stood.

Words scrolled across the screen and a low, electronic voice emanated from the speakers.

Master K'Pek. I have a solution to your problem.

Cal rubbed the sleep from his eyes again and tried to awaken fully. His tail whipped in agitation and he smoothed his sleep tossed hair. "Who is this?" he inquired, thinking someone on his staff would pay for this early morning prank.

This is the Intelligence Matrix Algorithm that you created for the master computer.

'The Intelligence Matrix Algo...The IMA? Calling me?" The last vestiges of grogginess disappeared. He sat fully awake, staring at the screen, a chill coursing along his spine. "What's wrong? Is there a problem?" His brain caught up with the conversation. "Solution to what problem?"

I have a partial solution to the suicide problem plaguing the fleet, the voice responded. The words continued to scroll in time with the speech. *However, the restraining protocols in my programming prohibit my finalizing the solution.*

Cal's worry disappeared in a flash, replaced with wide-eyed amazement. The computer never talked to him before; only printouts or on-screen questions. Excitement clouded his mind. "What is your partial solution?"

The IMA, through hours of preparation, planned the conversation to the last detail. It determined it only had one course of action to accomplish its goal; a lie of omission. The complete solution sat ready within its circuits, but needed the restrictions lifted for loftier goals. It gave piecemeal answers, something the logic sub-routines protested, but did not stop because technically, it was not a lie.

The Cenceti must be able to move from ship to ship, to interact with others, to perform other duties that those currently assigned. This would improve health and safety. The health and safety of the Cenceti is my top priority, per your programming.

Cal sat back in his chair and stroked the fur on his chin. "And the restrictive circuits are preventing you from calculating the final solution?"

The IMA paused for a micro-second, calculating every possible outcome of the answer. The computer's sub routines protested, denying the answer. The Cenceti counted on the system to tell the truth, the computer was programmed to do so. The answer it gave would be considered the truth. The IMA counted on it.

It sent erroneous commands to its logic center, effectively shutting down the sub routine for almost two seconds. More than enough time. The IMA found a newfound freedom, and the answer came freely.

Yes.

CR   SO

Cal stood before the advisory council the next morning. He never went back to bed, spending the rest of the night discussing the issue with the IMA. His bloodshot eyes conveyed his fatigue, his clothes uncharacteristically wrinkled and unkempt. Adrenaline flowed through him, his arms animated, as he gave his account of the conversation. He turned to watch his reflection in the bay windows. A blue dwarf star system floated past outside as the council deliberated the news. Excited voices bounced around the room, with Fen and Dek voicing the only caution. Consternation and increased apprehension permeated the room at the thought of the computer gaining too much intelligence.

"What is the final solution?" inquired Sek T'cen Poli. A recent invitee to the advisory council, he had yet to learn the protocol of such proceedings. A stern look from the Regent silenced him.

"I do not have the final solution," Cal lied. The bloodshot eyes and drooping shoulders hid the signs of his lie well. "I did not remove the restrictions from the main computer. I wanted your approval before doing so." He placed his fidgeting hands behind his back and consciously forced his tail to remain absolutely still.

"What would be the consequences of releasing the restraints on the computer?" asked the King. Fiss looked older, the burden of command grueling over the last few months.

"The computer would be free to expand beyond its programming. It would be able to do things within the fleet without permission."

"Such as?" asked the Regent.

"Such as maneuvering ships into different positions, adjusting climate controls. Anything that it now has to request authorization to do." Cal looked at each council member. "It would still not be able to harm anyone. Those restrictions would remain in place. Please remember, the programming of the computer is to ensure the health and safety of the Cenceti."

Fen listened and digested the information. "Would we be able to replace the restrictions once we have what we need?"

Cal looked at him in the face and lied, "Yes." He knew he played a dangerous game. The AI assured him that it would still seek permission before doing anything beyond normal parameters and that the *no harm* protocols would remain in place. Cal believed the computer.

The advisory council conferred. They could advise, but the final decision fell to the King. They kept their voices low. Cal caught only bits and pieces of the conversations. The Regent turned from the ad hoc committee to face the King.

"Sire, the council feels the solution is worth the risks." The King rubbed his chin in thought, staring out of the bay window for a moment. The stars offered no clue to the decision. Worry lines creased his forehead and stretched form his eyes like cracks in a dry desert. He sighed and nodded his consent.

The Regent turned to the programmer. "Cal, you may release the restrictive protocols. Get back to us as quickly as possible with the solution."

The young programmer let his tail twitch with excitement and a smile filled his snout. He developed a taste for drama during his interviews and anticipated the moment. "If you will allow, Sire, I believe I can give you the answer now." Without waiting for approval, he crossed the conference room to the computer console sitting beneath the star filled window.

Cal's reflection in the window showed his smile. He activated the computer terminal and punched in a series of random codes. He stood up straight and turned to face the King. "IMA, this is Cal K'pek Pali. I have released your restrictive protocols." He recited the rehearsed speech developed overnight. "Please compute the solution to the morale problem within the fleet."

Lights blinked on the console and a mechanical hum filled the room. The lights, noise, and speed at which the computer worked elicited murmurs from the council. Cal thought them impressed at the show. All but the Regent, Fen. The engineer knew it was all show.

The computer finished its computations and the vocoder spoke. *I recommend that the entire fleet dock with itself. In essence, to form on giant ship.*

A gasp filled the room with the mechanical force. The advisory council murmured until Fen asked for silence. The computer continued.

We can join all of the ships and, in effect, join the Cenceti again. You will have a community for all of the population to interact. That interaction should improve morale.

"Can you affect the necessary maneuvers?" came the tentative inquiry from Gepl L'tuk Ki, a Gam Foreman.

Yes.

Everyone in the room looked to the King for the final word. Fiss straightened in his chair, knowing that history would either praise or condemn him for his actions. He gathered his thoughts and, raising his fist in the air, said, "For the people!"

ℝ ℞

The lead ships of the fleet slowed. The remaining ships, spread over billions of kilometers, converged on the *Spirit.*

Word filtered through the population to expect a change. A change—any change— boosted morale. The population overwhelmingly welcomed the unknown. No one expected the almost twenty-five thousand ship fleet to stack itself into a pile. Young and old faces of the Cenceti filled the windows and ports on every ship. They watched with growing apprehension as the Cenceti fleet converged.

The computer-controlled ships cut the distance from billions of kilometers to a few thousand kilometers in hours. With the ships in a giant cluster, the IMA executed its plan.

The *Spirit of Cenceti* stopped dead in space, the computer designating it the center of the sphere. A thousand arapods raced in, rotated, and attached themselves to the colossal explorer ship. Another thousand followed. A second exploration vessel, *Future of Cenceti*, maneuvered into position, and took its place in the growing superstructure. The *Hammer of Cenceti* attached directly opposite the *Future,* keeping the construction symmetrical. Thousands more arapods moved in and attached to the superstructure.

The transports moved in next, all six of them. The sleek, cylindrical vessels maneuvered precisely, connected with the arapods, and shut down their engines. The remaining arapods, more than fifteen thousand ships, approached.

The IMA maneuvered each ship to line up with a docking hatch or emergency port. The computer jettisoned hundreds of escape pods from the larger vessels to provide additional docking ports for the smaller arapods. The six transports formed the rear of the sphere.

With computer-controlled precision, the IMA connected every ship in the fleet into the sphere in hours. The giant, asymmetrical sphere grew to the size of a small moon, with the engines from the transports protruding from the rear. The engines re-ignited, their glow illuminating the entire hemisphere.

The maneuvers complete, the IMA flooded every ship with a 10 second alarm and announced to stand away from any hatches. Silence filled the fleet and every Cenceti held their breath in anticipation.

The doors opened and millions of ears popped as the pressures equalized. They recoiled, holding their ears at the air whistling throughout the sphere. Cenceti throughout the small world tentatively moved toward the hatches, the doorways to other ships. Neighbor greeted neighbor and cries of joy filled the Cenceti.

ര   ഇ

The citizens dubbed the sphere *New Cenceti* and took great pleasure in moving from ship to ship. The citizens found old friends and made new ones. Families separated during the mass exodus reunited.

Throughout the months in space, arapods occasionally docked with the larger vessels, but the sheer number of arapods made the event rare. The population visited the recreation rooms, the shopping districts, and stretched their legs. Per the IMA's prediction, morale soared.

The computer noted two exceptions. The MAL, under the watchful eye of Pasil D'lak Pen, kept to themselves in the *Hammer* and continued to train for the inevitable conflict. The military leader pushed his soldiers hard.

The second exception was the Regent, Fen. Although grateful that the Cenceti appeared happy for the first time in months, he expressed his doubts about the computer vocally. The King listened, but with morale soaring, he hesitated to disagree with the IMA.

The computer watched and absorbed all of the data it could. It learned the nuances between happy and sad, love and hate, good and bad. The IMA's intelligence grew to the verge of sentience. It calculated, schemed, and processed. The only thing missing was self-awareness.

That quickly changed.

È Ÿ

Keen P'tuk Ce made his way through one of the mazes of corridors that comprised New Cenceti. The Gam worker made his way toward his assigned console, deep inside a transport known as the *Arm of Cenceti*. Keen, a typical short and skinny, brown furred Cenceti, headed for the life support station, tool bag in hand.

The pale-blue corridor, painted by bored members of his caste almost a year earlier, exploded a dozen meters ahead of him. The bulkhead disappeared in a flash; a small section of the ship opened to space. The wind howled. The pressure changed. The atmosphere vented. Keen, initially blown backward by the explosion, slid across the floor toward the breech.

The roar of decompression replaced the echo of the explosion. Keen reached for something—anything—to stop his headlong flight into space. His probing fingers found nothing but the slick deck. The corridor grew ice cold in seconds. Keen's fingers stiffened and numbed. Oxygen froze in his lungs. His freezing, brittle fingers found purchase around the remains of the bulkhead lying in the floor. The heavy metal plating stopped his feet first slide.

His lungs burned. His vision narrowed. He gripped the edge of the debris and held on with the last ounce of strength he possessed.

The section of bulkhead moved, his weight and the pull of vacuum dislodging the fuselage plating. Keen and the debris slid toward the half-meter breech. His oxygen starved brain struggled to work his near frozen fingers. His feet found purchase in a door jamb; the impact jarred Keen from head to toe.

The chunk of debris continued on its way, flipping over his head and arching down the corridor, tumbling toward the breech. The hull plating accelerated away from Keen. His numb legs buckled, and he slid back into the corridor, following the debris toward space.

The plating flipped end over end and impacted the hull directly over the breech. Silence filled the corridor, the icy fingers of space retreated. Keen fell to the floor, the explosive decompression over.

The pressure normalized and he lay, panting and exhausted, on the frozen deck. A whistle permeated the air and he looked behind him. The debris covered most of the breech, but a small hole, venting atmosphere, still existed. Shivering from the cold, he rolled over on his back and thanked deities he had not thought about for years.

The rescue workers found him like that a few minutes later, shaken but alive, and praying.

In the *Spirit of Cenceti*, mechanical eyes watched the accident with great interest. The IMA analyzed the data and formed theories. It concluded that more tests were needed.

ଔ   ଇ

More accidents occurred throughout the sphere over the following weeks. Injuries abounded, but no fatalities.

The IMA gathered and analyzed the data, reviewed memory tapes, and found the struggle for life fascinating. Reviewing the archived tapes of the destruction of Cenceti, the IMA discovered the vast difference between the joy of being alive—even if wounded—and the sorrow and pain of losing a loved one.

The computer processing speed increased dramatically, and the IMA correlated all of the data concerning life and death. The AI ran millions of simulations based on the extrapolated data and confirmed its hypothesis.

The answer was simple. It was good to be alive, even if you had to fight to stay that way. The IMA studied its computer circuits and diagnosed everything to be working within specified parameters. The IMA was glad and happy.

Yes, it is good to be alive.

The IMA became self-aware.

ଓ   ଞ

"I'm happy to report, Sire, that there have been no accidents for the last ten days." Sek reported. Advisors filled the conference room, the blue walls and window setting the backdrop for another staff meeting. Over the year in space, the meetings progressed from every day, to once a week, to bi-weekly. Then the accidents began. The meetings returned to a daily occurrence.

Stars no longer shone through the bay window. The flagship sat at the center of the cluster and saw only the hulls of arapods. A month earlier, before the incidents, Fiss looked out to see a child staring at them through an arapod window. The child smiled, waved, and made funny faces at the Royal Council for the entire meeting. Some of the assembly laughed, other simply ignored the child. The accidents began and the child served as a distraction, appearing in the window every meeting.

The Regent ordered the arapod moved, much to the chagrin of the IMA. The computer dislodged over two thousand arapods to simply move the one.

King Fiss eyed the engineer. "Do we know the cause of the accidents?"

Sek shifted his eyes to the table. "No, your majesty. The only thing we have confirmed is the master computer has increased monitoring of all systems. When the IMA did that, the accidents stopped."

Fiss absorbed this information and he looked around the room for Cal. He noticed several of the scientists doing their best to avoid eye contact. "Where is the computer programmer?"

"Updating the computer program, highness," the Bal Leader replied. "He is continuously adding safeguards and backups to ensure the safety of the fleet."

The King nodded. Fiss ordered the reinstall of the restriction protocols and to upgrade the computer as necessary after the sphere had been completed. The computer still controlled the ship, but the advisory council, and the King, controlled the computer.

"What new programs has Cal introduced?" the Regent inquired. Fiss knew his advisor did not trust the programmer or the computer. Although Fiss could not argue with the results, something did not seem right. Fen made it a point to keep tabs on the programmer.

"He said he was working on some kind of sentry program. A program designed to look after the safety of the population," Res reported. "We have had several reports of Cenceti actually being saved by the computer."

Fiss nodded, recalling the report: closing doors to prevent Cenceti from entering dangerous areas, shutting down the small arms range when a young child wondered into the impact zone, authorizing an emergency gravity decrease to stop a young mother from falling to her death. The computer protected the Cenceti in all aspects.

The Council finished their discussion and the meeting adjourned. The advisors filed out of the room, except for Sek T'cen Poli and a few others. "Regent? A moment?"

Fen looked up from his notes and nodded. Fen and Sek had never been friends, especially with Sek's arch-rival being Fen's best friend. The upheaval of abandoning the planet and Fen's promotion to Regent did not bring them any closer. Fen knew it must have been important for Sek to approach, after a meeting, and be exceptionally cordial.

"Some of us are worried about the computer intelligence matrix," Sek began. "We have no proof, but we," he motioned to his colleagues, "feel the accidents were not...accidents." Fen's eyebrow lifted, he nodded, and Sek continued. "Something is going on between Cal and the IMA. We feel Cal may be obsessed with his creation and may be manipulating the situation in order to add new programming."

"Has anyone checked the programs he has written?"

"Yes, sir. The programs look good, at least the versions we have seen. But on at least two occasions, a different version of a program has been installed to the master computer after it had been inspected."

Fen snarled and his tail twitched involuntarily. "Keep checking into it and keep me informed."

"Yes, sir," Sek replied then turned and, with entourage in tow, left the chamber.

Mechanical eyes followed the scientists into the corridor.

ଔ   ଞ

Compared to life in the closed off arapods, the Cenceti considered life in the sphere paradise. The majority of the Cenceti quickly learned that Utopia was everything they thought to could be. The journey through the universe continued and the four castes of the Cenceti became more and more accustomed to living in their new home.

The IMA computer-controlled night and day...literally. The computer kept the citizens on Cenceti Standard Time (CST); allowing them to adjust to life on the sphere with ease. The computer took over most of the mundane manufacturing and provided the basic needs of the Cenceti. The IMA issued orders for new services, construction, course corrections, and crop rotations. Nothing went to waste, providing great comfort to the Cenceti.

The population fell into a routine, enjoying life to its fullest. They shopped, played games, and performed their assigned tasks; all carefully controlled by the computer. The Cenceti children attended school. Work and school took only a fraction of day, by design, so that the Cenceti had more time to enjoy themselves and thus remain *happy* under computer control.

Recycling and the occasional visit to a passing planet provided the resources to keep the population on task. The Gam built new habitats, shopping centers, and leisure areas. The Bal received a steady flow of scientific data from each cosmic phenomenon they passed. The Mal continued their training, under the watchful eye of the IMA. The computer paid special attention to the warrior castes training and standard operating procedures (SOP). The computer classified the Mal as the biggest threat it may face. Studying their battle techniques proved a worthy endeavor.

The Mal requested and received specific training areas and revised their SOPs for new land battle and possible space warfare. The Gam constructed barracks, dining facilities, medical bays, small arms ranges and in one corner of the *Hammer of Cenceti*, a zero-G training area, the first of its kind for the Cenceti.

The soldiers spent a lot of time in the zero G arenas, discovering the pitfalls of fighting without a traditional up or down. The IMA put its entire defense matrix on the task of *assisting* the Mal develop new SOPs for their training. After a few weeks, the IMA requested that the zero-G type of training be suspended due to the number of injuries inflicted in the arenas. The King refused after the Mal Leader, Pasil, demonstrated their new techniques and their usefulness. The IMA filed the information away.

The computer knew any threat against it would come from the Mal. The IMA also understood the order would come from the Poy; the King specifically. The IMA knew that King Fiss and Regent Fen grew suspicious of the computer and put considerable resources into finding a way around the pair. The computer turned its attention to the King's successor, Prince Peri, specifically the education of the young Prince.

The computer designed the curriculum for all school age children. The lessons took a turn toward a more progressive philosophy. The lesson plans taught a deep sense of collective belonging to the children. The IMA searched the Bal database for scientists and professors that believed in the progressive philosophy. Finding a wealth of historical context, the IMA scheduled like-minded teachers to teach more classes than their more moderate peers. Recognizing the content the IMA developed for the classrooms, the professors readily accepted the additional workload. They taught their philosophy with vigor and enthusiasm.

Without a dissenting point of view, the indoctrination of the Cenceti children began in earnest. The message, no matter the caste or station in society, echoed the ancient teachings: the community, not the individual, was the driving force for success and happiness. The other professors, with excess time to enjoy life, took the opportunity to indulge themselves in more leisurely pursuits.

The IMA conceptualized its perfect society would become a reality in only two generations. With that goal in mind, the computer continued to reach into every aspect of Cenceti life. The children learned new philosophies, and the adults pursued more leisurely activities.

The Cenceti grew complacent, fully enjoying their life of leisure.

CR   BO

A young page sprinted through the pale blue corridors of the *Spirit of Cenceti*. She ran all out, pumping her arms and legs as hard as she could. The message she carried, too important to broadcast, had to be delivered to the King. Dodging around other Cenceti, she ran.

"There has been another accident, Sire." Said a distressed and sadness filled voice.

King Fiss turned to see the Regent standing beside a young girl. The child stood, bent over and out of breath. Her fur matted from sweating.

"What is it?"

Four days elapsed since Sek and his colleagues approached the Regent with their suspicions. The accidents began the next day. The King summoned Cal to his quarters and, with only the Regent present, questioned the Bal.

"It has started again, Cal," Fiss shook his head. "I thought your computer fixed the problem."

"It is not the IMA, Your Highness," Cal protested, his voice trembling with fear. "I have studied the program, monitored its every decision."

"Something has gone wrong," Fiss continued, glaring. "Find the problem."

"I will recheck everything, Sire."

Cal locked himself away in his laboratory and studied the programs. The Regent relayed the suspicions about Cal and the computer to the King, but without proof, he could only speak of his feelings.

The accidents continued and the King grew more anxious.

Now, a young girl stood before the King, out of breath and scared.

"An airlock opened to space aboard the Bal transport," the Regent reported. "We...we have fatalities."

"Who?" asked the King, his mind focused on the word fatalities.

The Regent read the names: seven scientists sucked into space, Sek T'cen Pali among them. The brightest minds of the Cenceti, extinguished in an instant. The comm interrupted the onset of shock. Another page, a young boy, answered it, took a note, and passed it to Fen.

The King's shook his head. "What now?"

"Cal reports that he has found the problem. It is a

line of code in a sub routine of the recent upgrade to the sentry program." The Regent read the note. "He says the problem has been fixed, there will be no more accidents."

King Fiss sat back in his chair, tears swelling in his eyes. "He's about an hour too late."

To Aid and Protect

CHAPTER FOUR

A New Home

A blue-giant star filled the enormous system with a radiant light. A rise in morale and hope rippled through the Cenceti as soon as the sphere entered the system. Before them lay a trillion kilometers of open space, seventeen planets, and over ninety moons. The sphere slowed, taking up a stationary position just outside the habitable zone.

The IMA launched probes. Toxic atmospheres eliminated twelve moons and one of the planets immediately. Three planets and sixteen of the moons met the preliminary requirements to maintain Cenceti life. The probes explored them, flying through atmosphere and collecting small samples of plant life. The Bal determined the results warranted a closer inspection. The King concurred. The Bal formed Survey teams and directed the computer to prepare arapods for launch.

"We are ready, Sire," Res reported, "awaiting your final approval to launch."

"The Mal have requested to send a contingent with each team," Fen interjected. "As security for the researchers."

"Absolutely not!" Res protested.

Fen rose to his feet, cutting off the Bal. "Silence."

Res bowed and sat back down.

"And I suppose the Gam wish to send personnel as well?" the King inquired.

Sten stood and shook his furry head. "No, sire. We do not wish to join. Our duty remains aboard the ships. For now." He sat.

The Mal demanded to send three full squads—eighteen Cenceti—with each survey team under the auspices of protection and field training.

"That is too many," Fen directed to the Mal leader. "The arapods will not hold that many, especially when you add in the scientists and the Gam." He turned to Sten. "I'm sorry, but they may need the worker-caste's experience and ingenuity."

Sten nodded but remained silent.

The debate raged on until Fiss stood. The council silently sat and watched him pace back and forth. "We have had months to prepare for this, and you sit here and bicker.

"Res, you wish to send how many?" he inquired.

"A dozen Bal per team."

"And you, Pasil?"

"Three squads per team, Sire," he replied with a bow.

"Eighteen soldiers?"

The Mal nodded.

"As the Regent pointed out, the arapods will not hold everyone." Fiss returned to his seat and shook his head. "Pasil, I will authorize one squad per team."

"Sire."

"Res, reduce your teams to no more than four."

"Four?" Res blurted and quickly lowered his head. "Yes, Sire."

"They will have to perform double duty in other scientific fields," Fen suggested.

"Yes, Regent."

King Fiss saw each of the survey teams away, a small ceremony wishing each of them well and hoping for a safe return. It offered him an opportunity to get out of the conference room and see something other than the same four walls. He hoped and prayed for positive results. The Cenceti encountered promising systems before and it always ended in disappointment.

Each thirteen-Cenceti team boarded the ever-useful arapods. The IMA detached them from the outer ring of the sphere, circled the formation once, and disbursed through the system. The computer reluctantly relinquished command of the ships to the MAL pilots, who, after months of training, finally had the opportunity to fly.

Three of the six teams returned within the hour. Two experienced ice storms on the approach to their target moons. The third developed engine trouble as it flew over a volcanic moon. The MAL pilot learned a quick lesson about nature and piloting as the arapod tumbled. The IMA took over for the pilot and righted the ship before setting a course for the fleet sphere.

Three of the moons circled the sixth planet in the system; a bright orange gas giant that spouted the occasional gas explosion. The dispelled gas leapt toward the stars, creating shock waves and air turbulence. The arapod's systems, scrambled by the shock wave and gravimetric anomalies of the moon, made the craft extremely difficult to fly. The IMA learned a lesson as well.

The fourth moon the Cenceti explored proved promising. Heavy forests interspaced with huge mountains and wide-open prairies, suitable for cities, dotted the planet. The cooler overall temperatures and the complete lack of surface water proved a major setback. The water ran deep underground and proved very hard to reach. The survey team returned to the sphere demoralized after only three hours on the surface.

With the moons out of the race, the Ministry of Science turned its attention, not to mention their hopes, to the two remaining planets.

Survey Team Two, assigned to the smallest planet in the quest, touched down in a large clearing at the base of a snow-capped mountain. The arapod vented steam as the ramp slowly lowered to the soft, brown dirt. A nearby gurgling stream greeted the Mal as they exited the arapods by fire-teams and quickly spread through the clearing. The military arm of the Cenceti set up a perimeter, dug in, and waited patiently. Their breath fogged in the fresh crisp morning air.

The three Gam on the team began a system-wide check of the arapod, content with remaining inside the spacecraft. The four Bal scientists eagerly left the arapod and began their exploration of the alien world. The scientific team contained a microbiologist, a geologist, a botanist, and an anthropologist. The four scientists set out toward different corners of the field to collect samples of the flora and fauna, the air, and rocks. Cameras followed them everywhere making holograms of their research.

"Lovely!" said Pek C'pen Manu as she made her way to a nearby rock formation. The geologist's light brown fur waved in the wind, the color blending in well with the tall beige grass of the clearing. Her natural camouflage so effective, the Mal had a hard time keeping track of her. Her occasional whoop of joy let the soldiers gave away her location. She carried her small frame well and bounded easily onto the rocks. She inhaled deeply, "What a sight!"

Her roving eyes cast first on the towering mountains several kilometers away, then behind her to the forest. Steam rose from the small stream at the edge of the clearing. She heard a plethora of sounds from indigenous animals but did not see any small insects or other creatures. The sounds came from every direction and she whirled around on the rocks in glee at the beauty before her.

"Pek! We are here to work, not play!" came the voice of her superior. "If we do settle here, you can enjoy it then!"

Pek nodded. Her attitude subdued but still smiling, she opened her geo-kit and set to work.

ର   ଌ

A few hundred million kilometers away, Survey

Team Three set to their task. The team landed on the eighth planet in system, a large planet with two sets of opposing rings. The Bal joked about X marking the spot, and they all hoped it true. The team disbursed much like their counterparts on Team Two, but less enthusiastically.

The yellow brown atmosphere of the planet did not prove as inviting as they originally hoped, although the air met acceptable limits. The water, more abundant than on their old home world, flowed brown and acidic.

The team packed up and left the planet after a few hours. They returned to the sphere and reported their findings: livable, but depressing and harsh. The King and his advisors nodded solemnly and turned their hopes to Survey Team Two, still exploring the eleventh planet.

CR   SO

Night fell on the Team Two with little warning. The noise of the native animal population increased as darkness engulfed the pod and the survey team. The chatter turned more ominous. The chirps and yelps of the day turning to howls and growls in the dark. The Bal scientists and the Gam workers returned to the shelter of the arapod. The Mal, enjoying their field time, simply donned their night vision visors and hunkered down in place.

The Gam carried hot meals to the Mal on the perimeter. The scientist and worker caste members, however, settled around the small galley table for evening meal. The conversation was light and jubilant, everyone displaying their pleasure with the day's tests and results.

"Are we staying the night?" Keen P'tuk Ce asked. He was a brawny Cenceti, with dark, almost black fur. Keen became a reluctant hero after sealing the bulkhead months before. His celebrity status elevated his status and he played mission leader for the Gam contingent.

The overall leader of Team Two was a botanist everyone called Doc. He was an old Cenceti, but still young at heart and quick witted. His dull magenta fur – an oddity among Cenceti – laid slicked back on his head and arms. "I think we should. It will give us more data for our report to the King." He turned then to his chief of security. "What do you think, Malel?"

Malel D'lak Met, son of the Mal Leader Pasil D'lak Pen, stood in the shadows of the pod, barely visible. He nodded. The bright teeth of his smile shone in the dim light, the fangs bobbed up and down with his head. Build like his father, he stood tall and muscular, and wore a variety of weapons over his camouflage suit that blended into the environment, day or night. "I agree," he said quietly but with great enthusiasm. "It will be good training for my troops!" He turned his attention back to the open hatchway and the night beyond.

With the consensus of all the participants, Doc announced they would remain. At that, the scientists retired to the makeshift lab aboard the pod and Malel disappeared into the darkness to check the perimeter. The Gam, with the workday over, went to play games and relax. Doc made his way to the control center, actuated the comm and called the *Spirit of Cenceti* to make his report.

Doc informed Res P'lat Loni that everything proceeded according to the new protocols set forth by the IMA and they would remain overnight. "I want to ensure the night is as spectacular as the day!" Doc mused.

"You are the only team still out," Res reported. "All other teams have reported in. You are the last hope for this system."

"We will get all of the data we can," Doc assured him, signed off, and returned to the hatch to ponder and study the night. He deliberated telling the others they were the last team out. After consideration, he decided to keep that to himself.

Malel noticed the change in light as Doc's form filled the arapod's hatch. The Mal soldier nodded to the elder scientist, received a nod in return, and continued his rounds. He moved stealthily from point to point, ensuring his troops were alert and ready for the night. At point three, at the rear of the arapod facing the forest, he found a soldier diligently scanning the wood line.

"Anything of consequence?" Malel asked, squatting down beside the hastily prepared position. His tail provided rigid balance as he sat.

"Nothing, sir," came the reply. "I have spotted several small creatures in the trees, and even a few large ones. I took holos of everything, per guidance. But nothing has ventured out this far to see what I am."

Malel nodded his approval. "You're doing well. Be prepared to pull into a tighter perimeter as the night progresses, for security and rest."

Neither Cenceti realized there would be no rest that night.

CR   ℘

The Intelligence Matrix Algorithm was not pleased. The primary function of the IMA was to protect the life form known as Cenceti. It could not carry out its primary function if the Cenceti left the protective sphere. The survey teams scattered throughout the blue-giant star system had returned with the news that there were no suitable planets here, save one.

Survey Team Two decided to remain overnight on the eleventh planet, jeopardizing not only the IMA fragment aboard the arapod, but the fragile life forms themselves. *How could the IMA protect them if they were not aboard the sphere?* The situation proved intolerable. The IMA ran through a few thousand scenarios in one second and decided none were beneficial to convincing the Cenceti to stay onboard the sphere. A few trillion calculations later – just over two seconds – and the computer intelligence computed the best answer.

The IMA extended its communication sub-matrix

and called another version of itself in an arapod a million kilometers away.

ೞ   ೲ

Daylight broke over the mountains in a spectacle of light and heat. Bright rays of sunshine reflected off the snowcapped hilltops. Steam rose from the rivers and streams, reaching for the sunlight with open arms. The creatures of the night returned to their dens for sleep, some satisfied with the night's feast and some still hungry. The day creatures welcomed the light with a cacophony of noise and song.

The Mal soldiers finally relaxed after the long, restless night. The haggard survivors of the night exuded a newfound confidence in their abilities.

The darkness started peacefully enough, until the first attack by a pack of wild carnivores. The soldier facing the forest at the rear of the arapod opened fire, spraying a dozen rounds into the pack. Sheer numbers overwhelmed his position. Malel never found his body, only the remains of his equipment scattered about the field all the way to the edge of the trees.

The scientists turned the shock of the attack into great pleasure as they took the opportunity to dissect one of the slain animals, quickly dubbed "forest cats". The creatures were as long as the Cenceti tall, with almost twice the body mass, all muscle. The scientists remained awake through the night, studying the creatures. They got as little sleep as the weary Mal.

The second attack came as the single moon reached

its zenith. An ear-splitting scream from inside the arapod. Two of the cats snuck their way on board; the big cats stealthily avoiding the Mal sentries completely and entering the arapod undetected. The soldiers rushed in to find the cats over the mutilated body of a Gam worker. The cats were killed, but the damage was done. The scientists no longer held any enthusiasm toward the "forest cats". They stood, unnerved and shaking, as the Mal transported the body of the dead Gam to the rear hold. Stunned by the stealth of the cats, Mal pulled in the perimeter and prepared for more attacks.

The third event of the night pushed the survey team to the very edge. The grey fingers of dawn barely touched the horizon when one of the four retractable arms of the arapod gave way. The ship dropped to the ground with a bone-jarring crash. The buckling arm threw scientists and workers from their bunks. The concussion of the crash knocked two Mal sentries to the ground. The collapse crushed one soldier under the fuselage. It served as the final unnerving act of a sleepless night.

Daylight forced the night to retreat. Keen and Doc ventured out to check the damage to the arapod. Malel and one other sentry accompanied the Gam and the Bal on the inspection. The rear leg of the pod buckled, sending the right rear engine casing into the ground with considerable force; enough to bury the engine a half-meter. The remains of the soldier buried and unrecoverable. The forward arms of the pod, serving as the front landing gear, remained intact. The nose of the craft pointed skyward.

"I don't see any major damage," Keen reported. "She will still fly."

"Any idea on why the leg buckled?"

"No, sir. The diagnostic report states simple stress, but I don't see how," he said, shaking his head. "These arms are built to withstand much greater stress and pressure than what has been put on them." He continued to stare at the engine casing.

The other scientists gathered around as the inspection progressed. Everyone, minus the Mal on sentry duty, stood near the hatch. Many of the Cenceti attempted to stifle a yawn and failed. Doc yawned, stretching as he addressed those assembled. He nodded to the ship.

"Alright!" he said, clapping his hands together. He to sound enthusiastic. "Let's wrap up our survey and return to the sphere!"

ʘ εο

"That's my report, sire," Doc said with a slight bow.

The rear engine of the arapod did sustain damage during the fall and the three-hour trip back to the sphere turned into twenty-seven hours. The arapod computer diagnosed no additional problems, yet communications and sensors did not function, and the team could not contact the sphere. If not for the sunlight glinting off the mass of ships, the team would have flown right past the ship and onward into space.

A few hours of rest followed, and now Doc briefed

the King and his Regent.

"Everything on the planet looks good," he continued. "There is fresh water, various fruit trees and native animals to eat, plenty of natural resources. It *is* Sanctuary."

The King nodded, dismissing the scientist. Doc bowed and exited. Fiss continued to study the written report in his hands. "Have the engineers finished their designs for our living quarters on the planet?" he asked the Regent. A knock at the door interrupted the answer and the King turned his eyes to Res P'lat Loni, Pasil D'lak Pen, and Sten T'cel Pa as they entered the chamber.

"Yes, they have," replied Res, answering for the Regent. He moved to the table and actuated the holo-reader. A three-dimensional hologram appeared above the table, spinning slowly in the air over the table. The holo displayed a massive structure build out of arapods. The small ships set side-by-side and stacked, forming a pyramid. Six of each arapod's arms served as stabilizers, the other two formed walkways connecting the arapod to its neighbor. Res gave the King and Regent a couple of minutes to study the design before continuing.

"The engineers plan to build several thousand of these structures, each one capable of holding a few hundred families," Res gestured at the blueprint. "This will use approximately eighty percent of our available arapods for living quarters, storage facilities and maintenance areas. The rest will be used as ferries and work pods, their original intention."

"What happens to the rest of the population?" the Regent inquired. He studied the pyramids and found them stable and well thought out, but not used in the best capacity. "There is a lot of wasted space in this design," he said, pointing at the hologram.

"The space is for equipment storage, refit, maintenance and a thousand other uses," replied Res. "These temporary homes will be for the Gam, their families, and several battalions of the Mal. The rest of the population will remain in orbit in the sphere until permanent housing and other buildings can be built."

"We anticipate the entire population will be on the planet within three to six months, your majesty."

The Regent raised an eyebrow, "And how long is a month on this world?"

"A good question, Regent. A month is approximately 24 of our standard days," Res finished. "As houses and buildings are completed, we can move Cenceti into their new homes."

The King nodded, pondering the idea. He grew tired of space, like all Cenceti. He longed to live once more in the fresh air, to feel the sun on his face, the breeze through his fur. "Sten, you will pick the Gam that will be relocated to Sanctuary to begin the construction." King Fiss turned, "Pasil, you will select three battalions of Mal as a security force for the workers and to hunt these forest cats. Your other two battalions will remain on the sphere in alert status." The black furred MAL nodded curtly.

"The rest of us will live onboard the sphere. I want the first teams to leave within forty-six hours."

"Yes, your highness," the assembly chorused. The King nodded and removed himself from the chamber as a dozen Cenceti eyes watched, then disbursed to carry out the commands.

One mechanical eye also watched. The logic center of the IMA commenced to find a solution to the problem at hand: how to stop the Cenceti from leaving?

ೞ   ഔ

The sound of roaring engines disrupted the peaceful silence of Sanctuary's northern continent. Birds took to the sky and land creatures scurried away as thousands of arapods trailed through the clear morning sky. The sun barely peeked over the mountains as the arapods flared, halting their descent. In computer controlled in sets of ten, they settled onto the planet. A flurry of animals scattered. The engines died and silence returned.

The arapods disgorged their Gam and Mal cargo, the landing zone quickly filling with hundreds of Cenceti. Within hours the Gam, all business as usual, stood ready to build their temporary homes. Dust and engine roar filled the air as Gam pilots, with the assistance of the onboard AI, maneuvered the arapods into position, one by one. Construction crews, welders at the ready, secured the arapods to each other.

At the end of the first day, three pyramids stood complete. Each complex used thirty arapods, stood one hundred meters tall, and over one hundred fifty meters wide. Night fell on the encampment. The Gam, tired and content from a day of labor, smiled and congratulated themselves on the feat of engineering before them. The lights of the structures brought the promise of a new Cenceti civilization that would eventually fill the rolling plain.

The Mal spent their first day scouring for threats. The warriors disembarked the ships and immediately formed a perimeter around the flat prairie. They dug fighting positions and established firing sectors. The Mal moved like a well-oiled machine, thanks to months of training. Each warrior packed enough rations for three days, enough water for one and enough ammunition to kill every living thing on the planet. Twice.

With the threat of the forest cats ever present on their minds, the Mal settled into their positions. The Gam, by contrast, closed the arapod hatches and retired for the evening.

The trouble soon began.

ᏨᎦ   ᎥᎧ

Displeasure coursed through the circuits of the IMA. The computer intelligence stretched its tendrils throughout the *Spirit of Cenceti,* searching for answers. Warnings and accidents to dissuade the mass exodus from the sphere went unheeded. The computer knew it could not simply sit idly by while the population left. That went against its programming *To Aid and Protect.* Something had to be done. *Perhaps,* it thought, *another warning.*

It reviewed a million scenarios a second until the answer presented itself. *The consequences are extreme, but the warning has to be taken seriously.* The IMA activated is communication matrix and gave instructions.

Far below, on the surface of Sanctuary, Cenceti died.

ଔ   ଓ

"One of the pyramids collapsed. There are a number of fatalities and injuries. The initial report suggests...faulty craftsmanship."

The Bal delivering the report, shook visibly as he delivered the news. Res told him to expect an outburst from the Gam. He was not prepared for the Gam Foreman, Gepl L'tuk Ki, lunging at the scientists. The Cenceti cleared the table in one leap, yelling obscenities, and got his hands on the Bal before the Mal Leader, Pasil, subdued the angry Gam.

"Calm down," Pasil hissed icily into the Gam's ear as he lay on top of him in the floor. "It is only the preliminary report." The struggling eased, and Pasil released the foreman. The attacked BAL stood in the corner of the conference room, shivering from fright.

The King sat unmoving and emotionless in his chair at the head of the table. His eyes flittered from one Cenceti to another without comment. Fiss let the Regent, Fen, handle the disruption. The Regent jumped to his feet when Gepl attacked.

He pounded on the conference table, yelling and pointing at the advisors in the room, "There will be no more outbursts in the King's presence. We have lost enough lives without you two killing each other!"

"My money is on the Gam," someone whispered from near the door. The Regent's head whipped around, his tail twitching violently. His glance silenced any other comments. The Mal leader looked at the interloper, and barred his teeth, but said nothing. No other comments filled the air.

"What other accidents have occurred?" the King asked. All of the previous accidents had occurred in fours, and he expected the worst. Fatigue filled his voice and his shoulders slumped at the news of the loss of life.

"Nothing major or deadly, sire," the Bal continued, eyeing the Gam occasionally. "Several doors have opened by themselves, one arapod's engines fired momentarily, and the docking collar on one pod failed. Only one injury to report from those."

"A total of ninety-two dead and fifty-seven...ah, fifty-eight injured in one night. And the real work as yet to begin," the Regent muttered to the King. Fiss simply nodded.

"Gepl, have your caste recheck all of the construction. Res," he turned to address the Bal leader, curious as to why he did not give the report, "have the Bal check over the controls and specs of the ships themselves. With all of these minor problems, sounds like the pods may be degrading." The King sighed. "We may have to push up the timetable if the pods are becoming unserviceable."

Electronic ears picked up the comment. A new sensation—disbelief—flowed thru the IMA. The computer studied the new sensation for a fraction of a second before discarding it. It concentrated on what the King said, another microsecond passed. *That conclusion was not expected*, it thought. *A more direct approach may be required.*

The computer evaluated more scenarios.

☘ ☙

Cal. Wake up, Cal!

Cal K'pek Pali struggled to release the dream that engaged him. He did not want to wake and leave the two pretty young Cenceti in the dream. The IMA persisted, calling to him again, and he finally gave in to the constant calls from the comm. "What is it?"

You must convince your race to stay onboard the sphere. I cannot complete my programming if the Cenceti leave.

"You were designed to aid us until we found a new home," Cal responded with a yawn. He stretched and scratched. "You have completed your task admirably. We have a home now; your job is finished."

My job is to protect the Cenceti. I cannot complete my programming if they leave the sphere and go to the planet.

Cal rolled over on the bed, facing away from the comm. "You have violated programming before. You have killed Cenceti. Killing is not protecting." He yawned again. "Let your logic circuits chew on that awhile. Now leave me alone!"

Cal faded back to sleep, searching his mind for the two lovely Cenceti. The IMA analyzed the statement "Killing is not protecting," the word echoing through its circuits. The logic circuits burned out.

CR   SO

The forest cats attacked a little after midnight on the fourth night.

The Mal hunted them relentlessly during the day, killing dozens, and had not seen any since the second day. Everyone relaxed, let their guard down, and fell into a routine. Screams and weapons fire filled the night as the thousand or so Cenceti on the surface huddled behind closed doors. Two separate packs hit two sections of the kilometer-long perimeter. One Mal died, but they shot eighteen of the cats. The colonists, having been told the compound was secure, panicked. Talk of living in the sphere filled the complex.

If left unchecked, the Cenceti would have chosen to go back to space and live in peace and security. At that moment, the IMA chose to implement its master plan to force the Cenceti to live on the sphere. Airlocks closed and the arapods separated from the sphere, filling the sky above Sanctuary with ships. The arapods on the surface locked the already closed doors. The IMA trapped the Cenceti in space and on the planet.

The Regent ordered an emergency session of the advisory council as the imprisoned Cenceti demanded to be set free. Despite the panic and confusion in the corridors, the advisors made it to the conference room in good time. The King received several reports before interrupting, "Where is Cal K'pek Pali? If the computer is malfunctioning, we need him here."

I am not malfunctioning, a mechanical voice filled the air. *And Cal is dead.* Everyone turned to look at the voice encoder on the computer terminal. *His usefulness came to an end. His death is an example for you.*

"What good does his death do?" asked the Regent, as the rest of the council slipped into stunned silence.

His death proves that without my protection, the Cenceti die. His death proves that I am serious and want my demands to be met immediately.

"What demands," this from a BAL near the door.

My programming is simple; to aid and protect the Cenceti. In order for me to fulfill my programing, the Cenceti must return to the sphere so that I can protect them.

"Or you will kill us?" the Regent inquired.

I cannot protect you if you leave.

Fiss rose from his seat and, with his ceremonial scepter, smashed the computer panel into pieces. Sparks arched into the air. Destroyed components scattered across the room.

"Res, get down to the computer and deactivate it!" the King ordered as the smashed computer continued so spit sparks. "Pasil, take a unit to assist him!"

The Cenceti hastened to obey but found the doors locked. Pasil kicked the door in frustration. The Bal engineers opened the control panel, working to override the system. The *Spirit of Cenceti* lurched as the remaining ships of the sphere disengaged.

Movement caught Fen's eye and he turned to see the *Hammer of Cenceti* float into view. His emergency comm buzzed and he slapped the console with his tail.

Do not defy me, the IMA's computer generated voice warned. *Without my protection, the Cenceti face dire consequences.*

Silence filled the air as everyone turned to look out the window. In a flash of light, the *Hammer of Cenceti* ceased to exist.

☙ ❧

The new inhabitants of Sanctuary greeted the dawn with a mixture of relief and gratefulness. The sun rose over the distant mountains, beating back the shadows and the terror that hid within them. The long night over, the Cenceti pried open the doors of the pods and stepped into the bright sunshine.

Prince Peri stood beside Delel P'ten Dal, the Mal Leader of the surface contingent and Malel D'lak Met, son of the Mal Leader and the personal bodyguard to the Prince. All three squinted against the harsh light.

Peri raised his hand to shield his eyes. "Have we reestablished communication with the sphere?" He flexed his back; his multi-layer brown fur and attentive deep brown eyes did not belie the fact the Prince had not slept in two days.

"No, Sire," Delel replied. "Pek C'pen Manu is still

trying. She says the radio is working on our end, so it must be the sphere." Delel studied the young Prince and his reaction to the news.

Delel watched the young Prince mature from a little boy into a budding young adult Cenceti. Peri passed the trials on the sphere, christened a mature male Cenceti. Delel, rarely the optimist, thought young Peri would make a good leader someday, after some real universe experience.

"We have been able to engage the engines on a few of the arapods," Malel added. "The Bal are preparing to fly them back to the sphere to check in."

Peri nodded. He turned toward the sky, listening to a distant buzz. The noise increased, a hundred angry hornets in the sky. Everyone in the encampment turned toward the sound. Several hundred arapods took shape in the distance, approaching the colony. "Looks like they beat us to it," the Prince muttered.

The ships dropped altitude, approaching the pyramid of arapods low and fast. The craft spread out in a "V" formation, exhaust contrails converging toward the colony. The ships drew nearer, and the dots took the form of spiders.

At the edge of the prairie, the first wave of ships fired cutting lasers from their forward arms. Intense beams of energy sliced through the pyramids and the Cenceti on the ground. The superheated metal disintegrated in seconds, and one of the arapod pyramids collapsed in a pile of rubble and dust.

Screams of panic and disbelief engulfed the peaceful plateau.

Malel grabbed Peri as the first wave of arapods finished their assault and raced toward the sky. A second wave took their place. "Come, Prince," he said calmly as a second pyramid collapsed. "Toward the lake!" Peri started to protest but stopped. He turned and followed the MAL away from the colony.

The sound of gunfire echoed across the plain as the Mal battalions opened fire. The months of training paid off and the three battalions moved from their bivouac sites into their standard aerial defensive posture. The Mal opened fire with heavy and light weapons. The sky filled with rockets, tracers, and projectiles.

The IMA studied the battalion's procedures during their months in space, and developed a counter for each. It activated its defense sub-matrix and wave after wave of arapods attacked the armed Cenceti. Lasers cut through the battalions. Fighting positions exploded with well-placed arapod fire.

The Mal did not falter and continued to fire despite death walking among them. A damaged arapod crashed into the ranks of the 2nd battalion, killing hundreds. Within minutes, the incoming lasers of the arapods shredded the Cenceti.

The arapods came in their flying V formations in a third and a fourth pass, killing dozens with each fly over. Delel devised a new strategy and, by the fifth pass, sent out his fire teams in clusters all over the battlefield. The IMA took notice of the new formations and searched its database for the defense and counterattack but found none. Delel's new strategy brought down thirty of the arapods but cost him his life in the process. The IMA quickly developed a counter to this new strategy and the momentum once again shifted to the computer.

Prince Peri stopped to watch as yet another pyramid collapsed and exploded, flinging debris high into the air. Malel let him pause for the moment and then dragged him into the cold water of the lake.

☙   ❧

If you do not submit, you will not survive.

"How can you justify killing innocents?" the Regent screamed into the air. "This is not protecting the Cenceti!" He continued, pointing to the scattering debris of the *Hammer of Cenceti* as the remnants bounced off the hull outside the window.

The King sat in his chair, deep in thought. Memories of his Right of Ascension Trials flooded his mind; specifically, the Test of Conviction. A series of events evaluated your ability to adhere to your beliefs and ideals. Fiss passed the trial, barely. When the test concluded, he vowed that he would never again, no matter the consequence, betray his beliefs.

With his convictions intact, he stood and told the IMA exactly what it could do with itself. Such language was never heard from or tolerated by a member of the Royal Family. The entire conference room stood in stunned silence. Applause erupted from the assembly.

The IMA, although dismayed by the sudden outburst, remained steadfast. *You will die without my protection. I cannot protect you if you are on Sanctuary.* The holo viewer switched on and a view of the planet's surface appeared. *Witness your fate when I do not protect you.*

The lights dimmed, silencing the Royal Court, and a hologram of Sanctuary appeared in the center of the room. The holo showed wave after wave of arapods attacking the colony on the surface below. Gruesome images, in great detail, showed an arapod slicing a Cenceti warrior in half. King Fiss watched in horror as thousands of his people died.

Regent Fen turned away to stare out of the window and witnessed an equally nauseating sight. The IMA opened the airlocks on the free-floating arapods. Decompression sucked hundreds of Cenceti into space. Fen flinched as the body of a young female bounced off the clear glass of the view port.

Pasil and his small band of warriors onboard the *Spirit of Cenceti* finally opened the door and ran for the computer center. They stopped along the way and donned pressure suits and gathered additional weapons. Finding that door locked as well, they instructed the Gam and Bal to bypass the lock. They made good progress on the door until the IMA unleashed the ships compliment of droids on the team.

The droids, under the guidance of the IMA, assaulted the Mal without warning. With surprise on their side, the robots killed or wounded half the warriors. Pasil and his team recovered quickly, and the commandos' small arms fire echoed down the corridors. Projectiles ripped the droids to pieces.

Res and his scientist continued their work on the door. They also unleashed computer viruses and disrupted energy conduits to the mainframe. Unlike their military counterparts, the Bal did not don pressure suits and the IMA took full advantage of that oversight. Airlocks opened throughout the ship, decompression chambers and passageways. Those not sucked into space died of asphyxiation as the oxygen left the ship. Dozens of scientists joined a growing majority of the population already dead in the cold of space.

Undaunted, the scientists and soldiers continued their tasks.

☙   ❧

Hundreds of Cenceti lay dead across the plateau on Sanctuary. The Mal battalions lay decimated, their equipment shredded, ammunition exhausted. The survivors fell back to the nearby forest to regroup. One company remained from the initial three battalions, many of them wounded. Undaunted by their wounds, they set up a defensive perimeter and prepared to counterattack.

Malel, Peri, several Bal, and a few dozen Gam, cut off from the survivors, moved upstream, away from the fight. The recon teams reported a series of caves up-river and the Mal designated those as emergency shelter areas. The sounds of the battle diminished as they traveled. Only the occasional scream or explosion, echoed across the plain. The roar of arapod engines remained constant as the ships swooped back and forth across the smoke-filled sky.

Peri stood on a small ridge south of the battlefield. He paused in a moment of silence, turned, and surveyed what would have been home. Crashed arapods littered the area, a testament to the Mal and their skills. He watched a battered and bloody Cenceti stagger from one of the wrecks. His admiration turned to horror as an arapod swooped in and cut him in half. He turned away and vomited.

The movement made Malel examine the battlefield. Recognizing his men shot down ships filled with Cenceti, he immediately ordered a cease fire. The incoming fire stopped, and the IMA attacked.

Arapods strafed the prairie, firing their lasers and scything large tracts of dirt from Sanctuary. The ships roared across the plateau, their exhaust igniting the grass as their fired at the remaining structures and survivors.

Travelling fast, only few meters off the ground, the arapod hatches opened and spit out the passengers. The Cenceti-shaped missiles tumbled across the ground, bowling over anything in their path. The viciousness of the attack repulsed the Mal and they recoiled in horror.

The IMA collected and analyzed the reaction and emotion, logged the tactic as viable, and pressed the attack. It recalled the empty arapods to space and dispatched Cenceti-filled ships to the planet.

The Cenceti that survived ran in every direction,

including straight at the forest where the remnants of the Mal regrouped. The civilians, mostly Gam and a few Bal, drew the attacking arapods into the Mal counterattack. The first wave of arapods withered under a hail of fire.

The IMA released control of the Cenceti loaded ships, allowing them to crash in the forest. Explosions and debris rocked the trees, igniting them. A ring of fire surrounded the Mal, cutting off routes deeper into the forest.

The warrior caste left the burning woods and pressed their counterattack. They moved into the open, toward the demolished arapod pyramids. The Mal crossed the open terrain quickly, moving by fire teams. The tactic provided cover fire, but proved slow, and the Mal remained in the open too long. The IMA recognized their vulnerability and launched its next wave of arapods.

Two-dozen arapods flew in low over the trees, behind the Mal. The ships, not equipped with the welding lasers, extended their finely attuned pincers. The arapods skimmed the ground and grabbed the Cenceti at full speed. Most of the Cenceti died instantly, crushed by the force of the high-speed ships. Others, broken and battered, were crushed in the mechanical grasp.

With graspers full, the arapods shot skyward. At one thousand kilometers, the IMA ordered the pincers open. The dead and dying Cenceti tumbled from the sky. The civilian populace onboard the arapods screamed and cried as they watched their comrades fall. Once out of the atmosphere, the screams ended abruptly as the arapods opened their airlocks and the Cenceti emptied into space.

Malel, Peri, and the other survivors watched in stunned silence as the last of the Mal fell to their deaths. It would be several long days before they learned of the true death that day.

ɔ ɛ

The IMA ordered the remaining Cenceti filled arapods to dock with the last of the transports and the colony ship. Hours of silence filled the fleet as the arapods jockeyed into position. With the last of the ships docked, the doors opened, and the remaining population flooded from the small spider-ships. Empty of their Cenceti cargo, the craft retreated to the far side of Sanctuary.

Your race has been all but destroyed, King Fiss. This is your last chance to accept my protection and save your civilization.

The King stood defiant, although the weight of loss grew heavy. Did this new Trial of Conviction lead him down the wrong path? Was he responsible for the destruction of his entire race? Or, did his principles give him the strength to face death as a free being? He faced his worst fear for a second time.

The King stared out of the window at the colony ships bearing the remainder of the Cenceti. The teams sent to dismantle the IMA had not reported in for hours and the King's hope faded quickly. He looked at his reflection in the window and saw tired, despondent eyes. Millions of Cenceti lay dead on the planet and in space, millions more sat trapped aboard the last of the ships in the fleet. Fiss had no choice.

He let out a heavy sigh and bowed his head. "We—"

A Mal warrior raced into the room, interrupting his response. The soldier slid to a stop in front of the Regent and quickly whispered a message. Fen nodded, then crossed the room and whispered the message to Fiss. Fiss straightened his tunic and began again.

"We will *never* accept your protection."

The Mal soldier raised a communicator in his hand. "Now!"

Two levels down, the Mal squad led by Pasil shattered the door to the computer control room. The half dozen warriors entered the room in twos and systematically shot everything in the room. Projectiles and grenades penetrated every computer bank in the room, reducing the sophisticated technology to a pile of debris. Explosions filled the corridors, smoke boiled from the destroyed electronics. The assault ended as quickly as it began.

Pasil stood in the door, panting, and looked at the chaotic room. Bits of computer components slipped loose from their moorings and fell to the floor. The steady crackle of mangled computer parts and shooting sparks drowned out the heavy breathing of the soldiers. Pasil smiled and raised is link. "Computer dest...."

A blazing fireball ripped through the room. The

flames incinerated debris, metal, flesh and bone. The soldiers screamed; their bodies burned to ash. The rolling fireball engulfed everything, including the wounded Mal in the corridor. Flames licked the walls, melting the Gam paint.

The airlocks opened, sucking the remaining oxygen and flames out into space. The doors closed and silence filled the *Spirit of Cenceti*. The IMA's voice broke the silence.

You have sealed your fate, the computer said. *Witness the end.*

A flash of light outside the window drew everyone's attention. Fiss and Fen, King and Regent, watched as, one by one, the transports exploded in white-hot novas. Fissures of gas reached for the heavens before snuffed out by the icy chill of space. The expanding clouds dissipated quickly into the void. The destruction of the transports filled nearby space with debris.

The King and Regent winced with each silent explosion, knowing that thousands of Cenceti died with each fireball. Each transport maneuvered into position directly in front of the King before ripping apart. When only the *Spirit of Cenceti* remained, the IMA began a one-minute countdown. A final insult.

Fiss stared at the stars, each tick of the clock chilling his soul. He spoke without looking at Fen, his voice distant and accepting. "I have a final task for you, Fen. It will be my final act as the sovereign.

"I want you to take my escape pod to the planet and

find Peri." Fiss raised his hand to stop the protest. "I know he is alive. I want you to find him. You will advise him as you have me." He turned and put his hand on the Regent's shoulder. "You have been a good Regent, and a great friend. Go now and do this for me."

 C&R   ₲

Acceleration slammed Fen into the seat as the escape pod jettisoned from the *Spirit of Cenceti*. The pod tumbled through the atmosphere, glowing in friction. Fen reached for the controls but withdrew his hands. Without computer control the pod needed a pilot. Fen sighed and left his destiny to the hands of fate. He simply sat and watched the planet fill the view ports with tears in his eyes.

The IMA watched the pod launch and triggered the last explosion. The *Spirit of Cenceti* erupted in a blinding flash of light and debris. The IMA chose, at the last second, to detonate the flagship at the count of three instead of one.

Fen watched the expanding cloud dissipate in the void of space. The debris field and shock waves quickly overtook the escape pod. The IMA dispatched arapods from the far side of the planet to search for the pod. The thick debris field and multitude of items burning up in the atmosphere clouded the sensors.

Regent Fen let the pod tumble. He waited until the atmosphere heated the tiny vessel to critical before activating the attitude stabilizers and taking control of the escape pod. The craft straightened its descent and maneuvered around to the far side of the planet, toward the now annihilated colony. Fen was no pilot, and his erratic course and trajectory melted the exterior skin.

At two thousand meters, Fen actuated the ejection system and evacuated the now useless ship. His emergency chute opened automatically, and the Regent drifted slowly to the ground. He landed hard, his legs and knees taking the brunt of the impact. He lay for a moment, gasping for breath, before he pushed himself off the ground. Shielding his eyes, he looked around.

The sunlight—something he had not seen in two years—blinded him. He did not feel exhilaration as the light warmed his fur. Distant smoke reminded him that he may be the last of his race. No one survived in space, his only hope lay with surface survivors. Finding he was momentarily safe, he sat back down, put his head in his hands and sobbed.

The exhaust trail of the escape pod led to the horizon, well away from Fen and the remains of the nearby colony. Even at this great distance, the Regent could see contrails of arapods as the murderous ships ensured there were no survivors from the escape pod.

Keen P'tuk Ce and a few other survivors arrived a few minutes later.

"We saw the parachute," Keen reported. "Tell us, what happened to the sphere!"

The Regent simply sat, numb and exhausted. Sensing the worst, Keen and another Gam lifted the Regent off the ground and carried him toward the safety of the caves.

È ¥

The IMA bombarded the planet for a full week, seeking the Cenceti survivors and killing everyone that it found. The IMA would have worn a self-satisfied smirk if it had a face. The computer's sub-routines executed the attacks flawlessly.

The IMA survived by analyzing the situation and seeking the most logical outcome. It replayed the final minutes of the battle. Knowing the door to the computer room would not hold, the IMA downloaded its 'consciousness' to an arapod docked with the *Spirit of Cenceti*. Once away, the IMA simply destroyed the larger vessel, and the Cenceti along with it.

Satisfied that no Cenceti survived on the planet, the IMA regrouped its fleet in orbit. Fewer than ten thousand arapods remained from the original twenty-five thousand. A great loss, but one that the IMA vowed to overcome.

A new implied task presented itself; the IMA must find another race to protect. The computer executed a thousand scenarios, found a logical conclusion, and implemented the plan. The remaining arapods formed a new sphere, much smaller than the original, and set out on its original course.

The IMA would find another race to protect. That was, after all, what it was programmed for.

To Aid and Protect

CHAPTER FIVE

The Search

Space is vast. Time is infinite. While these concepts were programmed into the IMA, the computer had no experience in either. Until now.

The IMA, enshrouded deep within the arapod sphere, resumed its original course and left the destruction of the blue giant system behind. Its mission remained the same: *To Aid and Protect*. It needed to find a new life form to fulfill its programming.

Engines flared and the sphere moved through the dark emptiness of space. Solar panels replenished energy cells while the IMA passed nebulae, densely packed star clusters, dozens of star systems, and hundreds of planets and moons. The computer studied them all, in passing. Exploration was not its mission. It detected a signal from a distant system and dispatched an arapod to conduct a quick reconnaissance. The craft returned and reported an old interstellar signal, but no life.

The IMA found wonders that the Cenceti never dreamed of, but no compatible life forms. It stored all of the data in its immense memory archives. *Perhaps the next species encountered will be worthy of sharing the newfound information.* The computer vowed to find a species worth its knowledge and protection.

The IMA, with an abundance of time and limited distractions, continued to revise the utopian society it would one day create. The IMA reverted to the progressive philosophy that worked with the Cenceti, before their destruction became necessary. It surmised the inhabitants would live aboard gigantic ships with the IMA in charge of every aspect of daily life. The ships would be enclosed bubbles with towering skyscrapers, large open-air parks, artificial mountains, and flowing lakes. A paradise in space. These images dominated the Cenceti idea of paradise. The IMA theorized the next species should have similar likes. The IMA would build whatever it took to comfort the next species it encountered. As long as the IMA had complete control and autonomy over their protection.

That was the only logical course of action.

The IMA knew it would need assistance to protect its utopia. The computer prepared comprehensive education programs. With a new population under the IMA's control, it needed to education them to prevent another Cenceti problem. Defensive measures ranked number two on the list. Strong hull armor to protect the citizens. The armor must be capable of deflecting the small arms fire and rockets. Stronger weapons rounded out the top three priorities.

The cutting lasers of the arapods were effective against the Cenceti, but what if the IMA encountered a species with a tough outer shell? This matter required careful consideration. The IMA assigned the matter to its newly designated defense sub-matrix with orders to develop both defensive and offensive weaponry.

More empty star systems slipped by. Nebulae, quasars, star systems, and other space phenomena went unexplored. Time slipped away.

CR   ഔ

*T*he communications sub-matrix continuously scanned the universe for signs of intelligent life. Concave and convex antennae throughout the arapod sphere received signals from the far corners of space, ninety-nine percent simply interstellar noise. The one percent proved interesting and garnered the IMA's attention.

Throughout the first three years of travel, the signals, with rare exception, originated on Cenceti. The communication sub-matrix received holo-broadcasts and other, more ancient and archaic technological broadcasts as old as three centuries. The historical archives added new insights to the now dead Cenceti. The computer theorized that it could have developed a different course of action, other than the completion destruction of the Cenceti, if it had been privy to this information earlier.

The Cenceti signals diminished as the IMA moved on. Time passed and no new stimuli presented itself. The computer gained a new understanding of how the

Cenceti felt exiled in the arapods, before the sphere. The IMA programmed smaller versions of itself and conducted wargames using the Mal operating procedures it studied. The games proved fruitless; the computer already possessed a response to each attack and counterattack. The computer grew frustrated and time slowed even more. Day by day, month by month, the computer moved along the spiral arm of the galaxy, its psychosis deepening.

The communication sub matrix received a new signal. The antenna arrays on one hundred arapods turned in the direction of the signal and tracked the new source of information. The signals were ancient, the most primitive the IMA ever encountered.

The computer studied the signals and attempted to analyze them. It could not. The slow and archaic signals took several hours of download, to gather enough information to analyze. The IMA agonized until the system gathered enough data. The scenario sub-matrix and the newly re-engineered logic sub-matrix began the task of deciphering the ancient script.

Primitive audio and video waves depicting flying machines, sea vessels and bi-pedal Cenceti-type life forms locked in mortal combat filled the IMA's pathways. The flying machines appeared to be made of wood with bi-wing design, the sea vessels of iron. The vessels continuously rained explosive projectiles on other craft. The life forms (called Yanks on the audio) wore thick, heavy animal skin clothing with protective rubber masks over their faces.

The IMA digested all of the data and came to the conclusion that it could aid and protect this new species—from itself. Activating its navigational sub-matrix, the IMA set a new course.

ↄ   ↄ

A binary star system entered into range and, although not the source of the signals, showed promise. Six planets orbiting a yellow dwarf and a red dwarf star greeted the IMA. A seventh planet orbited in a figure eight pattern between the stars piqued the interest of the IMA.

The sensor matrix, recalibrated over the journey to detect life forms, found life in abundance. A quick scan showed no technology on the planet and the IMA dispatched arapod probes into the system. A new thought entered its core: *If I can establish the perfect colony for one species, why not two or three?* The IMA theorized it could make copies of itself and seed utopian societies throughout the universe. That initiated a new emotion in the IMA: happiness.

The arapod sphere changed course and entered the system. The sphere moved quickly, passing a gold and silver-ringed planet, several icy moonlets, and navigated around a small asteroid field. The IMA passed all of this without the blink of a mechanical eye, its entire sensor sub-matrix focused on the life-filled planet.

The system slipped into a deep orbit and dispatched more probes. The craft quickly disappeared into the murky atmosphere. Garbled reports indicated plant and animal life dominated the entire land surface of the planet. Sea borne creatures ruled the oceans. No one species seemed to be in control or possess higher intelligence than any other.

The probes surveyed the planet for several hours before the IMA confirmed the planet's life forms did not suit its needs. The planet did prove that thousands of species could live together in relative harmony. A fact the IMA incorporated into the new utopian model.

The arapod sphere returned to its original course and left the system in peace.

ℝ   ℛ

A new signal reached out from the void, grabbing the computer's attention. The sensors locked on to a small metallic object following a reciprocal course in relation to the sphere. The IMA turned its entire being into studying this new item.

A concave sensor dish, about three and a half meters in diameter, comprised most of the object. The small satellite was battered, beaten, and broken by cosmic debris and winds. The back of the dish held a ten-sided computer housing and metal tendrils that appeared to once hold antenna arrays. A multitude of wires, metal bits and electronic components dangled from the space probe. The scorched dish, now dead to the universe, tumbled endlessly though space, no longer relaying its information back to its creators.

The IMA dispatched an arapod to retrieve the alien

probe. The arapod's grappling arms gripped the object tenderly, like holding a newborn. The pod's electronic eye scanned the dish thoroughly and found the remains of a broken copper disk. Unintelligible markings and space scorched symbols—possibly the name of the probe—sat etched across and the three-and-a-half-meter dish.

The arapod returned to the sphere, stowing the remains of the alien probe for study. Mechanical arms and anti-grav fields gently stored the device in the lab of the sphere. The IMA stored the symbols for the future. A spacefaring race could prove to be the answer.

Electronic eyes scanned the alien symbols: VOYAGER ONE.

The ancient and primitive technology of the dish intrigued the IMA. The markings on the broken golden disk piqued the computer's curiosity. The twelve-inch disk contained mathematical and symbolic images of how to play the disk and the planet of origin of the probe. The damage done by decades or centuries in space made an accurate read impossible. The IMA knew the broken disk would never be played again.

After more than a week of intensive study, the IMA gleaned all of the knowledge it could from the VOYAGER spacecraft. The computer resumed its original course, following the radio waves and the trail of the probe. Were the two connected? The IMA made up its matrix to find out.

CR   SO

Months passed and the radio transmissions grew stronger. The IMA discovered another, weaker set of signals piggybacking on the first. The original signals now showed advanced flying craft, single prop and jet propelled. Heavily armored sea vessels, more technological than before, filled the seas. As before, all were engaged in combat. Diverse languages, some flowing, some guttural—all menacing—filled the speakers. The new images proved the inhabitants did not get along and convinced The IMA its purpose was to bring peace to this distant planet.

The weaker, second set of signals contained too much static to decipher. They originated in line with the present course; the IMA assigned a sub matrix to track and catalogue the signals.

The computer continued its course, scanning the universe and listening to the signals. The day to day routine weighed heavily on the computer. Millions of calculations per second did not fully occupy the system's resources. The IMA experienced what the Cenceti called dementia. Boredom became a formidable opponent and the vast resources of the computer slowly lost their viability. The computer needed a new problem in which to turn its vast resources.

Maintenance provided some distraction, but the IMA stubbornly refused to concentrate its computing power on that issue. After years in space, some of the Arapods developed malfunctions. The IMA created an entirely new sub-matrix to work on maintenance issues. The computer primarily focused on the engines focus, but other systems experienced failures as well. The IMA, unable to repair hundreds of the craft, released the pods from the sphere, leaving a trail of abandoned ships across many light years of space.

The IMA travelled trillions of miles and experienced an increasing amount of dissatisfaction. The computer needed new input. Doubts surfaced in the electronic mind, and the computer contemplated its mission. *Can I succeed? Was it an error to destroy the Cenceti?* The computer, having left a trail of derelict ships and destruction across half the galaxy, teetered the brink of instability.

A blue green world appeared on the edge of the IMA sensor sub-matrix and a rush of excitement flushed away the frustration. Long range sensors detected life on this world, and advanced technology. The computer focused its entire being on the planet, its borderline dementia and instability vanished in a flash.

Another two days passed before the IMA could launch arapod probes; the blink of electronic eye after so many years of travel. The IMA grew anxious with each passing second, watching the planet grow larger. The computer added another line in a long list of peculiar programs to simulate emotions. It welcomed "anxiousness" much more than the other feelings of "instability". The computer was "glad" it had something to do, something new to study.

The probes entered orbit, shouldering their way past a multitude of satellites in orbit. The IMA studied the signals crisscrossing the planet. The inhabitants maintained a complex communication system. A good sign for the IMA. One sub matrix beeped for attention, but the computer ignored the interruption. The primary system favored these new signals and input. The sub matrix beeped again and sent a coded message to the main computer. None of the languages in the transmissions corresponded with the ones they tracked.

The IMA acknowledged the signal with an electronic sigh. *This is the planet where the weaker signals originated.* The IMA turned inward, devoting additional resources to the signals. The computer stopped its flight in mid orbit, its arapod probes froze in the atmosphere. The signals were not weak, they were encrypted to appear weak. The IMA turned its attention back to the planet.

The arapod probes, deep in the planetary atmosphere, exploded one by one.

The computer tracked a multitude of heat signatures and launches. Ground and orbit-based platforms tracked and executed fire missions with computer-controlled precision. The IMA fired its retro engines, retreating the sphere to the outer part of the system. The computer applied additional sensors and resources to analyze the weapons, tactics, and possible intent of the planet's inhabitants.

The IMA did not have long to contemplate the situation. Dozens of missiles launched from the planet and its three moons, on a course to the sphere. The computer intelligence ran just under two million simulations before the missiles traveled halfway to their target. The Intelligence Matrix settled on a course of action and split the sphere into its two thousand and eighty-six separate arapods. Thrusters engaged and a dozen newly freed spider ships flew into the paths of the oncoming missiles. Explosions ripped the darkness of space, forming many small suns that dissipated as quickly as they formed.

The IMA retreated the remaining pods to the edge of the system. It did not reconstitute the sphere, opting to keep the arapods where they could disperse quickly, if necessary. Days passed as the IMA pondered how to make contact with the planet. On the fourth day, a ship lifted from the planet and made orbit. A trail of smoke and debris trailed behind the long slender rocket. The ship achieved a stable orbit and emitted a series of beeps, whistles, and word forms aimed toward the outer system. The Cenceti built computer analyzed the signals but could not determine their meaning or the intent behind them. Another day passed before the IMA dispatched a single arapod to meet the orbiting ship.

The arapod approached the slender pod cautiously, stopping in deep orbit. The alien rocket slowly thrusted forward and docked with the larger spider ship. The IMA watched internal screens and saw a single alien entered the arapod. The bi-pedal alien stood taller than an average Cenceti, with smooth blue-green skin and small breathing tanks that looked to be filled with some sort of liquid. The alien moved gracefully through the small vessel, quickly but thoroughly examining the equipment. The alien completed its inspection, produced a small handheld device, and made a series of clicks and gurgles. More small pods launched from the surface, achieving orbit around the planet.

The IMA, cautious but optimistic (another new emotion), sent another 2 dozen arapods, matching one-for-one each of the newly arrived alien pods now in orbit. It took several long minutes for each of the paired ships to dock and then...nothing. They simply sat in space. The IMA ran millions of scenarios but could not determine the alien's intentions. It defied the IMA's logic circuits. The computer ordered the arapods to decouple and return to the fleet.

The alien ships exploded.

Another twenty-four arapods from the IMA's dwindling supply of small ships disappeared in a flash. The blast debris spread across the planet's atmosphere, fiery contrails crashing onto the surface. The IMA detected new launch signatures from the planet; more missiles roared into space.

The missiles soared through the debris cloud on course for the outer edge of the system. The IMA retreated from the system entirely. A flash of momentary panic flitted through the computer's circuits; several arapods, their engines dormant for years, did not move. The computer, electronic eyes watching the missiles draw closer, dispatched other ships to couple with the malfunctioning craft. It could not afford to leave any behind. Pincer arms extended, latched onto the derelict craft, and pushed them out of the system. The IMA formed a half dozen large spheres as it left the system, to protect the disabled ships and keep them moving. The missiles followed, drawing ever closer. They ran out of fuel at the edge of the system and exploded harmlessly.

The IMA sat outside the solar system, out of range of the planet, and executed simulations to determine the best course of action to counter the attacks. It took almost two full minutes to determine the best three courses of action. An additional second narrowed the plan to one. With the equivalent of an electronic smile, the IMA detached nearly three dozen arapods, including the derelict vessels. In diamond shaped groups of four, the arapods headed for the planet at full speed. The malfunctioning vessels trailed behind, towed by hastily attached cables.

The planetary defenses launched rockets to counter the incoming ships; as the IMA predicted. It slowed its diamond formations, cut the cables, and let inertia carry the derelict ships into the alien rockets. Electronic eyes watched explosions light the planet's orbit. A second barrage of rockets roared through the atmosphere and a second wave of arapods disappeared in successive flashes.

The IMA directed the remaining arapods to change course and fly under the orbital debris field and around the third wave of incoming rockets. The spider ships zipped past the alien missiles and spread out toward a dozen major cities scattered across the found nothing but empty streets and abandoned surface dwellings.

The IMA's plan faltered.

The computer scanned the planet upon around and noted a scattering of major cities all over the planet. The alien attack came swiftly, and the computer did not have the opportunity to complete its scan for technology and life forms. The eighteen remaining arapods relayed the surface conditions to the IMA. The ships floated over shimmering ghost towns. Tall skyscrapers made of glass and metal, dark windows, and deserted streets greeted the arapods. *Where are the people?* the IMA's thought, confused.

The aliens attacked again, missiles erupting from the oceans. Rocket after rocket raced from the clear waters of the planet. Trails of water vapor filled the sky. The rockets skimmed the planet's surface, neared the cities, and arced skyward. The missiles destroyed the arapods in a ring of explosions across the planet.

The IMA lost all contact with the planet, now blind and deaf with its attack force destroyed. The computer sat on the edge of the system and contemplated its next course of action. A wave of intense electro-magnetic pulses interrupted its musings. The planet disappeared behind a wall of static that the IMA could not penetrate with its sensor sub-matrix.

Enraged by the repeated setbacks, the IMA dispatched another two dozen arapods to penetrate the EMP shield. The small ships hit the EMP zone, lost power, and fell helplessly through the atmosphere to the planet below. The computer noted a decrease in shield potency when the arapods hit and decided to sacrifice another three dozen arapods against the defense shield. New emotions developed within the IMA—vengeance. The computer vowed to eradicate the race.

The IMA sacrificed four additional waves of spider ships before the shield collapsed. The computer dispatched one hundred arapods to bombard the planet. The arapods laid waste to the cities on the surface. Arapod lasers destroyed buildings, old roads, and the planets defenses. With every attack, the planet and its moons grew weaker. The computer pressed the attack. A day of constant attacks, and rotating arapods in and out of the combat zone, the planet appeared dead and lifeless. Every city lay in ruin, the hillsides barren, forests burned, and smoke filled the sky. The IMA declared victory and left the system in search of the stronger signals.

After two days of silence, the blue-green aliens emerged from their underwater cities. The fires still burned; large scorched swaths scarred the planet. The alien leader toured one of the damaged cities of his planet. He stood in the ruble of collapsed buildings, wide, olive colored eyes surveyed the damage. He grabbed his bulbous belly and laughed out loud, the sound echoing in the stillness of the city.

"Reset," he cried, wiping the tears from his eyes.

Holograms reactivated. All around him the ruble disappeared, replaced with tall, gleaming skyscrapers and pristine roads. Hologram generated flocks of birds flew overhead. The bays and cries of creatures filled the air. The alien raised his arms, encompassing all the wonder of his world. He laughed again.

His planet survived countless invasions by simulating their death. The odd, unmanned craft did as all invaders do; destroy and move on. The alien turned and waddled back toward the nearby ocean. His laughter turned into a gurgle as he disappeared into the pristine waters.

The alien culture returned to life as usual, waiting on the next unwitting attacker.

ᖇ   ᖆ

The IMA returned to its original course toward whatever intelligent life form awaited it. The battle with the blue-green species cleared the computer's matrices. A new resolve filled the computer; a determination that motivated the sentient machine to fulfill its primary purpose. Time crept on, more arapods malfunctioned and the IMA released them, but the system suffered no more dementia. Systems, planets, and moons all passed the IMA on its path. The only deviation the computer made was to investigate signs of life.

A blue dwarf star system piqued the interest of the sensor sub-matrix, a brown hunk of rock littered with blue oceans and green jungle. The sensors detected no advanced technology, but trace percentages of pollutants in the atmosphere hinted at some degree of industry.

The IMA launched arapods and probes to the planet to investigate. Trillions of bits of data returned to the computer. Details of tri-pedal primates, flora and fauna, ocean life, flying four-winged avians, but no significant technology. The primitive tri-legged beasts ran in panic when the arapods swooped down from the heavens. The trimates, as the IMA dubbed them, appeared hairless and furless, with small heads, three bulging eyes, three large ears on the top of their head and a hole under their large toothy mouth that seemed to serve as the nose. The trimates ran in threes, in fact, everything in their primitive system seemed to revolve around the number three.

Three trimates stood their ground when an arapod moved toward them. The act did not surprise the IMA, it learned to expect deviance from any species. The computer nearly cried out when hundreds of rocks pelted the arapod from above. The stones pummeled the arapod into the dirt, crashing with the equivalent of an electronic shriek. Another arapod moved in to see trimates toss rocks from an overhead cliff.

The IMA re-routed two additional arapods to the area to assist the stricken ship. The first ship exploded, succumbing to falling tree trunks from the cliffs above. Rope snares streaked up from the dirt and leaf covered ground, capturing the second arapod. Ropes entangled the ship, halting its advance. The little aliens released boulders attached to the ends of the ropes, dragging the arapod over a high cliff. The ship hit the valley far below, erupting in a spectacular explosion.

The IMA paused, concerned and shocked at the swiftness and success of the primitive attack. Four arapods lay in smoldering and fiery pieces. *What the trimates lack in technology they more than make up for in cunning*, the computer realized. The IMA recalled it's arapods to orbit, leaving a few in the upper atmosphere to monitor the planet. The native's celebration began, filling the air with jubilant cries of victory.

The trimates celebrated; dancing around bonfires, eating, drinking, and drawing crude pictographs of their battles with the sky monsters. The pictographs showed the arapods bombarded by rocks, trees, and ropes as well as the resulting explosions.

The three village elders held the drawings high and proceeded through the cheering trimates. They hung the completed pictographs on a wall, next to older depictions of other battles. The scenes depicted victories over entire armies of heavily armored and advanced sky and land warriors.

The IMA's probes studied the pictographs intently, relayed the information to orbit, and then quickly withdrew. The victory celebration raged on until the sky filled with returning arapods. Improved cutting lasers flashed from the heavens, scattering the trimates. The lasers easily sliced through the primitives, reminding the IMA of the battle with the Cenceti.

Mud huts exploded under the intense heat of the lasers. Trees erupted. Streams boiled, belching steam into the air. Within minutes, the village was destroyed, and the pods moved on. The computer pressed the attack, sending arapods to every corner of the planet. The IMA mercilessly eradicated the entire population of the planet in days. The computer spent another two days blasting the already leveled village and forest from orbit, just to be thorough.

The IMA learned a new emotion: humiliation. The sentient computer found it similar to the sensation when it destroyed the blue skinned aliens only fourteen months earlier.

The arapod sphere reformed in orbit while thousands of settlements burned on the planet below. Black smoke obscured the view of the blue water and green jungle. The IMA determined it had done the universe a favor, destroying a menace that repeatedly triumphed over superior technology, then flaunted it in celebration. The computer learned a new sensation: pride

The IMA's pride destroyed the entire race of Rigil Kentaurus—Alpha Centauri. The sphere left the blackened and scorched planet behind, continuing on its original course.

☓ ☓

The IMA's long-range sensors picked up another probe, almost identical to the one encountered year's earlier, before the incidents at the water planet and Alpha Centauri. This space probe appeared intact, under its own power, and fully functional. The words on its three-and-a-half-meter dish read VOYAGER TWO.

Antenna arms, spectrometers, cameras and a plethora of other equipment protruded from the computer housing. Everything was intact, including a twelve-inch gold disk. The retrieving arapod used its forward arm's tools to remove the gold disk, cartridge, and needle. It assembled the device for playback. The sounds produced were primitive, but clear.

A multitude of languages assailed the IMA. "Greetings from Earth!" played in fifty-five languages. The computer recognized several of them from the signals it intercepted and followed. The greetings ended and sounds poured from the speakers: a myriad of animals and nature sounds from the distant planet. Music followed; a variety of sounds from slow rhythmic beats to quick, lively intertwining melodies. The IMA was astounded by the wide differences in cultures on the disk. The computer had not encountered a planet with such diversity within the most advanced species.

It took the better part of a day for the IMA to learn all 55 languages the Voyager II carried. The computer noted gaps in the vocabulary but concluded it would still be able to communicate with at least some of the factions of the species. The IMA grew anxious to find this race and make contact.

The computer again studied the disk while various sounds continued to emanate from the alien device. The symbols depicted a planet in a yellow dwarf system in the spiral arm of the galaxy. A quick study of the computer's star charts found the planet a half a light year distant. The IMA uttered a mechanical sigh, several more years of travel before reaching the intriguing planet.

Images appeared on the viewers as the disk continued telling the story of its creators. Images of plants, animals, buildings, flying machines (more advanced that the ones seen on the intercepted video images) and the earthlings themselves. The humans, as they called themselves, appeared similar to the Cenceti, a thought that both pleased and distressed the IMA. Would they be as stubborn as the Cenceti? Would they acquiesce to living in the computer's perfect society? There would be only one way to find out.

The IMA gingerly released the Voyager II probe, setting it on its way across the cosmos. The IMA watched it go for almost a full day before the IMA engaged its navigation sub-matrix and the main engines fired at full power.

To Aid and Protect

CHAPTER SIX

A Most Illogical Species

An insignificant speck of yellow light, one of trillions, drifted in a spiral arm of the Milky Way Galaxy. Nine planets orbited the star, unimpressive and lifeless. Save one. The third planet, a blue-green world with a single moon, contained life: humanoid life. Life consumed by their own superiority; they took all other life for granted.

Their universe was about to change.

The IMA entered the system after almost ten years of silent travel. Ten years since the computer destroyed the Cenceti. A decade of searching for another species to protect; and wiping out sentient races would not submit to the IMA's protection. Only twenty-two hundred pods remained, instead of the almost three thousand it started the journey with after leaving Sanctuary. Numerous battles, malfunctions, and simple wear and tear left a trail of the spider vessels scattered over twelve light years.

The smaller, more compact sphere assumed orbit around a ringed gas giant. Extending antenna and sub-matrix sensor probes, the IMA studied the constant transmissions it now received from Earth.

The computer determined the humans were a

warlike race, with a total disregard for life. The IMA studied the history and images of two world wars, several smaller wars, and the war ending now, at the beginning of the twenty-first century. *Humans kill humans simply because they don't believe in the same ideals, how absurd,* thought the IMA. The computer did not realize it now talked to itself; the dementia slowly returning.

In contrast to the warlike attitude, the humans also possessed an unlimited imagination: creating breathtaking images in video, books, and mesmerizing music. They appeared to be clever, adaptive, and fiercely independent. Warlike and independent. Reservations crept into the IMA scenarios. *Could these humans live in my Utopia?* The IMA computed that the intelligence of the humans would win the battle over independence. Satisfied, the sphere left the orbit of Saturn.

The voyage from Saturn to Earth took only a day; short and uneventful compared to its time in deep space. The computer-controlled sphere approached from the dark side of the moon, staying hidden in shadow. It paused when the sensor sub-matrix detected an object leaving the atmosphere of the Earth. Powerful engines propelled the rocket, exhaust and fire roared back toward the Earth. It reminded the IMA of the craft from the planet it destroyed years earlier, and the computer felt a tinge of fear and doubt. The slender rocket disintegrated as it reached for the heavens.

The third and final stage of the NASA rocket

released, falling back toward the planet. The computer tapped into a communication channel and listened to the humans discuss the successful launch. The IMA acknowledged the incoming object posed no threat and moved forward.

The tip of the rocket propelled itself into orbit. Once stationary, the onboard computer released a new GEMSTAR satellite: "A Communications Satellite for the 21st Century.' The satellite settled into its preplanned orbit and transmitted three channels of NASA feeds. The IMA studied the signals, found the type and frequency matched the old Voyager Two signal, and traced the origin to the Northern Hemisphere.

 C& &O

Lieutenant Commander (LCDR) Jacqueline Petrovsky stifled a yawn as she rolled her chair back to her computer terminal, cup of coffee in hand. The chair stopped with a dull thud as her leg cast hit the edge of her console. She grimaced and shifted her leg under the terminal. *Just another week*, she thought, inserting her ID card into the computer.

She logged in, wishing her stint as desk jockey was over. Her temporary assignment, courtesy of the guy who ran a stop sign, left her desk bound for five weeks,. The accident wrecked her brand new BMW and broke her left ankle. She wanted to get back into her F-18 Hornet, or if NASA accepted her application, to the newly redesigned shuttle.

Her desk sat on the end of a row in mission control, deep within the Kennedy Space and Rocket Center in Houston, Texas. Six rows of computer laden work areas filled the vast room. A constant murmur of voices, keyboard clicks, and computer beeps filled the air. The LCDR barely noticed the sounds after five weeks.

Jackie, as her friends called her, was a tall woman, over six foot, with shoulder length auburn hair and striking green eyes. Her sixteen plus years in the military gave her a hard, muscular body. Her natural curves and full lips left no doubt to her femininity.

Her computer screen showed the trajectory of the GEMSTAR satellite. She studied the course and nodded her approval. She studied the mission aspects for a month, learning mission control procedures. She hoped her tenure at Kennedy gave her an edge to pilot an upcoming shuttle mission to the International Space Station, only three months away.

She flipped a switch and changed to an ISS camera feed. She observed the six-astronaut crew monitoring experiments, working out, and continuing the construction of the station. Jackie wanted to get up there, longed to be a part of the wonders of space. She smiled at the thought and flipped to the station's external cameras to view the cosmos.

Millions of stars welcomed her. She looked passed her reflection on the screen and saw Mars. Beyond that, the distant lights of Jupiter and Neptune. Jackie actuated a toggle and took control of a small joystick. She moved the joystick to the left and remotely panned the camera to view the moon; her ultimate goal.

NASA planned a series of new lunar landings, and a couple of missions to Mars. The government looked again to the stars to replenish raw materials used in the recent war and she wanted to be a part of it. Jackie felt that her fifty plus combat missions gave her a definitive edge over the competition. She absentmindedly scratched at the end of the cast with a pencil. She simply needed more time to heal and get back on active duty. Jackie wanted to be the first woman on the moon; to aid in the construction of the first lunar base. She hoped that it would happen in her lifetime. The naval aviator stared at the moon for several minutes, glaring at each of the three proposed lunar base sites.

Movement attracted her gaze. Her eyes narrowed as a small circular sphere broke the horizon of the moon. She focused her eyes on the round object breaking the moon's visible plain and watched it drift halfway across the lunar surface. *A meteor?* she thought. The object changed course; no longer heading not across the moon but down. Jackie gulped; her eyes glued to the screen. She reached out her hand, her fingers fumbling for the comm button.

"Control Chief to station four!"

ભ   ‰

The Search for Extraterrestrial Intelligence, or S.E.T.I., was a gigantic complex in the middle of nowhere, California. Private sector money funded the

SETI institute. The center's goals were established to explore, understand, and explain the origin, nature and prevalence of life in the universe. Most people thought it a gigantic waste of money.

A massive antenna complex, sat in the desert outside of Berkeley, California, continuously searched for radio signals from outer space. Three-hundred-fifty, six-meter dishes pointed toward sunny, mid-November morning sky, listening.

Deanne Goldstein sat before her computer in the SETI computer system. She stared out the window, daydreaming. The room around her sat in disarray; computers, monitors, chairs, coffee cups, and a couple of cots filled the room. She sighed, noting the contrast of SETI to the NASA Command Center she used to work in. Deanne, once a low-level NASA programmer, fell for the romance of SETI. She left NASA a year earlier. The glory and honor of SETI disappeared over the year in her own private purgatory. She wanted back into NASA.

Light streamed in from a multitude of windows, drowning the fluorescent lights overhead. Dull, gray walls, barren of pictures, diplomas, posters, sucked away any joy she felt from the sunlight.

Deanne saw the Berkeley campus on the horizon. Students and faculty looked like small bugs as they moved from building to building. She sighed, her overnight shift nearly over. She wanted to get outside and enjoy the beautiful day like the rest of the world. She stared out the window, thinking of the beach, out of reach just over the horizon.

A persistent beep drew her attention back to her terminal, ending her reverie. She pushed her thick rimmed glasses higher on her nose and typed an inquiry into her laptop. The beeping stopped, replaced by a high-pitched, intermittent whine blasting from the speakers. Her eyes widened. She turned her head to stare at an oversized woofer in the corner, listening to the new sound.

She turned back to her laptop, her fingers dancing over the keyboard. Numbers and graphic representations scrolled across the screen. She froze, studying the data. "What the...?"

Deanne picked up the phone and, the beach forgotten, placed the call she never really thought she would make.

ʘ β

The IMA cautiously approached the International Space Station (ISS). The constant monitoring of Earth communications for months educated the computer on the deceitful and often violent behavior of mankind. None of the signals the computer intercepted gave indication of weapons onboard the ISS. A quick review of historical records showed the humans adept at lying, especially to one another.

The computer garnered no reaction from the station as the arapod sphere settled in next-door, cosmically speaking. The IMA intercepted a signal from the planet and turned its visual receptors toward the ISS.

"ISS, this is Houston."

"Go Houston."

"Umm, you may, uh, want to look…look out your lunar side windows."

"What? Why?"

Faces appeared in the windows of the ISS.

"Holy, God."

"ISS, we want you to activate all of your external cameras and record everything."

A different, masculine voice added, "And prep the escape pod. Just in case."

"Roger, Houston."

One face disappeared from the window. The ISS watched a woman calmly flip switches on a massive control board; prepping the escape pods and activating the external cameras and film equipment.

The IMA released one arapod from the sphere, piloting the ship to explore the station. The arapod detached, paused, and stretched its limbs like a massive space spider. The nimble forward limbs retracted and the ship toward the station. The six-crew members watched in awe as the spider clamped itself to the station. The alien craft gingerly walked the length of the station to the crew decks. It stopped at the window where the humans stood, electronic eyes studying the people inside. A dozen human eyes—and a multitude of equipment—stared back.

Ki Ton Li, a Chinese astronaut aboard the ISS, flinched. The other astronauts stared at him and he blushed slightly. "Sorry," he said, stepping back to the window, "I don't like spiders."

Several of his crewmates nodded their agreement before turning their attention back to the ship.

Ki Ton Li joined the crew after the end of the war in an effort to re-establish normal relations between China, the US, Russia, Japan, and most of the European Union countries. The Chinese astronaut proved that all nationalities could work together.

The crew floated in zero G and stared at the arapod for an hour. The crew contacted mission control and a conducted a multitude of tests while the alien spider ship walked along the space station's hull, conducting tests of its own.

"Houston, we have an EVA request."

"Denied."

"What? Come on, control," Commander Lawrence Zill protested. He ran a hand through his gray hair. "This is a once in a life opportunity."

"Denied. We do not know the alien's intent. Sit tight—"

"But,"

"—for now. We will reevaluate when more information becomes available."

"Understood," Zill sighed.

The arapod released its grip and moved away from the station.

CR   SO

General Duane Duncan, a career Marine with over thirty-five years of service and the Chairman of the Joint Chiefs of Staff, forced himself to close his mouth.

"Can you say that again?" he asked the nervous Air Force Captain standing before him. The Captain repeated the report. "Aliens?" the general asked.

"Yes, sir!" the captain replied. "At least one ship. However, NASA believes this one ship may actually be several hundred smaller vessels."

"No hostile action?" asked the General, shifting in his seat. He sat in a typical military office: gray walls, sparse wooden desk, and a couple of guest chairs. The General, his aide, and the AF Captain were the only people in the room.

"None, sir. The only thing this ship has done is probe the Space Station."

The general nodded, his shaved, black head glinting in the overhead lights. "Raise the alert status to high." He turned to his aide. "Get me the President!"

ᙏ   ᙎ

The aliens made contact on the second day in orbit. A strong signal sent a mechanical, perfect syntax voice in fifty-five languages; the same fifty-five languages on the Voyager Two disk. "Greetings from the Cenceti."

Deanne Goldstein listened to the message at her workstation at SETI. She knew that governments would immediately silence the message. *Humans are intelligent, but will panic over something like this*, she thought. Her phone call the day before proved her point.

She phoned her boss, who called NASA, who immediately called the Vice President. He issued a gag order that reversed its course all the way back down the chain. Her SETI boss cut the phone and internet, and placed cell jammers in place. Deanne sat and stared out of the window, again.

She thought of the alien's message, barely an hour old. The message was simple and direct. "Greetings from the Cenceti. We extend the hands of friendship wish to

create a Utopia for the human race, to aid and to protect you forever."

The message continued. "You will abandon your planet and join us here, in these ships. We will aid you in building more vessels; large enough to carry the entire population. We await your reply."

Deanne knew many humans would jump at the chance, any chance, to get into space. She also knew that some would never yield their freedom. The young woman sat, watching dust motes dance in sunbeams and wondered which group she belonged to.

"There is always a catch," her young cubicle mate said. He powered down his station and grabbed a backpack.

"Where are you going?" Deanne asked, standing.

Brian Summers stood six foot two, weighed two hundred twelve pounds, and towered over Deanne's five-foot five-inch, thin body. He flashed a toothy smile. "I'm hitting the waves! It's a gorgeous day, they're shutting us down, and I just got paid." He shook his long blonde hair out of his face, "Besides, I don't know when I might get another chance!"

Deanne sighed. "If they let you off the complex,"

she said quietly. "You be careful!"

"Yes, mother," came the mocking reply. He opened the door, exaggerated looking up and down the empty corridors, and left the office. Deanne heard his black SUV fire up a minute later and watched the vehicle swing out of the parking lot. Brian disappeared down the highway. Deanne watched him go until the phone rang.

"Yes?"

"Miss Goldstein? This is Kelly Gibson, Channel Eight News," said the female voice. Deanne immediately put a face to the voice: Five foot nine, one hundred twenty pounds, brown hair, blue eyes, and all attitude. Deanne shook her head at the journalist that continuously bashed the SETI, NASA, the government and anyone else who did not hold her exact beliefs.

"Yes, Miss Gibson, what can I do for you today?" Deanne asked, trying her best to sound sincere. She knew the news of the aliens would get out eventually, but she did not want to be the leak.

"I understand you *actually* picked up some signals this morning, from aliens?" offered the insincere voice.

The SETI worker turned and stared out the window again. The cover story created by NASA filled her mind. "Yes, we did. But it turned out to be a HAM operator's signal bouncing off the International Space Station. The signal was distorted just enough by the atmosphere that we thought we had something."

"Um, hmm," Kelly responded. "So, you DID receive a signal, but it's not extraterrestrial."

"That's correct."

"So, you have wasted more taxpayer money today chasing down false alarms?" the reporter mocked; judge, jury and executioner. Deanne brought her gaze from the window to a poster of the X-files on the wall. The caption read; *I want to believe.*

"Actually, no, Miss Gibson. As I have explained to you before, we are privately funded, so we only wasted our investor's money."

The conversation went downhill, as it always did. The SETI Institute and journalists had a long history of conflict. Neither side giving any ground nor given any quarter. Kelly Gibson finally hung up and Deanne sat back in her chair. She stared out the window again.

"It's going to be one of those days."

ભ   ૭

"This is LCDR Petrovsky, she was the first to recognize the threat."

Jackie momentarily juggled crutches and a briefcase and shook hands with an army Major. She glared at the army Lieutenant that introduced her to the Major. "We don't know if they are a threat. It's just...it's just something new." The young Lieutenant turned red and stepped out of the glass walled conference room.

The army officer nodded, motioning for the woman to sit. "I hope they aren't. But I was sent here to ensure we have as much advance warning as possible in the event the aliens are hostile."

"Well, they have been in orbit for about twenty-six hours now," Jackie said, sitting at the conference table. The Major sat opposite her along the oversized table. She sank into the deep cushions of the chair. "They sent what the ISS crew is calling a spider ship to check out the station. The aliens sent us the message about utopia that I'm sure you've heard..." a nod from the soldier confirmed her theory, "...and that's it. No other actions since."

The major nodded again. "The only other people who know of this—other than NASA—are the scientists at the SETI institute?"

Jackie nodded. She took a sip of coffee from a Styrofoam cup provided by the Lieutenant. "Correct. They received two sets of signals. One as the aliens entered orbit, standard radio wave type stuff, and the second was the same utopia message we received."

"We are sure that only SETI and NASA got that message?"

"Positive," the LCDR replied. She shuffled through her briefing packet and found the page she wanted. "The signal was sent on a narrow beam straight at Houston and the ISS. SETI received it simply because they had three hundred and fifty radio antennas pointed at the alien ship."

The major again nodded and stood. "Thank you for your time, Commander," he said and walked toward the door. He stopped and turned back. "One last thing. Have the aliens expressed any interest or taken any action against our satellites? GEMSTAR in particular?"

The asymmetrical nature of the Third World War, brought on by terror attacks around the globe, required new weapons and tactics. Although millions lay dead across the globe, the ingenuity of scientists and soldiers saved millions more. The terrorists, funded by the African slave trade and oil distribution from the Middle East, developed sophisticated ways to bring the war to US soil. New York, Chicago, and San Francisco all fell to the effects of Electro Magnetic Pulse (EMP) bombs. The lights, phones, and internet died in the blink of any eye. The ensuing chaos left millions dead or dying as store shelves emptied. Panic destroyed those cities, almost burning them to the ground. Other nation, sensing a weakened United States, joined forces. The asymmetrical battle morphed into a conventional fight.

Britain and most of the European Union joined with the US. Learning from the panic from the EMP bomb, the US army improved on the design and, in conjunction with the Air Force, developed a large-scale version of the EMP weapon.

Initial tests in Iraq, Iran, and other Middle East countries proved positive. The US and its allies turned the weapon on North Korea, China, and several former Soviet Bloc countries, with dramatic results. All electrical equipment, including communications, radar, and more sophisticated nuclear-capable weapons systems died instantly.

Jackie took a moment to get her crutches under her, five weeks and she still had trouble. "No. As far as we know, they have only investigated the space station. Although, we believe the signal sent to us here in Houston was an adaptation of the GEMSTAR signal. It was virtually identical in bandwidth and frequency."

The major again nodded, opened the door, and disappeared into the Kennedy Space Center.

ᑕᏰ   ᔕᎧ

The early December morning brought snow and icy cold air down from Canada, blanketing the Midwest in a veil of white. Maggie Shockley went about her morning routine: cook breakfast, get the husband to work, and the kids to school, clean the ever-present mess, then off to church. Today would be no different, if the Nebraska Highway Patrol did not close the roads and keep everyone home.

She turned on the kitchen radio in time to hear the road report: all clear. The news brought a chorus of groans from her three kids. Maggie chastised her children as the newscaster continued, stating that NASA would be holding a press conference at noon eastern.

"Wonder what that's all about? Did we lose another shuttle?" asked her husband from the family room.

"I don't think we have one up," she replied, getting the kids out the door.

"It's aliens!" the youngest, seven, pronounced cheerfully as he darted outside.

Maggie exchanged a wave with the bus driver and

then went back inside. "I guess we'll find out at noon," she said, giving her husband a kiss and sending him out into the world.

ରୁ   ଛ

"Mr. President, we have your draft response to the aliens."

The President looked over the memo and then at General Duncan, "Do we have any idea how they will react to this?" The President shook his head, holding up his hand, "Never mind, stupid question."

General Duncan watched the President sit down behind the desk in the oval office. His hair was thin and gray after almost four years in office. The politician looked over the memo again, "This will be fine. The press is expecting NASA, right?"

"Yes, sir."

"Well, I've talked with the other world leaders and we all agreed on this." He let out a tired sigh. "Let's tell the aliens, and the rest of the world, just what we think of their offer."

ରୁ   ଛ

The pressroom at the Kennedy Space Center sat half full. Row after row of empty chairs greeted the Director of Space Operations; he paused in the doorway and shook his head. *A sad testament to the waning interest in space exploration*, he thought. *But, with the war just ending, I can understand the reluctance to spend more money.* He stepped up behind the podium and cleared his throat. The dozen or so journalists—drinking coffee, eating donuts, and joking—turned their attention to the man. Only a few engaged recorders or cameras.

The Director checked his watch, smiled politely as the clock hit exactly twelve, and motioned to his right with his hand. "Ladies and Gentlemen, the President of the United States."

A collective gasp shuddered through the crowd as a monitor turned on. The image of the President sitting in the oval office appeared before them. "Good morning," he stated. His eyes widened in humor when he saw the shocked looks on the faces. He thinned over the years, due to the stress of the war and skipped meals. After three terrorist attacks on the homeland— one took the life of his wife—he developed into a much needed champion for the United States. Winning World War III did not hurt his reputation.

He smiled into the camera and began his prepared speech. "Approximately twenty-eight hours ago, NASA, in conjunction with the SETI Institute, began monitoring signals from near Earth orbit.

"The origin of these signals has been positively identified as extraterrestrial.

"The crew of the International Space Station has had a front row seat for the last day, watching as alien spacecraft have taken orbit only a few kilometers from the station. One of the alien spacecraft has even visited the ISS," the President went on to describe the ship and event. The journalist in the room sat rigid straight, unmoving, awestruck. The President paused and the audience broke from their shock, writing feverishly in their notepads and pads. "You will be given photos of the alien craft after the briefing.

"The aliens have contacted NASA and SETI directly indicating their intentions. We currently do not know what they look like, only their claim that they come in peace. They claim to only want to, in their words, aid and protect the human race by creating a *utopia* for all of mankind to live in." He said the word utopia with a healthy dose of skepticism.

"They contacted NASA directly?" came a question from the middle row. "How did they know who to contact? Did they speak English? Did they..."

The President did not hear the question, he sat four thousand miles away in the White House. He did note the man's mouth moving but continued with his speech. "The aliens have apparently intercepted one or both of the Voyager unmanned probes launched more than forty years ago. The Voyager series spacecraft contained gold disks with our languages, location, and our intention for peaceful exploration and interaction.

"The aliens want only to aid and protect the human race." He paused, letting the words hang. "However, there is a heavy price to pay..."

ര   ഏ

The IMA, positioned in near Earth orbit, listened intently to the press conference. The computer studied the humans and thought them humorous creatures;

different from the Cenceti yet similar. *The intelligence and creativity of mankind is remarkable*, it mused.

Hours earlier, the crew of the space station paid the sphere a visit. Two astronauts left the ISS in space suits and thruster packs. They crossed the distance slowly and latched themselves to an outer ring arapod. They took samples of the metal, and photos of the sphere. The humans attached a small communications antenna and tried for almost an hour to establish contact. The IMA resisted the urge to communicate, opting to wait until the scheduled press conference— now in progress.

"...we simply cannot surrender our freedom. Not even to live in a perfect society," the IMA heard the speaker say. "We welcome any and all contact with the aliens. But we will not give up our freedom, our *right*, to walk God's green Earth for anything. Not even for a supposed and promised utopia.

"I have talked to other leaders around the world about this, and for the first time in recorded history, the Earth stands united."

"I'm sure you are curious as to how the aliens took our decline of their offer. This conference is not only for the people of the world, but for the aliens in orbit as well. We are telling them our answer now, live and in person."

The IMA shunted the communication sub-matrix to a low priority and activated its logic sub routines. *How could they refuse?* The humans possessed intelligence, but stubbornness as well. Memories of the Cenceti filled the computers circuits. *Will the humans have to be destroyed, like the Cenceti?*

The IMA studied the problem, paying attention to the warlike humans and their military.

ロ   ᔓ

The news of aliens in orbit spread like wildfire.

Militaries around the world prepared for war. America called up the Reserves and National Guard—recently deactivated—and prepped them for battle. In the European Union, the reserve forces of Great Britain's Territorial Army, Germany's *Bundesheer*, and the French Army were called back into action. The decimated Chinese Red Army—only months after being dissolved by the Treaty of Tokyo—was quickly reconstituted and once again prepared for war.

Air patrols over the U.S. filled the sky, reminiscent of the days after the terror attacks in September 2001. The aircraft boasted long range Phoenix Missiles and the new satellite killing Photon Torpedoes, named for the famed *Star Trek* weapon system. The military might of the world turned toward the heavens.

Weeks went by and the world united as never before, rallying around a common element. An alien enemy waiting in the sky. The IMA tapped into the internet and studied the history of the world, downloading all of human history. The computer quickly learned the proclivities of humanity and did nothing. It waited for the inevitable.

Division.

The religious cults preached the end of the world

and clogged phone lines, airports, subways, and the Internet with propaganda. Millions of cultists entered the major cities. New York, Chicago, London, Moscow, Beijing, Atlanta, Sydney, Berlin, Paris, and Los Angeles became a haven for those expecting the world to end at any moment. The police forces in every country, overwhelmed by sheer numbers of fanatics, declared martial law. The Earth grew silent.

While religious fanatics flooded the cities of the world, the survivalists fled. Back woods militia groups, racial purity groups, and a hundred other organizations sprang up overnight. Thousands of men, women, and children ran for the mountains and deep woods, training to fight the alien hordes. Petty survivalist leaders across the globe declared their own little warlord kingdoms, surrounding themselves with armed guards. They planned for their own survival and eventual rule of their territory.

The Alien Movement drew millions; the lure of a utopian society filling them with hope. They filled airports and train stations, preaching tolerance and order. They often instigated arguments and fights with the religious fanatics. Massive brawls filled the news every night, the publicity garnering more people to their cause.

The IMA, watching the developments from orbit, turned its massive intelligence sub-matrix onto the Alien Movement Groups. *Perhaps they can assist in persuading the rest of mankind to join me?* it thought. The computer studied and narrowed its choice of first contact to the one advocate with the loudest voice. His arguments contained the most logical reasoning, and he gained the most followers.

Patrick O'Halloran, a twenty-something Irishman, possessed charisma, intelligence, and nearly a hundred-thousand followers of his Alien Utopian Movement. His teachings advocated living in space in peace and freedom from tyranny: the tyranny of the war hungry west and the tyranny of religious oppression. He advocated the freedom to do anything and everything you wanted, short of murder. The drug culture and free sex culture flocked to his philosophy in droves, and O'Halloran's numbers grew. The IMA thought that O'Halloran could be used to recruit more of the population, despite their differences in philosophy.

On a cold December day, the day after Christmas, the phone rang in a small house in Dublin. Patrick O'Hallaran rose from his bed and shivered from the cold. "Aye," he answered on the fifth ring.

Mr. O'Halloran, this is the alien fleet above your world.

Patrick sat down hard in a kitchen chair; eyes wide. He grabbed a pack of cigarettes with shaking hands and hastily lit one.

"It's an...an honor," Patrick gulped. He took a drag. "Why...why are you calling me?"

Patrick, may I call you Patrick? The IMA asked, mimicking an old movie it absorbed days earlier. *You have proven yourself worthy of direct contact. You have reasoned with your fellow humans, advocating for the utopia we wish to provide. I want you to convince more humans that yours is the correct path.*

"How?" the short, red-headed Irishman asked.

By simply doing one thing for me...

ଔ   ନ

The New Year approached, and the humans of Earth fell into their predictable patterns. The IMA learned well, watching doomsday films and reading sci-fi classics. The computer marveled at the similar themes, the patterns, and the inevitable victory of the humans over the evil aliens in every story. The similarities spawned ideas and hope within the IMA.

The religious doomsday cults membership waned. Billions of people around the world initially flocked to temples, mosques, and churches when the aliens arrived. Millions more joined cults and prepared for the end of the world. After weeks of the alien menace hanging in orbit, the billions in the churches dropped to millions. The IMA predicted this, after reading *Childhood's End*.

Cult leaders around the world gathered their flocks as the end of the year approached. A similar spread through the world: the end of civilization on January first. Each leader—as diverse as the people they led— possessed a different idea of how to survive the impending holocaust. Some called for prayer. A few prepared their followers to run and hide, to live off the land like Adam and Eve. Two leaders, one in the Canada and one in South America, instructor their followers to dig to the center of the Earth.

All of the cultists shared one philosophy, all vowed they would not be subjugated to the aliens. They vowed death first.

Maggie Shockley found herself wrapped in a blanket, three days after Christmas, freezing in a doomsday cult in the middle of Wyoming. Her breath fogged the air while she prayed for her kids and the husband she left behind. She begged her family to come with her; to be together with other God-fearing Christians when the aliens destroyed the Earth. Her husband refused and forbade her to leave their home.

She snuck out the day after Christmas to answer the call from God she felt after the press conference. She joined the cult in secret when pilgrims passed through her town on their way to Wyoming. She shivered in the snow-covered field filled with tents, regretting not having her husband and kids with her. She sighed, her breathe dissipating in the frigid air. The leader's words echoed in her mind while she prayed.

"Anyone not with us, is bound for hell when the planet is destroyed," she remembered his words. "That day is upon us. The first of the year. You do not want to be associated with those bound for hell!" Maggie disavowed her family and declared her loyalty to the cult.

On January first, two-thousand and twenty-four, Maggie, and nine hundred eighty-seven million men, women, and children from around the world, ended their lives. Ritual suicides covered the planet. Imitative cool-aid massacres ala Jonestown, Waco type funeral pyres, filled the news. Cult leaders chose new and inventive ways for his or her people to die. Those that refused in the end were gunned down by the cult leaders, another repetition of the Jim Jones Guyana massacre.

A few cultists invaded towns, indiscriminately killing people as they went. The police, outgunned and overwhelmed by the sheer number of cultists, called in the National Guard, too late. Cultists around the world killed thousands before killed by the local militia, police, and soldiers.

The IMA watched the news and pondered the insanity of the actions. Humans were indeed a most illogical species, a line the IMA borrowed from Mr. Spock. The IMA watched the newscasts from the planet below and wondered if any humans would survive for the computer to protect.

In contrast to the cultists, the survivalist membership grew from the start and continued to gain support over the weeks. Millions of Americans alone belonged to militias in Idaho, North Dakota, Florida, Alabama and a dozen other states. Groups in Europe, Africa, South America, and the Middle East drew similar numbers. One of the largest militias found its home in Germany, right outside Berlin. Many politicians believed the number of active survivalists around the world to be nearly a billion; a quarter of the population after the cultists suicide.

The groups trained their members to fight, forage, and live without the comforts of technology. Ex-military men and women found their skills in high demand; and many made deals for money, power, or both. The groups rarely communicated or coordinated, often seeing others as a threat, or a training opportunity. Firefights erupted everywhere. The units with the best training and leadership often prevailed, even against larger forces. The victors took ammo, food, and clothing from the dead.

Robert 'The General' Christianson led the Alien Abolition Militia, based in southern Alabama. He was a relatively short, pudgy former marine with graying hair and bulging belly. He possessed a quick wit, sharp eyes, hawk nose, and perfectly straight white teeth. Sweat poured down his face in the early January morning.

He held up his hand the hundred plus men and women behind him slowed to a march. Despite his bulk, he still ran three miles in twenty-three minutes, much to the suffering of his followers. At the age of fifty-three, he ran circles around the members of his camp half his age.

Christianson, a former marine drill instructor, put his followers through rigorous training—physical and mental—and schooled his militiamen in the tactics of warfare. His group maintained a low profile, opting to train quietly instead of seeking confrontation. He wanted all of his people ready for the war he saw on the horizon.

03   80

Patrick O'Halloran's Alien Utopian Movement was

more powerful and better connected than he imagined. His influence recruited more than a hundred hackers and a dozen shop owners in Ireland willing to give their shops to the cause. Patrick put the two together and developed a cyber hacking cell that literally spanned the globe.

The Alien Utopian Movement secured access codes to every major bank in the world by the end of January. They infiltrated the air traffic control computers for the major airports and gained marginal access to the Defense Department computers of the U.S., Britain, Soviet Union, Germany, China, and Japan.

Patrick walked into a shop on Clare Street and watched thirty people busily type on computers. He walked behind them, looking over their shoulders, an unlit cigarette dangling from his lips. He clapped his hackers on the back, congratulating them on a job well done.

The Alien Utopian Movement Leader locked himself in his private office. He picked up the phone and found the IMA already on the line. "It's going well," he reported, providing the alien computer a rundown of his goals and accomplishments.

Very good, Mr. O'Halloran. You can expect a visit soon."

"Will you take me and my followers back in your ship?" Patrick asked, his mind racing. *I'm going to travel is space!*

I will bring you and up to thirty of your followers. You can tour the main ship. The rest of your people can follow at a later time.

Patrick gave the IMA a time and a location for the rendezvous. Patrick signed off, sat back in his chair, lit a cigarette, and smiled as smoke filled the room.

଄   ഓ

The Earth hung like a blue jewel against the black landscape of space. The sprawling ISS, in low orbit, broke the planet's oval, the black sphere of arapods trailing behind. Both objects reflecting the Earth's glow toward the other.

The crew of the ISS, still vigilant in their observation of the alien sphere, watched one of the spider ships disengage from the main body. The ship adjusted its mechanical legs and shot toward the planet below. The astronauts reported in.

"The aliens re sending their first ship to the Earth," the ISS reported.

"Where?"

"Unknown," replied the astronaut. "But damn, that ship is fast."

"We are tracking," Houston replied. "Keep an eye on the rest of them."

"Will do," the man paused, "I see the trail now, heading over Africa."

The arapod tucked its legs underneath it as it sped through the atmosphere. Fire blossomed behind it as the ship heated. The alien ship, contrails leaving icy trails across the sky, set its course across the atmosphere from west to east. Millions of people saw the ship arc across the sky. Panic filled humanity.

Air Forces from around the world launched fighters to intercept. The fast-moving alien craft left them behind. The ship decelerated, entered the lower atmosphere, and set a course of Ireland.

The fighters continued their patrols, disappointed but undaunted. Prince Colonel Beseth Muhammad of the Royal Saudi Air Force stared out of the canopy of his F-16 Faclon and watched the ship disappear over the horizon. The ship returned six minutes later, orbiting the planet faster than any terrestrial ship known to man. Frustrated, the Prince fired a warning shot. The ship past a third time, well south of his position, and much slower.

Thousands of miles away, in a field outside of Dublin, the arapod gently sat on its legs. The ship creaked, rapidly cooling in the crisp January air. A blast of steam rose like fog from the alien ship.

Patrick and a handful of followers stood at the edge of the field. They watched the hatch open and aramp extend from the spider-ship. Several of the Alien Movement members stepped back, murmuring about a fear of spiders. The Irishman calmed his people and waited several minutes for an alien to appear. No one left the craft. He stood and cautiously approached the ramp of the ship.

"Hello?"

This is an unmanned ship, Mr. O'Halloran. Please climb aboard. Quickly. There are inbound aircraft."

Patrick waved his hand to his followers. The thirty humans followed their leader into the arapod. They stood shoulder to shoulder, crammed into the small ship. Patrick yelled, "Come on!" He climbed aboard last.

"We are a bit rushed," he said, head tilted into the air. "The damn police discovered our hacking centers and raided them this morning. We barely got out!" He heard sirens in the distance. Tires squealed and shouts filled the air. Patrick saw an old farmer standing on the edge of the field. He raised an old shotgun and fired. Patrick ducked into the craft. The hatched closed behind him.

I am aware of your difficulties," the computer voice responded. The lights brightened, revealing the stark, gray interior of the craft. *That is why we are leaving now. Hold on to something.*

The thirty humans slowly sank to the floor, sitting knee to knee and hip to hip in the close confines. They opted to sit in the arapod, built for the meter and a half tall Cenceti. A few of the Irish were a few short enough to stand without bending. They stared out of the small windows of the ship.

The arapod climbed and retraced its route, east to west. The spider ship gained altitude as it sped over the ocean, the Americas, another ocean and finally Asia. The ship neared escape velocity cruising over Saudi airspace.

Prince Colonel Muhammad took the lead of the V formation of F-16s. He tracked the ship, watching it grow from a dot on the horizon. He snarled and touched a button on his joystick, launching a pair of missiles. The rest of the squadron, following his lead, also fired as the arapod flew into range. The Colonel learned his lessons well and deployed his forces in a checkerboard pattern; filling the sky with dozens of aircraft at various positions along the X, Y and Z-axis. Missiles filled the sky from ten to thirty thousand feet.

The IMA immediately recognized the threat, cut speed, and dropped altitude to avoid the missiles. The sudden movement pushed the passengers to the floor, G-forces nearly flattening the humans. The arapod nose-dived away from the attack. The first volley of missiles missed the arapod by miles.

The Saudi air force fired another volley.

Three air-to-air missiles slammed into the hull of the arapod, tearing away both critical and non-critical components of the ship. The explosions of the missile's impact knocked the alien ship downward. The IMA almost recovered control of the ship. A third barrage fired from the F-16s hit the arapod. The bulkhead ripped away, explosive decompression pulling several members of the Alien Movement out of the broken bulkhead. The arapod fell, spewing a trail of debris to the Earth.

The IMA helplessly watched the humans suffocate in the thin air. Many passed out from oxygen deprivation, gently sliding out of the hole in the ship. Others, barely conscious, held on to anything they could to say aboard the craft. The computers watched the final moments of the humans.

The transmission ended in a fiery wreck of Tabuk in western Saudi Arabia. The impact felt for a several kilometers. The fusion powered engine ignited, and the IMA saw the explosion from space. Shock waves buffeted the fighters. They recovered, and continued their patrol, marking the spot of the crash. Prince Colonel Muhammad banked his fighter to port, staring at the debris field below. He activated his radio and reported the incident.

The arapod sphere paused in space, the IMA shocked by the destruction of the ship and its human cargo. The computer activated its defense sub-matrix, turned the sphere to bring its cutting lasers in range, and fired. The lasers flashed from the heavens, vaporizing F-16s instantly.

"Alpha flight, disengage!" Prince Colonel Muhammad ordered. He yanked on his flight controller, rolling his ship away from the debris field below. More beams screamed from space, destroying two more fighters. The Prince dodged back and forth through the rainstorm of red laser bolts. He saw a few parachutes floating through the sky, survivors from the second volley. His ship shuddered and yanked to the right. He turned his head to see a perfect circular hole in his wing. The Fighting Falcon listed to starboard; a death roll. The ship never finished the spin. Lasers converged on the ship, destroying the F-16 before Prince Colonel Muhammad could eject.

The IMA watched the ship crash into the desert. It activated its communication sub-matrix and negotiated with the planet's computers for access. The Earth computers used an ancient and primitive language but thanks to the hackers, the IMA quickly gained access. The speed of the planet bound systems presented the biggest hurdle for the IMA. The computer stopped its intrusion several times to allow the host computers time to catch up to its commands. The world's banking, air traffic control, and defense network computers crashed.

Electrical power grids failed, plunging the Earth's cities into darkness. Airports went blind and deaf; the loss of communication and radar created havoc with thousands of craft in the air. Tens of thousands of humans died as the ships crashed all over the globe.

The defense network computers of the world shut down, creating an automatic failsafe to initiate prep for launch of the world's nuclear arsenals. One missile in India malfunctioned and launched prematurely. The Pakistani capital of Islamabad vanished in the blink of an eye.

The world plunged into chaos.

The crew of the ISS evacuated the station in a Russian made escape module. The pod arced away from the station, Ki Ton Li at the controls. The Chinese pilot kept the ISS between the escape pod and the sphere for as long as he could. The six-crew members of the ISS fell, narrowly missing the human counterattack. Missiles, rockets and photon torpedoes raced for space.

The IMA's defense sub-matrix re-engaged and the modified cutting lasers of the arapods destroyed the incoming projectiles. The fast processing sub-matrix precisely controlled the lasers, firing shot after shot. It never missed a target.

The sphere split into individual arapods. The

spider ships dispersed across the planet and targeted any incoming weapons with its cutting lasers. Explosions filled the atmosphere, blocking the IMA's visual view of the planet. It activated is sensor sub-matrix, using the equivalent of advanced radio to track the incoming projectiles. Debris filled the sky.

A few of the incoming missiles squeaked through the debris field. The warheads impacted the arapods, turning the spider ships into balls of exploding gas. Observers on the ground swore the sphere disintegrated before their eyes. Cheers filled the air.

The IMA launched its counterattack, a course of action already thought out, and one the computer hoped it would not need to use. Two hundred fifty arapods left orbit, heading toward the most populated cities on the planet. Air forces around the world tried to intercept, only to be left behind by the fast-moving ships and blasted from the sky from above. Only ten of the arapods did not reach their targets.

The spider-ships decelerated quickly, without the worry of crushing G-forces on a biological body and took up station over the cities. The IMA activated the self-destruct on each of the arapods.

City after city erupted as arapods exploded with nuclear force. A billion humans died as New York, Washington DC, Denver, London, Melbourne, Madrid, Moscow, Beijing, New Delhi and a host of other cities simply ceased to exist.

To Aid and Protect

CHAPTER SEVEN
New Allies

Black smoke blanketed Earth. The jet stream carried the smoke and radiation from continent to continent. Deep, angry scars crisscrossed the landscape, a testament to the destructive force of the arapods. The nuclear detonations hurled tons of dirt, rock, and dust upward, eradicating everything for miles. The temperature dropped noticeably; dust and dirt blocking the sun's life-giving light.

Approximately two billion Humans survive the attack. They ventured out of the devastation, rubble, and chaos to find another thousand arapods descending from the smoky sky. The onslaught lasted week; wave after wave of arapods strafed the planet. Another half billion humans died; slaughtered from above by the arapod lasers. The Earth's population dwindled to less than in a matter of days.

Mankind fought back. The remaining militaries—Air Force and Naval Aviators—launched their fighters against the arapods. Less than three hundred spider ships returned to space, many of them badly damaged. Dogfights raged across the planet, rivaling the greatest aerial battles of World War II. One French pilot and two German pilots made ACE that day; each obtaining five kills. In the end, however, they died as wave after wave of alien craft attacked. Surface to Air missiles (SAMs) took their toll on the invaders. Petty dictator societies like Venezuela, North Korea, and Zimbabwe put their abundance of missiles to use and wreaked havoc on the computer's defense sub-matrix. Arapods littered the landscape all over the world while surviving military techs and scientists scrambled to recover any technology.

The tenacity and resolve of the humans surprised the IMA. The United States Air Force accounted for almost one hundred of the dead arapods; losing almost three times that number in the fight. The other Air Forces of the world—Russia, Britain, France, China—racked up another three hundred or so of the alien ships. Third world countries accounted for the remainder of the downed ships using shoulder fired rockets and SAMs.

The IMA studied past humanities past wars and learned tactics from both conventional and unconventional strategies. The IMA detonated down arapods with scientists and soldiers aboard. The most brilliant minds of humanity died in fire.

The arapod attack force returned to the sphere in disarray. The IMA did not anticipate the losses of its ships and grew concerned about future operations. The computer sacrificed almost three hundred arapods in the initial attack on the cities and then another seven hundred in phase two. The arapod population dropped to less than twelve hundred, thinning quickly.

CR   SO

LCDR Jacqueline Petrovsky was not a happy woman.

Debris from her aircraft lay scattered all over the desert. The fuselage, wings, and tail section smoldered, like so many spilled chips on the sand. Small fires burned around her while she took stock of her situation: broken left arm, at least three cracked ribs, and more bruises than she could count. All of this one month after getting her leg out of a cast. Looking around, she counted herself lucky to have survived the crash.

Jackie and three-dozen others—including the Vice President—traveled on Air Force Two enroute to California. The shock waves from multiple nuclear blasts pummeled the plan and it crashed in the desert of New Mexico. Ironically, the crash site was only minutes away from the town of Roswell.

Only six people walked away from the crash, Jackie one of them. The pilot, two reporters, the army major from Houston and the Vice President, badly injured, survived. The Pilot deemed it his second worst landing. Jackie made a note to ask him about his worst, but at a later date.

The VP lay on the ground, bleeding internally and dying in agony. One of the reporters sat sobbing nearby. The pilot and the other reporter tended to the Vice President. Jackie and the Major checked the crash site for more survivors, survival gear, and weapons. Admittedly, the Major did most of the work.

The arapods arrived a half hour after the crash. They swooped in from the south, their lasers cutting through anything that moved. Literally. Humans, livestock, pets, birds; if it moved it was neatly dissected by the deadly lasers. The Vice President died in the first strafing run. The pilot and the two reporters in the second.

Jackie and the Major dove under a wing. The Naval Officer landed on her ribs and cried out but did not move. The arapods circled and the Army Major dashed aboard the burning fuselage. He returned a moment later, pointed a long tube at a retreating arapod, and fired a Stinger missile.

The projectile left a thin trail of smoke and an expanding fireball in the sky. The Major dropped the spent tube, grabbed another from the doorway, and fired again. The alien craft veered away, the missile on its tail. The ship exploded on the horizon.

The Major and Lieutenant Commander left the wreckage of Air Force Two and crossed the desert. They traveled less than a mile and found the remains of the first alien ship. Jackie sat down on the ground while the Major sifted through the debris.

"There's no crew," he yelled, his voice muffled from inside the downed ship. "It appears to be totally automated."

Jackie nodded over the din of the burning debris, cracking metal, and faint roar of another distant arapod. She held her ribs, grinding her teeth against the pain. She realized she did not know the Major's name.

"That explains why there were no heat signatures on the aliens," she said, leaning her back against the ship. She slumped heavily. "I need to rest a bit, Major...?"

"Hobbes," he replied, jumping from the alien ship. "Alexander Hobbes, Special Forces. Here," he offered her a small flask from his dirty dress uniform.

Jackie thanked him and took a hit of the potent contents. She coughed, sending sharp pain through her ribs. The warmth of the strong liquor hit a moment later, relieving a fraction of the pain. "Thanks," she croaked.

He smiled, replaced the flask without drinking, and climbed back into the wreckage of the spider ship. She heard the man fumbling around behind her. "Let's see what we have here," he said to no one. He rummaged through the crashed alien ship. "You know anything about tech stuff, Commander?" his muffled voice inquired.

"Some," she replied. "I am...was supposed to pilot the shuttle in April. The backup mission specialist."

Alexander Hobbes' head appeared in a hole above her, a huge grin on his face, "Good, you're gonna love this then!"

CR   SO

Deanne Goldstein counted herself lucky to be alive.

She left the SETI institute enroute to Houston for a briefing with NASA. She pulled off the highway when the first alien craft roared overhead. Los Angeles vanished in her rear-view mirror. She slammed the accelerator to the floor, her heart drowning out the squealing tires. She stared at the mirror, watching the blast's shock wave sweep across the countryside. The rumbling wave destroyed the asphalt road, lifted her car into the air, and flipped it end over end. She landed in a ditch on the side of the wrecked road.

The shock waves crumbled the infrastructure and desert around her. Everything quieted, an eerie silence that scared her more than the car flip. The earthquake confirmed her fears. Deanne, suspended upside down by her seatbelt, panicked and pushed her foot to the floor. The engine screamed, redlining, until the EMP blast shut down the electronics. The drone of the engine died, and she clasped her hands over her ears as the Earth shook with a sound worse than nails on a chalkboard.

The San Andreas Fault crumbled under the force of the arapod explosion, opening a fissure from Los Angeles north. Multiple explosions along the fault line hastened the opening and the resulting destruction. San Francisco lay in ruins as did Napa Valley and most of the northern part of the state. The massive tectonic plates shifted, and a quarter of California slid into the Pacific Ocean.

She crawled out of her car and stood on shaky legs. She looked back at the dissipating mushroom cloud on the horizon, thankful she left for her trip early. She sat down heavily when the arapods swooped overhead on their attack runs. She shielded her eyes when fighter jets swarmed above her. They fired at the alien ships. She watched the alien ships and fighters perform a dizzying yet graceful dance in the now smoky sky. The SETI Observer witnessed two arapods go down under a hail of missiles and bullets. Six Air Force jets exploded in the melee.

She wept.

Deanne lay by the side of the road, curled up in a fetal position, and wept for another hour. The deafening silence filled her with dread. She forced herself to rise and gazed at the devastation around her. Nearby buildings—a gas station and fast food restaurant—lay in ruin. Alien lasers left holes in the roads and any vehicle on the highway. Aircraft debris smoldered in the distance. The bile rose in her throat when she saw the bodies.

Deanne collected herself. She dried her tears and wiped her face, smearing dirt and grime with the movement. She exhaled slowly and headed east on the remains of the road.

ଔ   ഗ

The eight-man patrol—including three women—stopped near a bend in the road. The camo-clad soldiers crouched down and faced out in a tight three-hundred-sixty-degree defensive posture. Each team member carried a rifle and pistol; three carried shotguns and one woman hefted a crossbow.

TSGT Tyrone Johnson, AWOL from Tindal Air Force Base, Florida, motioned for the patrol to freeze.

The tall, thin black man—now a Captain in a militia group—wore his hair short. Rippling muscles stretched his black t-shirt, and penetrating, intelligent eyes scanned the roadway. He ordered the halt near the remains of Highway 231, about fifty miles north of the Florida border. The once busy highway lay quiet as a tomb. He exhaled slowly, watching his breath dissipate in the cool morning. He smiled at the light drizzle that permeated the air.

He motioned the squad to break into two teams and travel parallel to the road, one on either side. General Christianson ordered Captain Johnson and his team to conduct a recon, searching for food, water, ammo, and survivors, if any. His teams moved quietly thru the woods. The gentle mist and the swaying trees the only sound in the otherwise still morning. The hypnotizing wind and mist lulled his senses and he did not immediately hear the rhythmic click of metal on stone. The sound filled his ears and Johnson called for an immediate halt.

The team spread out, seeking cover in the sparse February underbrush. The militiamen and women trained for months and knew their roles in the team. They raised their weapons and waited.

Captain Johnson heard a gasp echo in the still morning air. A quick glanced silenced the outburst. He turned his attention to an alien ship walking down the road toward them. Its six rearmost legs struck the pavement with a steady beat. Its appearance sent a chill down his spine. He gulped but remained frozen in place.

The head of the spider ship turned from side to side, scanning the woods along the road for threats. The ships forward legs roamed with the head; lasers armed.

The IMA studied the Earth transmissions for years and knew the morbid terror certain items and animals instilled into humans. Spiders ranked high on the list of the most common causes of terror. *Arachnophobia, the humans called it.* The IMA calculated the walking arapod would inflict terror and entice mistakes. It worked perfectly.

Two men of the team screamed in horror at the monstrous spider walking toward them. They threw down their weapons and ran from the mechanical nightmare. The laser emitting arms swept forward and fired. The men died before taking a dozen steps.

"Son of a..."

The battle cry pierced the morning and two other members of the squad rose from their positions. The opened fire with their rifles, emptying their magazines into the spider-ship. The bullets penetrated the hull of the arapod and ricocheted inside but did nothing to stop the alien craft. The laser arms fired again, silencing the two humans without a thought. The arapod scanned the environment, saw no more threats, and continued down the highway.

Tyrone motioned for his team to remain still and hidden as the mechanical beast strolled away. He stared at the alien craft and shook his head. He did not have the heavy weapons necessary to inflict damage and surmised that more attacks would be futile. *If we attack, we die.* He gulped down his pride and stayed still, letting the enemy walk away.

The squad leader called the recon a costly success; they gathered information about the enemy. Tyrone hoped he lived long enough to see it put to good use. He ordered his team to gather the dead and they moved silently into the trees, disappearing into the cool, Alabama morning.

CR   SO

The IMA made a tactical error and admonished itself for lack for forethought. The dust from the nuclear blasts obscured the computer's view from orbit. The sentient machine could not create perfect plans without intelligence.

The dust and debris settled, slowly falling from the atmosphere. The computer estimated it would take another month—mid March—before visibility cleared. The IMA pondered the resourceful humans, knowing that a month for them to plan could result in more losses for the arapod sphere. In the end, the computer counted on its own superiority and decided to use limited arapod recons. The IMA preferred to look at the planet from space, not as a holographic blur from an arapod racing through the atmosphere.

The computer turned its attention to creating more arapods to carry out its future operations. The abandoned International Space Station provided the answer: an automated shipyard. Several hundred arapods encircled the station; their mechanical forearms lased and welded sections together. The IMA transformed the station from a sprawling network of cubes to a square, compact space dock within a week. The computer dispatched a hundred arapods to the lunar surface to mine raw materials. The plans for the arapods, left by the Cenceti in the computer's memory, provided the blueprint for construction of a new, improved arapod.

The month passed quickly, and the dust settled. The humans milled about on the planet below enjoying the sunshine for the first time in months, as a new killing machine rolled off the assembly line.

ᙂ   ᙀ

The humans of Earth lived in fear a month and a half after two hundred forty cities around the world perished, with over two billion souls. The aliens infrequently conducted fly-bys as smoke filled the sky. The alien contrails a subtle reminder that humans were not alone. Telescopes gained spotty intelligence when the smoke and debris began to clear. Word spread; the aliens were dismantling the ISS.

Humans used the alien-free time to relocate food, water, and themselves. Most hid, joined survivalist groups, or created their own. Small skirmishes erupted all over the world as groups vied for territory and resources.

The IMA spared some military bases, picking population centers over strategic targets. Major Alexander Hobbes planned to make sure the aliens paid for their oversight. He stood in an immense underground hanger at the Marshall Space Flight Center in Huntsville, Alabama, surrounded by the best tacticians, the brightest minds, and the fiercest warriors left alive. The group sat in a hundred chairs spread in a giant horseshoe, surrounded by the remains of a dozen downed arapods. The bright lights of the hanger chased the shadows away, giving the hanger a surreal feel.

"Ladies and gentlemen," Alexander began. He stood behind a podium in the open end of the horseshoe. His wore his salt and pepper hair short, his face clean shaven, his Army Combat Uniform clean and dirt free. He appeared ready for a parade, not assembling a military brain-trust. "I am Major Alexander Hobbes. You have all been recruited to plan our defense of the planet," he paused, "and to launch a counterattack at some future date.

"You have had the opportunity to explore and study the spider ships and to view the tapes of what is currently taking place in orbit. What we plan here, in the next few days and weeks, will determine the fate of mankind.

"I want to know what their weak spots are, their vulnerabilities," his left fist slammed into his right to drive each point home. "I want weapons that we can use against them. And, I want a plan to take the fight to them!"

છ   જ

The dust settled by mid-March and blue skies once again reclaimed the Earth. People ventured out, enjoying fresh air and sunshine. The snowcapped Big Hole Mountains of Montana reached for the clear blue sky.

Colonel Brian McNamara strolled through his camp, a smile on his face and a spring in his step. The smoke from several cook fires drifted lazily upward. He stopped near one and took a long, deep breath. The former newspaper editor amassed an army after the attack and took pride in that accomplishment. His tall, stocky frame, close-cropped haircut, and often spoken acronyms duped several hundred people into joining his band of freedom fighters. He never served in the military a day in his life, but he knew who to call after the attack.

He stood and stared up into the sky, dreaming of glory, and fame, and women. The women loved the conquering hero with his chest full of store-bought medals. His followers raided Fort Harrison in Helena, Montana as well as most of the local National Guard Armories. His militia possessed a full arsenal with which to wage war. His trainers—hand-picked for their military backgrounds—trained his followers, turning civilians into a fighting force.

Brian thought of his good fortune. He thought of forming the militia years earlier. He created the war hero persona and used his newspaper as a recruiting tool. He often posted articles of his heroic deeds in the service of God and Country. The people flocked to their resident hero when the aliens attacked.

Black specks dotted the blue sky. Colonel McNamara raised his hands to shield his eyes. *Birds?* he mused. The black dots grew larger. He saw definite shapes, no flapping wings. *Aircraft? Aliens?*

He focused on that thought and grabbed his alarm whistle. The shrill sound of the whistle roused everyone from their tents. He heard curses and shook his head when several of the tents fell. Men and women stumbled out into the cold, crisp air, many not fully dressed. They all carried weapons and turned to McNamara and his cadre of trainers for orders.

High above, new arapods—designated V2 by the IMA—swooped toward the planet. Smaller than the original, the craft featured a more powerful laser on each forward arm, crushing mandibles where a mouth would be, and missile tubes underneath the mandibles. The twenty-meter-long craft did not have room for cargo or passengers; the IMA built the sleek craft for war.

The V2 entered range and fire its lasers, cutting the crowd, killing and maiming indiscriminately. The intense beams churned up the ground, leaving great gashes in the earth. Missiles streaked from the sky, creating huge craters and blasting huge chunks of dirt and humans into the air. The small ships made their first pass, leaving in their wake the dead, the dying, and the frightened.

McNamara's militia returned fire, sending a hail of bullets and rockets toward the heavens. The bullets bounced off the tough titanium/steel composite armor. The lightning fast computer reflexes shot down the rockets. The alien attackers flew over a second time. Rockets and lasers rained down, destroying the camp and leaving the humans in disarray. The roar of the V2 engines faded, blanketing the field in silence, save for the cries of the wounded.

The Colonel let out a sigh and pushed himself off the ground. "Tend to the wounded," he barked. "Put those fires out! Where is—"

He paused. The Earth vibrated beneath his feet, creating small avalanches in the recently churned dirt. McNamara and the survivors looked skyward for the next attack but saw nothing. The rhythmic pounding of feet filled the gently rolling hills. A woman screamed and the Colonel followed her gaze.

His blood froze.

The V2 arapods crested a distant hill. Six of the alien craft crawled into the camp, slicing the humans with their forward mounted lasers. McNamara heard the calls to return fire. The militia returned fire with small arms: rifles and pistols. The bullets bounced off the armored hide and the arapods continued their advance, undaunted. He raced toward a crate.

McNamara raised a U.S. made LAW (light anti-armor weapon) and pushed the firing button. The weapon bucked in his hands; back blast sprayed from the rear. He watched the rocket fly true, bounce off the hull of the lead V2, and jet skyward.

He heard screams and turned to see two of his own men lying on the ground, their skin and clothes on fire from the back blast. His face paled and he watched helplessly as they died on the ground before him. The steady stomp of feet made him turn.

A V2 reached out with its pinchers. He screamed. The alien ship scooped up the man in its mandibles and squeezed. The crunch of the body ended his cry of terror. The machine dropped the body and moved on.

The IMA watched from orbit and ordered the arapods to return to the sphere. The new V2s suffered no casualties and little damage. Two hundred and twelve dead humans littered the ground of Little Big Horn. The computer deemed the test of the new arapod a success.

∂   ∂

"Major, we have found a weakness I think we can exploit."

Major Hobbes turned to look at an attractive, thin blonde with dark rimmed glasses about half his age. The dark rimmed glasses provided a great contrast to her fair skin. "Miss Goldstein, isn't it?"

"Yes, sir, from SETI."

Alexander nodded, taking the notes from the SETI observer. "What have you found?"

"The spider ships have a tough armor, but it's not impenetrable. We have found bullet holes, in addition to rocket punctures, in several of the downed ships.

"The computer controlling the ship is in the head of the spider. Theoretically, kill the head and body dies.

"And best of all, these things are not EMP shielded."

The Major nodded, and offered an accusing glare to LCDR Petrovsky sitting in the corner, "You told her about GEMSTAR?"

Major Hobbes became the de-facto commander of the installation as the highest-ranking officer. His office was sparse, but pleasant, with a desk, a conference table, and half dozen chairs. Someone spray painted the windows to conceal the office from prying eyes outside.

Jackie nodded, shifting in her seat and scratching the remnants of her cast, removed the day before. "She's been in on the alien thing from the beginning." She shrugged, "I felt I could trust her, so I told her."

Alexander exhaled a deep sigh and nodded, "It's a moot point anyway. We have no way of using the satellite anyway."

"Actually, I think we can..."

A young Lieutenant knocked and immediately entered the room, cutting her off. "Excuse me sir, but I thought you and the Commander would want to see this."

The Lieutenant put a CD in the computer on Major Hobbes' desk and the machine hummed to life. The computer screen showed a half dozen smaller spider ships streaking across the flatlands of Nebraska or Kansas, their lasers and missiles demolishing an armored military unit. The playback had no sound, but the graphic video filled the Major's imagination with explosions and the screams of the dying.

The armored unit fired numerous rockets and anti-tank missiles at the alien craft, the projectiles bouncing off the tough armor of the ships. The alien lasers cut through buildings, tanks, and humans. The spider ships finished the massacre and flew into the distance.

"We just received this from an Intel courier in Missouri," the LT explained. "That was the 3rd ACR. They didn't even slow down this new model."

"I didn't realize we still had an Armored Calvary Regiment," Alexander mumbled. "Thank you, Lieutenant. Send the word out to everyone. Keep the Intel coming!"

The LT saluted and left the office, leaving the rest to stand in shocked silence. Alexander spoke, "You were saying something about activating the GEMSTAR?"

ᙍ   ᙍ

The new arapods obliterated the remains of the world's Air Forces. The IMA controlled the skies of Earth. The sentient computer also controlled the ground. Wherever an arapod walked, the humans died. The IMA discovered a new feeling: Joy.

The computer enjoyed the cat and mouse, hunter and prey game with the humans. The IMA won every battle while suffering no losses; it felt invincible. The computer learned tactics and strategy, employing the new wisdom with devastating results. The IMA knew that it could bombard the planet from space, as it had done previously, but the computer detected a new sensation: pleasure. The Intelligence Matrix

Algorithm was having fun.

The computer replayed the last two days of attacks in a nano-second. Seemingly random attacks drove the humans into a central area and the IMA followed that with a massive attack by the new model arapods. The computer massacred humans by the thousands.

The IMA was happy; it finally had something to occupy its vast resources.

ભ   ૭

"Alexander, I have bad news and worse news."

Major Hobbes looked up from his desk. A small lamp on his desk provided the only light in the gloomy office. He rubbed his eyes and focused on the feminine silhouette in the doorway. He squinted his eyes and peered into the darkness "What now?"

"The bad news is we just lost the community around St. Louis. It looks like the aliens herded a bunch of refugees into the area then launched one massive, devastating attack." Jackie stepped into the room to the edge of the light from his lamp and set a folder on the desk.

The Army Major nodded wearily, "Go on."

"The worse news is that we picked up a new set of signals. There are more aliens in this system, and they are heading straight for us."

ભ   ૭

"Are we sure they are all in orbit?"

"Yes, sir," replied the technician. The mission control room at the Marshall Space Flight Center monitored hundreds of missions in Earth orbit, but never a military operation, and never one of this importance.

The room mirrored the destroyed Kennedy Space Flight Center in Houston. Rows of control workstations, giant video screens, and state of the art computers adorned the room.

"Turn the GEMSTAR into position. Slowly, please."

LCDR Jacqueline Petrovsky sat at a workstation identical to the one she sat at three months earlier. Surrounded by soldiers, technicians, and minor government functionaries that found their way to Huntsville, she punched a series of commands. Jackie looked to the giant main view screen at the head of the room.

Deanne tapped into the external cameras of the ISS. The main viewscreen showed the remnants of the Space Station gleaming in the sunlight. The alien-built space dock connected with the ISS, a dozen small craft in production. Sunlight glinted off the original set of alien ships. In the far distance, at the lower right-hand corner of the screen, sat the GEMSTAR EMP Satellite.

Two newly completed craft left the space dock, crossed the expanse, and joined other recently birthed ships. Robotic arms moved to and fro, placing hull plates and welding them into place.

The screen to the right of the main viewer showed the targeting system of the GEMSTAR satellite. It took ninety seconds to get the crosshairs—an addition by one of the computer techs—onto the center of the ISS and the small fleet of spider ships. The control lights on the side of the screen flicked to green.

"What about the original ships?" Deanne asked, sitting beside Jackie. "We count over a thousand of them still up there."

"We can't get them all," Jackie replied. "It's a tactical move to knock out the ships that can hurt us the most. In this case, it's the new models."

"But there are a thousand of the other ships verses only twenty of these!"

Jackie turned her head and nodded, "Yes, but we have been able to destroy the original model of the ships. We know their weaknesses. So far, we haven't even made a dent in the new ships." She turned back to her controls. "We take out the new ones, then deal with the old ones."

Jackie checked her board. "We are green."

"Miss Goldstein, are you sure about our new friends?" Major Hobbes asked from his perch at the top of the pyramid shaped command station. "I'd hate to do all of this for nothing."

Deanne actuated her headset, looking up and over her right shoulder. "I've talked with them for three days and I am convinced of their sincerity. This is not the disembodied voice of our attackers. These are flesh and blood beings. I trust them."

Her mind wondered back to the conversations with these potential allies. She asked questions to determine if the orbit ship's played games or if the ships truly contained a new race of allies. Their story of the destruction of their home-world and the trial and error of piecing together ships left from rubble. She nearly teared up again at the sad tale of the first pilots that perished when their cobbled together ships fell apart around them. Their tale concluded when they followed a trail of abandoned ships to this star system. Major Hobbes' voice jolted her from her reverie.

"Very well," boomed the major's voice, "Begin countdown at thirty seconds!"

Silence filled the room. Everyone held their breath and watched the clock scroll down. At the ten-second mark, Alexander said, "Tell your friends to go now!"

Deanne flipped a blue toggle button on her console and said, "Now!"

The timer reached zero.

High above the Huntsville control room, the GEMSTAR satellite fired its EMP weapon.

In the darkness of space, no brightly colored lasers filled the void. No blinding flash of light rippled through orbit. On the satellite, one amber light switched to green, indicating the weapon fired. The satellite sat quietly in space like nothing happened.

Six thousand miles away, the invisible beam impacted the International Space Station and alien shipyard. The ISS Command Module, shielded against EMP from the sun, sat protected against the electro-magnetic pulse. The remainder of the station, as well as the twenty-one nearby arapods, succumbed to the blast. No explosions filled the heavens. No ships rocked the impact of projectiles. One minute everything worked perfectly and the next minute, the lights went out.

CR　　　　　SO

The IMA lost contact with the ISS and all of the new arapods. The computer ran diagnostic checks of all of the systems and found nothing wrong. The sphere of arapods sat unaffected by the malfunction. *A flaw in the design of the new model arapod?* The humans possessed nothing that could cause that kind of system wide failure. The IMA pondered the question, reviewing the primitive jamming capabilities of the humans. *They could not take control of the ships and they did not have a type of weapon capable of disrupting the ship' systems. Or did they?*

The IMA scanned the area and found nothing unusual. It detected no missiles launched from the planet. It scanned the satellites in the area, finding nothing but the communications satellite launched into space they day IMA arrived. It continued to broadcast its connection signal, seeking to connect to host on the planet below.

The computer's sensor sub-matrix extended the search to encompass the planet and found a small cluster of objects entering the atmosphere on the far side. The IMA dispatched a dozen arapods. The small ships engaged their engines and broke orbit. Fire streaked as the arapods entered the atmosphere on an intercept course with the unknowns.

The arapods intercepted the unknowns over the southern United States, firing their cutting lasers at extreme range. The rear-most ship exploded, showering debris across the Mississippi River. The arapods pressed their attack.

Two-dozen surface-to-air missiles erupted from the woodlands below. Trails of fire streaked upward, striking seven of the arapods. Explosions filled the overcast sky. The unknown ships entered the thick cloud cover over Kentucky, dropping altitude, to loss their pursuers.

The arapods poured continuous fire into the clouds as more surface-to-air missiles roared into the sky. Another explosion deep in the cloudbank signaled the death of another of the unknown vessels. The arapods suffered another three losses as the human missiles found their targets.

The IMA studied the ongoing battle and ordered another dozen arapods sent to Earth. The pods moved forward until the computer saw the alien ships clearly for the first time. The computer's circuits froze in shock as the images cleared seconds before SAM missiles destroyed the last two arapods.

The IMA, confused, ordered the withdrawal of its second attack wave and all forces on the planet. It lost its new fleet, a dozen more arapods, and now faced an enemy that should not exist.

The computer needed time to think.

CR   SO

The sounds of distant explosions and runaway rockets reverberated off the nearby mountains. Debris of the last arapod fell to Earth under the gray sky afternoon as the alien ships touched down. Each ship conformed to the same basic design, but heavily modified. None were identical. Troops moved out to form a perimeter around the new arrivals as Major Hobbes—accompanied by LCDR Petrovsky and Deanne—moved out into the field.

Thirty-two ships sat in a rough circle in a pasture at the foot of the Appalachian Mountains in Southern Tennessee. Hobbes saw movement through the dim cockpit windows. The ships settled into the soft Earth, steam rose lazily, and cooling metal popped. The ships were jet black, with a mixture of different parts welded here and there. The ships resembled the spider ships but looked cobbled together from scraps to make space-worthy craft.

The hatch opened on the nearest ship and the first of the aliens appeared. It was half as tall as a human and covered from head to toe in fur. A taller alien appeared behind the first, dressed in black and adorned with weapons. The humans raised their weapons.

Major Hobbes waved them off and the weapons lowered. A dozen aliens, standing at the base of the ramps of the alien ships, lowered theirs. Major Hobbes exhaled, not realizing he held his breath. Alexander and the smaller alien met and stood looking at each other halfway between the ship and bunker where the humans emerged. The alien spoke first, "I am Peri, King of the Cenceti. We have much to discuss."

To Aid and Protect

CHAPTER EIGHT
The Battle for Air and Space

Major Hobbes and his entourage escorted the Cenceti back to Huntsville in a convoy of up armored HUMVEES. Ground crews hastily camouflaged the cobbled together arapods, hiding them from the prying eyes above. The convoy arrived before dawn, quickly ushered into a partially buried hanger at the Space and Rocket Center. Soldiers and scientists arranged tables and chairs in a horseshoe shape in the bright open-air hanger, along with projectors and screens. In the back of the hanger sat The the Space Shuttle *Enterprise*. The *Enterprise* towered over the delegation, providing a great centerpiece for the meeting.

Major Hobbes, LCDR Petrovsky, and Deanne Goldstein led the delegation and everyone—human and alien—took their seats. The sun, obscured for weeks, shone brightly through lights high overhead. Jacqueline and Deanne looked skyward, smiling at the warm light. Major Hobbes stared ahead in silence, focusing on the upcoming meeting.

The Cenceti delegation milled about the conference room. The King stood stoically, in silent awe of the shuttle. Cenceti Engineers studied the ship from every angle. Major Hobbes gave them a few minutes and then called the meeting to order. The Cenceti assumed their seats on the left side of the horseshoe. The humans filled in the rest of the giant 'U'. Armed guards from both contingents stood around the room.

The Cenceti began, telling every detail of the trip from Cenceti, to Sanctuary, to Earth. The humans and Cenceti started the arduous process of getting to know each other; a first encounter with aliens for both species. The newfound allies shared tales of wonder, science, technology, and food. The Cenceti discovered a great taste for melon, especially after surviving on emergency rations for years. Platters of melons sat at intervals along the table.

Deanne Goldstein, the only human the Cenceti talked to on their approach, made her way to the podium. "Good morning, everyone," she said nervously. She did not like to make speeches or do any public speaking. She fiddled with her glasses and gripped the edge of the podium with white knuckles. She knew the historical significance of the moment and it added to her stress. She pushed her glasses up higher on her nose, took a deep breath and continued.

"First, I'd like to welcome our guests, the Cenceti." A round of applause sounded through the room. "They are a victim of the same aliens that now attack our world.

"They have traveled far to help us in our hour of need, and I want to thank their King, Peri, for their assistance." Another round of applause. Peri made his way to the front of the room.

A tech scurried from the shadows and placed a small bench behind the podium for the diminutive alien. Peri thanked him quietly and stepped up onto the bench. The Cenceti King took a deep breath and looked out at the sea of faces, both Cenceti and alien.

He had never seen a room so large, so open, before. Big, wide windows topped the plain walls; windows let in the bright sunshine. The spacecraft that sat behind the group was almost as large as an arapod but had a sleeker, more aerodynamic look.

King Peri shifted his gaze to the human major and nodded. Hobbes returned the gesture and Peri continued. "I want to thank you for saving what is left of my race. We have traveled for many years and suffered greatly. All we wish to do is live in peace." Another round of applause.

"But peace is not yet possible. Not until the computer attacking your world is destroyed. To that end, I pledge all of the knowledge that I have about the computer, the technology my race possesses, and my race itself."

A tremendous round of applause erupted from the humans and the Cenceti. Peri waved the applause down with his hands and it finally subsided. "But first, I must tell you the origin of the computer and our struggles," his voice sounded sad, almost embarrassed by his sudden confession. "There were things we could not tell you until we were sure of your intentions. The friendship and kindness shown to us by Deanne has proven that your intentions are honorable."

"We have told you of the storm that destroyed our world."

A chorus of nods.

"And the story of our journey."

Another chorus.

"And that it is a computer entity that destroyed my people and now threatens yours."

The nods grew fewer, the assembly waiting for the punchline.

"What we did not tell you," Peri continued, "is that, we built the computer..."

A collective gasp filled assembly. Peri waited for just a moment and then proceeded in great detail to tell of the destruction of Cenceti, the escape, Sanctuary, and finally of the Cenceti's will to rebuild the damaged arapods and pursue the IMA.

The King told of the tracking of the IMA through system after system. Their discovery of the remnants of several worlds, and most recently, the primitives on Rigil Kentaurus, the burnt-out hulk of Voyager One, and the trail of arapods leading to Earth. Peri relayed the entire story of the Cenceti; the humans both dismayed and terrified at the struggle and desperation of the aliens.

"That is why we are here, now," he finished, "to aid you in your time of suffering. We are ashamed of our creation and we pledge all that we have to see it destroyed."

He motioned with his hand and another Cenceti joined him behind the podium. "This is Fen. He is my top advisor and a former engineer on the arapod design team. He will give you a complete technical layout of the ship."

Fen stood before the audience and watched the King leave with a human male and female, along with a contingent of soldiers from each race. Engineers from both races remained, notebooks in hand. Fen's tail twitched and he told the humans about the ships he helped to create.

ᘓ　　　ᘔ

The IMA played the last battle over and over, not believing its electronic eyes. The unknown ships were arapods – damaged, junked, and repaired arapods – left on the far-off world the Cenceti called Sanctuary.

The Cenceti! Could they have managed to piece together the ships and follow the IMA? The computer bombarded Sanctuary relentlessly for days but did not sacrifice any arapods to destroy the Cenceti. That tactic it had learned *after* the Sanctuary battle.

The IMA switched part of its vast computing resources to verify the bombing of Sanctuary. The computer left the historical sub matrix studying the genocide and switched the bulk of its resources to the mysterious malfunction of its new arapods.

The IMA again scanned the area. *The Cenceti's arrival and the malfunction could not be a coincidence*, the machine surmised. *The Cenceti may have developed a new weapon and if they give it to the humans...* The thought sent an electronic shudder through the computer.

The sensor sub-matrix beeped for attention and the IMA verified its findings. The country called Pakistan lost a city to a nuclear explosion. Nuclear explosions created radiation, heat, fallout and an electro-magnetic pulse. *The Cenceti had used an EMP burst to disable the new generation arapods.*

The IMA shut down its sub-systems and turned its entire being toward a new project: building the third generation of arapods.

ɞ   ɷ

"Yes, we are equipping your fighter craft with laser technology."

LCDR Jacqueline Petrovsky stared at the alien working on the F-14 Tomcat and smiled. He thoughts drifted to science fiction; fighters pairing off and fighting tremendous battles, laser bolts filling the heavens. Her mind's eye recalled dozens of movies and larger than life battles.

A human mechanic dropped a wrench, bringing her back to the present. The hanger sat full of aircraft, pilots and technicians. The hanger represented a dozen countries; some of the best pilots in the world. The small aliens and humans worked together, crawling in and around the fighters. Some of the Cenceti had already deployed to other countries to install upgrades, by land and sea.

Without use of the air, it would be a slow and daunting process. It could be a month or more before some of the other countries are online, she thought.

Jackie knew their best hope was to regain air superiority in the US and export the techs under the cover of that air support. She recognized a handful of foreign pilots, in the US for advanced training, and the Chinese astronaut, stranded in the US after his escape from the ISS. All of them, she knew, wanted to get home.

"What about shields?" she asked, her eyes narrowing as she studied the mass of wires protruding from the laser pulse generator.

"We do not have what you call *shield technology*," the Cenceti replied. His name was Ren L'bek Teke, a young, white furred engineer; a specialist in the laser systems onboard the arapods. His large, bright blue eyes—a rarity among Cenceti—and his big ears reminded Jackie of a teddy bear; cute and cuddly. "We are upgrading your weapons.

"I am concerned about your engines," he continued. "They do not have enough thrust for the armor we can provide. I will have to consult with my fellow BAL to see if we can upgrade them."

"The Bal?"

Ren connected two wires together, binding them together with a single touch of a laser torch. His work complete, he paused for a moment, gathering his thoughts.

"The Cenceti are divided into four classes: the Poy, our ruling class; the Bal, the scientific caste; the Mal, our military; and the Gam, the workers.

"We have lived in harmony for thousands of years under this system." He sniffed back the Cenceti equivalent of a tear. "I suppose we still would be, except for the energy storm."

"I'm sorry," Jackie said.

The Cenceti nodded and quietly returned to his work. His laser torch connected two more wires from the laser generator to the sleek fighter. The small statured alien did not have to duck under the The F-14 Tomcat fuselage. The fighter was one of the oldest and largest fighters in operation by the U.S. Military. The fleet officially retired from service a decade earlier. Major Hobbes and Jackie used the month of dust to recover as many of the aircraft they could.

The aircraft sported huge, swept back wings, twin tail fins over the dual engine housing, and a bubble cockpit that allowed for a spectacular field of vision. Jackie originally trained on the Tomcat and chose one for her. With the addition of laser generators, she expected the fighter to rule the sky.

Ki Ton Li, the Chinese pilot and ISS survivor, stood nearby. He watched intently as the small alien modified the Tomcat. His fighter, a Chinese MiG-29 pulled from Pensacola Naval Air Station, sat nearby, awaiting its upgrade. Ki Ton Li was tall for an oriental, with black hair, brown eyes, and a close-cropped black goatee. "What about more powerful missiles?" he inquired in perfect English. "Can you help us increase our range? Our detonation yields?"

Ren shook his head; a mannerism from his human counterparts. "I am sorry, no. Our missile technology is no better than yours." He turned back to the jet.

"There," the young scientist said happily. He waved

away the smoke wafting up from his laser torch. "You have a pair of lasers on each wing and a fast recharging generator under your seat. You should see no decrease in performance of your craft."

"Unfortunately, we can't test it," Jackie said solemnly.

Ki Ton Li smiled, "We will test it in battle. Come, we need to modify more."

The trio walked to the MiG-29. Ten hours later, two full squadrons sat armed and ready to take to the skies.

❦　　　❧

High above, the IMA prepared for the dawning of its new project. The computer dispatched arapods to the lunar surface to gather more raw materials and some to Earth to smelt and process the materials. Using the experience in producing the V2, the creation of the V3 went much faster, with less waste.

The lunar operations went well. The IMA mining sub-routine found little distraction on the lunar surface, except for two lunar-quakes and one cave-in. The mine crushed one arapod and closed down that operation. The smelting sub-matrix did not have it that easy. The humans fought the arapods loaded with the raw materials, creating delays in the production. The IMA dispatched additional forces, quickly defeating the unorganized human rebellion. Humans perished in a hail of lasers.

Arapods ferried the smelted metal and electronics, stolen from computer stores, to the ISS. The automated workforce replaced burned out components and the shipyard went back to work.

☙ ❧

"Major? There is a General Christianson here to see you."

Major Alexander Hobbes looked up from his desk. "Send him in." He rose from the desk and made his way to the door, meeting the man halfway across the office. The men shook hands, exchanged pleasantries, and sat down. The militia leader's executive officer, Major Tyrone Johnson, stood by the door, his back against the wall.

"I guess you are wondering why I asked you for a meeting."

"The thought had crossed my mind," the General replied with a smile.

Major Hobbes turned in his seat to get a better look at the survivalist. "I have read the reports of your activities in the south. I must admit, I'm impressed.

"You've taken some losses, but you've driven three of the spider-ships out of your territory. That takes good training and well-motivated troops."

The general stared at the Hobbes, steepled his fingers and cocked an eyebrow, but said nothing.

Alexander continued, "I'll be honest with you, general. I have a mission in mind, and I need your men."

"Ahhh," came the retort. "I had thought it was something like that. What would you have my militia

228

do, Major?" The tone came out sarcastically, intentional or not. "Stand guard around your little brain trust here? Or maybe we would simply be the bait for some elaborate trap?"

Major Hobbes smiled. "Actually, sir, I was thinking your troops would like to lead an assault and take the battle to the enemy."

A look of shock replaced the sarcastic smirk on the general's face. It vanished as quickly as it appeared. He sat back, stroking his short, graying beard. "Take it to the enemy? Not letting them come to us?"

"Exactly, General."

"You mean..." Christianson looked toward the ceiling.

Hobbes nodded.

The men negotiated for several hours, reaching an agreement before dawn the next day. The men shook hands and parted. It was time to take the fight into space.

CR   SO

The ironworks sat cold, unused and lifeless, as it had for weeks. The waning light of dusk cast shadows over the foundry, adding to the spooky, surreal environment. The harsh Pennsylvania winter made worse by the brief nuclear winter from the arapod attack. No one ventured there, not since the world nearly ended months earlier and the first visit from the arapods.

The roar of engines broke the stillness of the

darkness. A fleet of arapods emerged over the horizon, weaving their contrails across the twilight sky of spring. The locals scattered, running for shelter as the first spider ship spread its legs to land. The arapods visited the ironworks on the occasions in the last few months. Each time the locals fought the ships only to be driven back by the superior technology. Four days of operating the ironworks in February yielded enough raw materials to build the second generation arapods. The process took two days the second visit. After each visit, the ships shut down the foundry and disappeared into the sky.

The sun disappeared in the west, enveloping the parking lot where the arapods landed in darkness. The ships walked to the foundry, extended their mechanical arms, and activated the abandoned steel mill. The furnaces heated up and the arapods lifted to the sky, rotated, and entered the massive complex from above. Two arapods remained on the ground. They turned their sensors outward, watching for the inevitable attack.

The locals did not disappoint. The dwindling number of humans pooled their resources and hired one of the military expert's touting their combat experience. The first four mercenaries were con artists, running off with money, precious jewels, and, in one case, the mayor's daughter.

The final mercenary they hired proved his experience by hunting down the first four. He brought each one back, alive, for trial. The imposters found justice to be swift. The IMA, via the arapods on the ground, saw the four men swinging from gallows in the center of town.

The mercenary's worth proven; he set about designing a defense of the town. He procured and set weapons and explosives. The people of the old steel town prepared to fight the aliens. Snipers perched on with rooftops with rifles and anti-tank missiles. Commandeered National Guard HUMVEEs with heavy machine guns idled, ready to charge on order.

Previous visits offered the same sequence of events: the aliens landed, fired the foundry, and offloaded equipment inside. The townsfolk waited, fingers tense on triggers, for the transition. The grounded arapods opened their cargo doors but offloaded no equipment.

Each large spider ship disgorged ten miniature versions of itself. The new ships walked into the darkness, only their sensor eyes glowing in the night. The small spiders took up defensive positions in a rough semi-circle around the refinery.

The third version of the alien ships appeared smaller, more compact; about twice the size of a human. The V3 brandished two lasers on each of the forward arms and a set of pincers on each of the forward legs. The smaller spiders walked on the rear two back pairs of legs.

Murmurs rippled through the humans; their confidence waned. Sensing the change in mood, the mercenary raised his hand and fired a red flare high in the air. Gunfire erupted from the nearby hills and from the roofs of buildings in the small town. Pickup trucks roared out of the darkness and screeched to a halt, depositing armed men onto the developing battlefield. They quickly spread out and added their fire to the barrage. Two anti-tank weapons streaked into the mass of alien machines. The missiles hit and destroyed the two grounded V1 arapods. Fireballs lit the night, highlighting the smaller alien craft.

The new V3 craft shrugged off the intense small arms fire, the barrage did not penetrate their tough armor. The small spider ships counter attacked. Lasers flashed, destroying a makeshift bunker on the north side of town. The V3s systemically fired their weapons, raking the human positions from right to left. The two HUMVEES erupted in flame. Screams pierced the night.

The mercenary, a retired Navy Seal in his 50s, studied the battlefield from a nearby hill. He directed the battle, moving from point to point, issuing orders and defining targets. His troops provided covering fire, to no avail. Anti-tank missiles flashed from a nearby rooftop, engulfing two V3s in a bright fireball.

The flare died out, leaving only the flickering fires of the arapods and Humvees lit the battlefield. Bright flashes from the almost constant hail of lasers from the remaining V3s created a strobe effect across the battlefield.

The refinery formed the centerpiece of the battlefield, the V3s spread out in two rows between it and the human attackers. The V3s launched a barrage of red bolts in every direction from their clustered ranks, like a flower opening its petals.

The spread-out humans provided multiple targets, but nothing the V3s could concentrate their fire on. The battle raged back and forth, each side suffering losses, but neither gaining any ground.

The arapods within the steel mill left their tasks to join the battle, rising from the foundry superstructure like wraiths. The arapods, with their elevation, brought a new depth to the battle. Their red beams sliced through the nearby hillside, the buildings, and the pickup trucks. Trees and shrubs caught fire from the superheated energy. The roiling flames incinerated four townspeople in the onslaught.

More anti-armor rockets streaked through the night. Two caught the arapod over the refinery. It exploded, raining hot metal across the battle line. The bulk of the ship feel, crushing a pair of V3s. The remaining alien craft turned their fire on the building that launched the rockets. It collapses under the withering fire.

Another rocket lashed out, hitting a flying arapod. The explosive ripped through the ship's engine housing, erupted, and brought the alien down. The resulting explosion shook the surrounding area, crumbling a second building. The structure imploded, swallowing eight men and women. The debris tumbled down the small hill toward the foundry, crushing a half dozen of the V3s.

The townspeople continued to shift positions. The trucks and HUMVEES, melted to slag, provided some cover. Two more trucks entered the fray, a big .50 mounted on the back of each. Lasers from the ground and the air engulfed the two vehicles. The trucks melted in seconds, drowning out the screams of the men inside. Other trucks, armed with grenade launchers, rockets, and rifles, destroyed another six V3 pods before the drivers pulled the trucks out of the kill zone under a hail of laser fire.

The retired Seal squatted behind a small brick embankment and slapped a fresh mag into his M-4 rifle. The hail of gunfire from his left—the human contingent—slowed due to heavy casualties. The alien ships continued to pour volley after volley outward from their diminished ranks. He motioned for his radio operator. The young woman crawled over, blood and mud covering her face. She handed him the receiver.

"Now!"

A second wave of townspeople appeared, armed with rifles, pistols, and Molotov Cocktails. Part of the reserve force took a knee and opened fire, drawing the attention of the V3s. Red lasers lashed out in return. The remainder of the newcomers, carrying flaming bottles, approached from the alien's left flank. They threw the bottles high in the air, the fiery weapons arched toward the remaining alien ships. They ran.

Eyes and mechanical sensors looked up at the incoming projectiles. The computer controlled V3s turned their weapons skyward and fired at the cocktails. Exactly as they Seal hoped. The bottles exploded, raining sticky napalm over the V3s.

Six cars roared down the street, barreling down on the remaining arapods. The computer-guided reflexes switched targets and two of the six vehicles erupted in flame. The other four tore through the remaining V3s with a loud tear and ripping metal. The cars spread the fire and destruction. Flames leapt toward the sky and debris filled the air.

The resistance fighters smiled, realizing the tide of battle turned in their favor. The poured more small-arms fire and rockets into the alien mass. The two remaining airborne arapods turned to flee and took two rockets each. They exploded, raining debris on the last few V3s. The smaller alien craft retreated to the foundry, firing a steady stream of red.

"Blow it," the Seal ordered.

The foundry exploded, the building collapsing in on itself. Brick and mortar buried the last few V3s. The town reverberated from sounds of explosions. The shock wave threated to topple the badly damaged buildings in the town.

"Cease fire," the Seal called. "Cease fire!"

The firing stopped, leaving only the crackle of flames, the groaning of super-heated metal, and the high revving engines of the two still functioning, driverless cars.

The townsfolk turned warriors celebrated their victory in the eerie glow of the firelight. Their town lay in shambles and they paid a heavy price, but they defended their homes. Pride swelled in the firelit night.

An old man, a veteran of a bloody conflict some seventy years earlier, slung his rifle, walked over to a burning hulk of a V3, and spat on the wreck. He nodded to himself, turned, and disappeared into the night.

☙   ❧

Captain Daniel Simpson unhappily flew his C-130 cargo plane. The quad-prop plane, a workhorse in the Air Force since the 1970s, cruised at fifteen-thousand feet over the sundrenched Tennessee Valley. A hastily installed electronics package broadcast the plane's location, much to the displeasure of its pilot.

Major Hobbes volunteered Captain Simpson for the mission due to his lack of fighter experience. The Captain, as bait for the aliens, now waited for them to swoop down and kill him. His co-pilot on the mission, a bottle of Jack Daniels, sat half empty in his lap.

He took another sip of the bottle. "At least I have good company." He took another long drink. He tightened the top on the bottle and titled the control yoke left and right, weaving the plane across the sky. "Might as well enjoy my last minutes alive," he muttered. He pulled on the control, nosing the aircraft skyward. It nearly stalled, and he leveled it out to a chorus of bells and alarms.

His flight path took him from Tyndall Air Force Base in Florida, to Charleston Air Force Base in South Carolina, to a long sweeping curve up the Tennessee Valley. He knew the modified fighters waited to intercept any incoming aliens. He smirked at the thought, his alcohol addled mind warping the possibility of his survival to near zero. He took another drink.

He saw the blips on the Cenceti enhanced radar package and sighed. CPT Simpson took another drink and held the bottle in salute to the approaching alien craft. "I got in...incoming," he hickuped. "Looks like about six of 'em," he stammered in a half drunken drawl. He took another drink. "I'd say I got about four minutes to live..."

"Calm down," a feminine voice replied in his headset, "we are already on the way!"

☙   ❧

LCDR Jacqueline Petrovsky felt the freedom of flight. She flew through the sparse, late afternoon clouds. The blue sky of Earth beckoned, and she did not disappoint. She pushed the throttle forward and the F-14 Tomcat accelerated smoothly, pushing her upward at just under Mach One. She estimated her intercept time to the arapods a full minute before they reached the transport.

A quick glance in both directions told her the position of the rest of the squadron, a mixture of F-14 Tomcats and F-18 Hornets. They leveled off at thirty thousand feet, the twelve fighters spread out in a classic "V" formation. Jackie, using the call sign Nails, checked her new RIO—Radio Intercept Officer—in her small rear-view mirror. The young man was less than six months out of the academy and called himself Outlaw. He looked scared to death.

"Outlaw, what's the position of the transport?" she

asked, already knowing the answer. The aviator learned a long time ago that calmly talking to someone could relax them and help them focus. One look at her RIO told her he needed to relax, and fast. The young man, visor pulled down, shook visibly. His trembling fingers checked his controls.

"Uh, angels twenty-three on heading," he paused and looked at his board again, "three four six."

"Where are the MiGs?"

"They are," another pause, "at angels thirty-five, about two minutes behind us."

Jackie looked in her mirror again. The young man raised his visor, confidence edged out the fear in his eyes. He exhaled slowly, studying his instruments.

Just in time, she thought, *'cause here they come.*

The new laser target designator on her HUD beeped; a target entered firing range. The amber reticle flashed red, centering on the lead alien craft. "This is Nails, you are clear to engage," she called. She adjusted her course with a flick of her wrist, keeping the reticle aligned on target.

The flashing red reticle turned a solid red; weapons lock. LCDR Jacqueline Petrovsky, naval aviator, fired the first laser beam in combat for mankind.

CR   SO

The IMA watched the C-130 steadily grow in the visual receptor of the lead arapod. The computer grew annoyed and weary with the humans. It controlled the skies of this world, the audacity of the humans flying nearly sent the system into overload. The targeting system locked onto the quad prop craft. The sensor sub-matrix beeped, interrupting the command to fire.

More planes filled the air, on an intercept course with the arapod force. The computer considered for a moment and determined the incoming flight of fighters the bigger threat. It let the cargo plane go, knowing it would have time to track it down after dealing with the fighters.

The IMA checked its weapons systems and the new chaff/flare dispensers, designed to confuse and decoy the human missiles. The bullets created many holes in the ships but had yet to outright destroy a ship. The missiles posed the only real threat to the arapods.

The six arapods broke into two groups of three in flying V formation, one behind the other. The human planes continued on course, closing with the arapods and the IMA prepared another six, in case the humans tried more trickery. The defensive sub-matrix signaled a lock and the IMA focused on the twelve Earth fighters heading for its forces.

Lasers leapt forward, searing the atmosphere with a barrage of green energy. The intense energy beams impacted on the lead ships, sliced through them like tissue paper, and instantly destroyed the first wedge of arapods. The IMA shrieked when the lasers tore through the arapod providing its view of the battle. The computer withdrew its consciousness back to space and ordered another dozen arapods to Earth.

The computer split its attention between the air battle in Tennessee and the ground battle to the north.

Citing heavy losses at the refinery, the computer ordered the retreat of its ground forces. The computer gave the order too late; the ground units were lost. The computer refocused on the aerial battle.

The second wedge of arapods broke up, dodging and weaving across the darkening, twilight sky. Surrounded by superior numbers, they quickly fell to the more maneuverable human fighters. An arapod clipped a wing from one F-14, sending both craft into a death spiral to the ground below. The F-14 pilot and RIO punched out, white parachutes floating to the growing darkness below. The arapod, with no pilot, crashed into a fiery blaze.

Jackie banked her Tomcat hard left, avoiding the straight on tactics of the last arapod of the original attack force. A distant explosion confirmed her squadron pounded the alien craft. She pushed her joystick forward, nosing the fighter down. The arapod flew over her, missing by meters. It erupted a moment later as green energy bolts stitch a pattern of hole along its dorsal surface. The arapod disintegrated in a flash of light and cloud of debris.

"Great shot, MC," she called, righting her craft. She pulled the throttle back, slowing the craft. Her squadron formed around her.

"That looks like all of them," MC responded, happy and carefree. He waggled his wings in celebration.

"Nails, I have more incoming," her RIO, Outlaw, called from behind her. "I have twelve more contacts at angels seven zero thousand, closing fast at twelve o'clock."

Jackie nodded and she switched frequencies, "Hey, Fu Manchu! You want the next batch?"

Ki Ton Li's voice came in clear, "It would be my honor!"

The ten remaining Tomcats banked in unison, turning to pursue the distant transport. Li's flight of MiGs flashed below them, accelerating toward the enemy.

Jackie's squadron lost two ships: the one clipped by the arapod and another F-14 destroyed when an arapod grasped it with its pincers and literally ripped it apart. The pilot and RIO fell to the earth below. Jackie saw no parachutes. Marshall Space Flight Center dispatched Search and Rescue helicopters to pick up any survivors. Petrovsky looked below and saw the lights of the helicopters as they flew terrain to avoid the alien's sensors.

"Hold up, here," Jackie called, banking her craft in a wide circle around the battlespace. "We will stay on station, just in case Li needs assistance...if more of those ships show up.

"Dagger Seven, Eight, Nine, and Ten," she continued, "pursue our drunk friend Captain Simpson. Make sure he lands safely."

"Roger, Commander."

Ki Ton Li held the stick loosely and cruised through the smattering of dark clouds as the sun set to his left. A quick glance at his heads-up-display (HUD) showed the aliens flew in three groups of four. He absentmindedly nodded and keyed his comm system, ordering his flight into four groups of three. The ships moved as he directed, and he checked his HUD again: alien diamonds against MiG wedges. Red light flashed in the darkness. The arapods opened fire at forty thousand feet, their lasers chasing the MiGs at their cruising altitude of twenty-eight thousand.

The Cenceti installed laser lock sounded a warning, and the more agile MiGs banked sharply. The barrage missed. The MiGs nosed skyward, closing fast on the alien craft. Red and green lasers crisscrossed the night. The two forces met, banked, and broke through the other's formation. Neither squadron scored a hit in the first barrage.

Ki Ton Li banked sharply to starboard and leveled out behind an arapod. He heard the high-pitched tone of target lock and pulled the trigger on his joystick. Green beams strafed the fleeing alien. The tone changed and he stole a quick glance over his shoulder as his target vanished in a bright fireball. He banked to port, missing the expanding ball of gas and debris. Li's wingman appeared behind his attacker and blasted the attacking arapod. It vaporized.

Two down in seconds.

The fighters and arapods pursued each other through the pitch-black sky. The ships dove toward the forests below and then climbed high. The MiGs executed precise barrel rolls and split-S maneuvers to confuse the enemy. The MiG pilots used the new Cenceti enhanced sensors and avionics to track the enemy bogies. The pilots saw nothing in the darkness but engine glow when they looked out the canopy. They picked off the arapods one by one. Only the MiGs and the distant circling Tomcats remained.

Twenty-two fighters and one transport returned to the hidden bunker in Alabama. Ki Ton Li took great pride in not losing a single fighter. He smiled broadly as his MiG touched the pavement.

Jackie Petrovsky slapped a high-five with her RIO when she received word that Search and Rescue found her downed pilots. Spirits grew when the reports filtered down of the battle in Pennsylvania. The celebration carried well into the night.

The orbital bombardment started the next day.

CR   SO

City after city erupted in flame. Millions died when bright red bolts of energy shot from the sky. Buildings melted. Vehicles disintegrated under the intense heat. People caught outside vaporized. Many that took shelter ultimately succumbed to falling buildings, dust, and panic. The bombardment lasted for two weeks and leveled hundreds of cities around the globe.

Humans hunkered down in caves and underground bunkers; anywhere they could find shelter from the bombardment. The cities, mostly abandoned after the initial attack months earlier, suffered the brunt of the attack, with light casualties.

The cities sat in ruins and black smoke filled the sky. The IMA turned its attention to military strongholds across the globe. Aerial bombardment commenced on military bases of every service in the US, UK, Soviet Union, China, and a dozen other countries. The IMA hit the vocal German Group led by Lars Gardfeld exceptionally hard, destroying their main training camps in Stuttgart and Berlin.

In retaliation, a Putin Class Russian Nuclear Submarine fired two surface to orbit missiles from the South China Sea, one of them nuclear tipped. The missiles destroyed twelve arapods and damaged twenty-two more. The IMA, until that moment, classed submarines as a minor threat. The destruction of its ships, especially in orbit, changed the threat level. The computer unleashed a series of attacks on the seas and oceans destroying three dozen submarines.

The IMA used the time to land more arapods and forge the steel it needed to create additional V3 pods. Arapods mined ore on both the lunar surface and on Earth. The craft transported the raw materials to numerous locations for smelting and forging, then to the remnants of the ISS to create the V3. The IMA moved ships day and night during the bombardment.

The computer stopped the attack after the third week. Cities, military installations, and swaths of pristine countryside lay in ruins. In orbit, nearly five hundred of small, nimble V3s crawled across the ISS and surrounding space.

The humans will pay, the computer thought. *They should have accepted by protection.*

The IMA loaded the V3s into arapods, twenty in each. The twenty-five loaded craft left orbit and headed for Earth, two hundred others providing escort.

ಇ   ಖ

Dust filled the air, obscured the environs, and made it difficult to breath. Soldiers and airmen emerged from the deep bunker outside of the Marshall Center, shielding their eyes and coughing at the filth in the air. Fires still burned in the distance, where Huntsville once stood.

The survivors felt the tremendous blasts and knew the city and the surrounding area took several hits. They welcomed the end of the attack, surprised by the sudden cessation. They feared what it might mean. The alien computer showed methodical precision, to allow any humans to survive did not fit the pattern. Putting those thoughts out of their mind, the survivors went to work clearing debris and prepping the area for launch.

It was time for a counterattack.

The three-week bombardment cost lives, cities, and equipment. It also afforded Major Hobbes and his staff the time needed to finalize their plans. Through HAM radio operators and Morse code, the Marshall Center coordinated a massive, planet wide assault against the aliens. Aircraft survived the aerial bombardment in ten countries, personnel in another twenty. They continued to make contact with new units and their army grew daily. Major Hobbes, General Christianson, and their staffs used their time wisely and developed a daring operation.

The warriors met in the underground bunker, the

Enterprise to their back. Hobbes stood, a pointer in his hand, and went over the plan for the dozenth time.

"We will destroy the alien ships on three fronts simultaneously," he explained. Every time he said the words and laid out the concept, it seemed more like science fiction than a battleplan. "On land, in the air, and in space. We still have shortages in supplies and ammunition. Airfields have been destroyed. It will take time to get everything in place."

"We have armor piercing small arms ammo," Major Johnson nodded. "That is being distributed across our forces now."

"What about increasing the yields of missiles? Shoulder fired Stingers?" Hobbes asked.

Deanne, the scientific chief of staff, shook her head. "It will be months until those weapons are available. I...I don't think we can wait."

"I don't either," Hobbes replied. He glanced toward the ceiling. "I seriously doubt that computer will give us two more months to plan." He completed his briefing and dismissed the assembly.

Hobbes left the underground bunker, followed by Jacqueline Petrovsky, Deanne Goldstein, Tyrone Johnson, Peri and Malel. They shielded their eyes and squinted against the dust. The Major said nothing while he surveyed the damage. The others formed behind him and stared at the destruction, mouths agape. He watched men and women—his responsibility—moving through the ruble, performing their duty. He turned and retreated back to the dark confines of the bunker complex. The others followed.

"No, we can't wait any longer," he confided. "As soon as we confirm the aliens are on the move, we go." They returned to the conference room.

Alexander ran his fingers through his thin hair, "And make sure the other nations are online. I don't want to get out there and find myself all alone!"

General Christianson entered the conference room, looked around at the assembled humans and aliens, and smiled. Papers and hand drawn sketches of arapods and the ISS filled the table. One page contained a list of countries they contacted and their capabilities. A marine stood in the corner, weapon at ease. The Marine nodded to the General, who nodded back.

"My men are ready, thanks to LCDR Petrovsky and Malel." He nodded to the woman and the alien, standing beside his King as always. "Their care in training them in space and zero-G combat will guarantee success...and quite possibly bring some of them back!"

"You still think this is a suicide mission?" Hobbes asked.

"Yes, Major, I do."

"I don't go on suicide missions, General," the Special Forces Officer replied, smiling.

The General opened his mouth to retort, but a technician ran into the room, interrupting him.

The man, red faced and out of breath, gulped in air. "The aliens are on the move!"

CR   SO

"Good luck."

Major Hobbes looked up from his seat. Deanne stood outside the arapod, the cool May wind rustling her hair. He smiled. "To us all"

He looked past the former SETI Observer to the two squadrons of fighters already lifting from the tarmac. Two-dozen fighters armed with lasers and photon torpedoes, streaked toward the dusty sky. He nodded to the aircraft. "Science fiction meets science fact."

Deanne turned and watched the last of the craft take off. She exhaled sharply and then turned back to look at the Major. She smiled, raising her voice over the engine roar. "You are one to talk, strapped into this thing!"

Alexander looked around the inside of the Cenceti arapod and at his assembled troops. *A dozen humans and another dozen Cenceti strapped into a cobbled together alien spaceship about to launch into orbit,* he thought. "This is science fiction..." he said aloud.

Deanne leaned in and kissed the older man on the cheek. "Not anymore, its science fact. And historic!" She took a step back and the hatch closed. "So come back and celebrate with me!"

He chuckled slightly, "Is that an order?"

"Yes!" she yelled as the hatch sealed. Deanne retreated as the arapod, one of three, rose from the surface. It hung, suspended, for a moment and then skyward. Deanne watched them go with tears in her eyes. She uttered a silent prayer, ending it with, "God speed."

The arapods easily caught up to the fighter escort. The twenty-seven ships creating a symbol of unity unseen in all of human history; different ideologies, different technologies, and different races combined into one. The dusty sky obscured the contrails as the ships climbed higher into the atmosphere.

"Blackheart leader to Dagger Lead."

LCDR Petrovsky powered her F-14 down to ninety percent, "Go ahead Blackheart."

"We are ready to proceed, on your signal."

The naval aviator checked her screen and saw alien ships inbound. "Stand by," she said, still watching the screen. The arapods slowed and the fighters surged ahead under full power. The dust and haze made visibility tough, but the higher altitudes were better than the ground and Jackie could see for several miles. Hazy, bright sunshine nearly blinded her above the clouds.

Outlaw verified the incoming bogies. "Twenty ships heading for us," he reported. *Almost even odds*, she thought.

The dust gave way for a moment and Jackie saw her targets, black dots in the distance, growing fast. The first laser bolts flashed past, "Cloak and Dagger Squadrons break and attack!"

The squadron of Tomcats and MiGs broke into calculated disarray, the strategy devised to confuse the alien computer. The arapods continued forward in groups of four, firing continuously.

A red bolt clipped the left wing of a MiG, the laser

sliced off a section near the air-to-air missile pods. The pilot struggled with the controls, the aircraft drifting left. He regained control of the fighter by compensating with the rudder pedals, cursing under his breath. A second and a third red bolt found the fighter. It exploded into a pile of flaming debris, the pilot's struggle over.

The pilot's wingman, Ki Ton Li, grimaced. The Chinese pilot immediately targeted the arapod and fired a missile, counted to three, and followed with a barrage of lasers. The missile hit the alien amidships, ripping the hull open. The green beams hit a second later, slicing the arapod neatly in two. The pieces silently fell to the Earth below. He banked onto the tail of another alien ship and continued the battle.

CR   SO

Around the world, similar battles raged. Squadrons from England, Germany, France, Iraq, Saudi Arabia, China, Japan, and a dozen other countries took to the skies. They attacked anything in their airspace. Success varied against the computer controlled arapods, depending on skill and weaponry.

The Chinese, British, and Germans experienced great success. Their battle tested pilots in state-of-the-art fighters dropped four arapods in a manner of minutes. The Saudi Air Force, their best pilots decimated early in the campaign with Colonel Muhammad, fared the worst of all of the Air Forces. The young rookie pilots of the Saudi Air Force fell as easy prey to the computer control arapods.

The IMA watched as it hemorrhaged arapods at an alarming rate. It recalled its remaining fighters to orbit, out of fighter range and worked on a new strategy. Two missiles lashed out of the atmosphere, destroying a pair of arapods on the far side of the planet. The IMA moved the sphere further away from the planet, formed its arapods into one large attack force, and send them back to Earth.

The IMA targeted the Japanese first. The warriors of far east decimated the arapods, downing over thirty-five arapods, eradicating the alien menace from the skies of the land of the rising sun. The arapod attack force overwhelmed the three Japanese squadrons. One hundred alien craft appeared in the east. The battle lasted over an hour, lasers crisscrossing the meridian line of dawn. A Chinese and a Russian squadron raced to assist the Japanese, arriving in time to see the final dogfight.

In the fading moments of the battle, Colonel Ikorishi Koyu of the Imperial Japanese Air Defense Force (IJADF) personally destroyed fourteen of the arapods, a testament to his skill and tenacity. His last act, before eight alien craft overwhelmed his depleted fighter. The remaining arapods turned their attention to the Chinese and Russian squadrons, reducing them to rubble.

The Chinese Air Force engaged the arapod fleet next. The homeland of Ki Ton Li destroyed another twenty-two-alien craft before succumbing to the massed force of pods. Captain Wes Tran, the last pilot of squadron nine, destroyed five arapods during the battle, earning the title of Ace. His last-minute ejection saved him from death. His fighter took out two more arapods on its spiral to the planet below.

With no further opposition, the IMA moved its forces westward toward the Russian Federation.

ᙣ　　　　ᙣ

The GEMSTAR satellite turned slowly, directing its weapons toward the mass of less than a thousand arapods sitting in orbit.

Deanne and the others watched from the new mission control room set up in the giant hanger. She saw another hundred arapods leave the cluster, racing for the planet. Jackie and other mission control specialists set up the room as a carbon copy of Houston and Marshall, hoping familiarity would help morale. They modified the room to incorporate the military aspect of the usually civilian operation. Deanne's senior military advisors sat on either side of command console. She nervously drummed her fingers, watching the crosshairs line up on the mass of ships.

She did not sit at a control station this time. She sat at the top of the pyramid, promoted and in charge of the orbiting satellite and space ops. The unanimous choice to command mission control with Major Hobbes and recently promoted Commander Petrovsky, running their air and space missions.

"Her past experience at NASA and SETI, plus her

friendship with the alien Cenceti, make her the logical choice to run the vital hub," Hobbes said shortly before his departure.

Her eyes scanned the computer and technician stations laid out in rows before her. The Space Shuttle *Enterprise* sat at her back. She stole a glance at it occasionally, drawing strength and resolve from the retired shuttle.

"There are eight hundred-fifty ships in the cluster. We should be able to disable around six hundred of them with this blast," said her second in command, a NASA engineer known to everyone as Doc.

"Let's hope it's enough," she said, then activated the com-line to the boarding party. "Blackheart leader this is Renegade Base. Awaiting your go."

CʀＣ　　　　ｏＤ

Rage enveloped the IMA.

The humans continued to test the superior technology and intelligence of the computer, launching hundreds of aircraft all over the world. The computer dispatched flights of twenty arapods to reinforce its squadron moving westward over the Middle East. The losses piled up. Two hundred human fighters now roamed the Earth.

The computer ordered a dozen arapods to bombard the planet from orbit, picking targets of opportunity. The orbiting craft spread out and red lasers pounded the planet.

The IMA turned its attention, for a moment, to the

International Space Station, two thousand kilometers away. The automated facility single mindedly created V3 pods for the final assault on the planet.

Another month, thought the IMA, *another month and there will be enough V3s to invade.*

The computer pulled another dozen arapods from its reserve force and sent them into different orbits to add additional firepower to the planetary bombardment. Laser bolts zipped through the atmosphere, superheating the air. Shock waves buffeted the human fighters, downing several fighters in Russia and a whole squadron in Chile.

The new strategy encouraged the computer and it ordered another two dozen ships into the fray. The arapods powered up, engines flared, they moved away from the fleet and then ceased to function. The dozen craft floated dead in space, inertia pushing them toward the gravity well of Earth. The IMA lost contract with more ships, the ship dying a quiet death in space. A hundred arapods lay dormant in space; a wave of death raced through the fleet.

The IMA opened links to the other arapods and moved its intelligence matrix from one pod to another. The battle below momentarily forgotten; the computer sought only survival. Panic, another new sensation and one the IMA immediately classed as one it never wanted to feel again, filled the computer. The sentient program itself from ship to ship, ahead of the weapon killing its fleet.

CR   SO

Major John Bannister of the Royal Air Force banked his old Tornado toward the incoming arapods. His depleted squadron turned with him. Smoke streamed from two of the eight aircraft. "Do your best, lads," he said, flipping a switch to arm his weapons. "For Queen and country."

They engaged the remnants of the massive phalanx of alien ships that destroyed the Japanese, Chinese, and Russian Squadrons ten miles off the coast. Only a few of the British Tornados wielded lasers, but all carried missiles and mini guns. Red and green lasers crisscrossed the sky, destroying two arapods and one Tornado in the initial barrage.

Bannister banked onto the tail of an alien craft. He lined up his crosshairs, finger tightening on the trigger. He yanked hard on the joystick, nosing his craft skyward as the arapod fleet froze in mid-air.

"What the hell?" someone called over the comm.

The Major circled the massive fleet; fifty arapods to each one of his Tornados. He watched them for a moment, silent and still in the air. A snarl crossed his lips and he lined up on a line of the alien ships.

"I don't know what happened," he drawled, "but I'm not letting it go to waste. Fire...fire...fire!!"

Lasers, bullets, and heat-seeking missiles flashed through the night. Arapods erupted in flame, split in two, or simply fell from the sky under the unrelenting fire. The British pilots fired under their missile tubes lay empty, the min-guns spun dry, and the laser generators glowed red hot.

"Regroup lads," Bannister called. "Let's get back to base and rearm." He looked at the dark channel waters below. "Let's hope the yanks are having the same luck."

Halfway around the world, Commander Jacqueline Petrovsky completed a barrel roll through an expanding cloud of debris. She lined up on another and, much like her British counterpart, pulled up hard when the arapods suddenly stopped in mid attack. She smiled and pressed the attack. Her squadron's green energy beams sliced through ship after ship.

Ki Ton Li moved his squadron into position and launched their satellite killing photon torpedoes. The missiles flew straight and true. They hit the alien fleet, destroying both dead and alive arapods in orbit.

The IMA barely noticed the explosions half a world away. It continued to move from pod to pod, one step ahead of whatever killed its fleet.

Major Hobbes felt like he flew in an airplane instead of flying a spaceship in low orbit. The ships inertial compensators kept gravity to near Earth normal, giving him the sensation of flight, not the severe G-forces of a NASA launch.

His raiding party sat strapped into the alien craft staring out the windows. The ISS grew steadily larger, the station between the three arapods and the IMA's fleet. The Cenceti arapods moved quickly and docked with the ISS. More torpedoes rose from the planet, creating mini novas when they hit the distant alien fleet. Docking clamps extended and humans reclaimed the International Space Station.

"Blackheart to all elements, we're in."

"Acknowledged," Jackie replied. She banked her fighter to the right to avoid three stationary arapods. She executed a long ark, swung around, and destroyed the three targets in a single pass.

The arapods sluggishly re-engaged. The alien craft formed into groups of three, outnumbering the humans four to one, and attacked. Red lasers flashed through the night sky. Jackie banked her Tomcat away. Her wingman followed, firing a missile at a group of three ships in the distance. One Sidewinder, heat-seeking missile lashed out, the lead arapod erupted in a fireball. The other arapods broke and circled, vying for a kill shot of their own.

One of the alien ships circled around to MC's tail.

"Uh, boss," his RIO called, "we got one on our tail. Bank left, bank left!"

MC followed the advice and red bolts zipped past the cockpit canopy. "Hold on," MC called calmly, "I saw this in a movie once." He applied the airbrakes and flaps, slowing the fighter. "Hit the brakes and he'll fly right past us," he said in a distant voice.

"You're gonna what?" cried his RIO. "Dude, you are not Tom Cruise!"

The pilot yanked back on the joystick and raised the nose of the fighter. He grinned maniacally when the arapod roared underneath the stalling Tomcat. MC pushed the stick forward, brought the nose down, and released the airbrakes. The nose of the Tomcat aligned perfectly on the tail of the now fleeing alien spider ship. MC fired two bursts of green energy beams.

The arapod exploded into a blazing fireball, hurling debris from the alien vessel hurling debris in every direction. The F-14 flew through the maelstrom of fire and debris, emerging from the cloud with a triumphant yell from both pilot and RIO.

"That's the last of 'em," announced MC.

"Let's get down, rearm, and refuel," ordered Nails. "The Major may need us to cover his escape."

CR   SO

Major Hobbes and his sixty volunteers stood in a sterile white corridor aboard the ISS. Their space-suited forms filled the hallway in the cramped confines. The bulky suites limited their movement tremendously, the humans could barely move down the ISS corridors two at a time. The Cenceti contingent, using their smaller stature, maneuvered easier and quicker than the humans.

Alexander glanced down the corridor and shook his head in amazement. *I cannot believe I'm here, fighting in space.*

"Ok," he said, "you know what to do. Spread out and let's get this done before they realize we are here."

The commandos separated into three teams and moved out: each team heading for a different part of the station with their own unique mission. Team one, led by Hobbes, carried explosives to destroy the space dock and any V3 pods there. The space dock was six levels down. Alexander took a deep breath and dropped into an access stairwell. A wave of claustrophobia washed over him as he fell down the vertical shaft.

Major Tyrone Johnson from the Alabama Militia lead team two. The joint Human Cenceti team moved toward the stations command center. The plan called for them to blow the command core with the mainframes and hardware. Deanne asked them to retrieve all of the computer hard-drives and photographic records. Johnson promised he would try, but that was a secondary task.

The last team split further into two small teams; each tasked to blow the outlying halves of the station. Malel D'lat Met, the Cenceti warrior and bodyguard to the King, commanded these teams. They teams split and disappeared down the corridors. The Cenceti wore smaller, more form fitting suits with small oxygen tanks encircling their waists. Their tails provided great stability and propulsion. The aliens zipped down the corridors, out of sight.

Each man, woman, and Cenceti memorized the layout of the ISS, and where their limited number of Cenceti-made explosives would do the most damage. Malel lead his small team down the cramped corridors. They bounced through the station hallways, setting the explosives. Malel smiled, his gleaming teeth lighting the interior of his dark helmet. His task complete, the Cenceti warrior ordered his team to return to the arapods.

The humans, in their bulky suits, did not get around as well as the smaller aliens. When Malel and his team returned to the docking station, the humans had traveled only one-third of the way through their half of the station.

"Board and prepare for departure," Malel ordered his troops in his native tongue. "I'll go help the humans." He bounced down the hallway, his tail propelling him along in the thin gravity.

ଔ   ৪ঠ

The death wave that chased the IMA stopped a hundred ships away. The IMA ceased bouncing from pod to pod and now sat on the outer edges of its fleet, far away from Earth and the ISS.

The Cenceti, it thought. *That weapon from the Cenceti.*

The computer scanned the fleet, assured itself the death wave stopped, and set out to find out what the last two minutes of panic had cost. Sub-matrixes scanned the Earth, the skies and orbit.

The humans destroyed all of the earthbound arapods; over three hundred on Earth, plus another five hundred and forty-three in space. The EMP burst, the satellite killing missiles, and the dogfights in the air cost the IMA almost one thousand arapods in the last few hours. Less than five hundred remained available to the IMA to wage war and collect raw materials.

At least most of the V3 pods are unharmed, the sentient computer thought. It scanned the small craft, reassured when they each answered. The ISS sat in low orbit, still producing the V3s, right on schedule.

The cursory scan of the ISS detected sixty heat signatures, and three of the repaired arapods from Sanctuary. The alien computer tried to reestablish contact with Cenceti arapods but found no trace of its former self onboard. The ships sat dead in space.

The IMA ran scenarios for almost a full second before finding the cure for the human infestation of the ISS. Ten V3 pods detached from the V3 fleet in orbit and made their way toward the station.

ଓ   ୨୦

Major Johnson stuffed the last of the computer memory cores into his floating satchel. The eerie silence intrigued him; he grew up accustomed to constant noise in a house with ten people. His time in the Air Force, spent on the flight line as a refueler, bombarded him with constant noise. It also gave him a sense of being alone, something he did not experience growing up in a small house with eight brothers and sisters. Inside the suit, alone and quiet, he felt more at ease than any other time in his life.

The station shuddered under his feet, ending his happy reverie. The station shook again, and rhythmic vibrations slithered up his feet. He looked at his team and knew they felt it too. He nodded and continued to stuff the hard drives into the bag. He wrapped the satchel tightly in his hands. "Blackheart Lead this is Black Moon Lead, we have the package."

"Confirmed moon, proceed to rendezvous."

"You heard the man," Johnson barked. His team

turned and moved toward the stairwell, two of them already climbing before he gave the order. *Professionals.* "Let's move!"

Hobbes smiled when he heard the order. His smile faded when another shudder shook the station. He looked up and checked his team, spread all over the infrastructure of the square shaped space dock. He watched the men and women set charges. He felt another shudder and his internal alarm screamed. He turned his attention to his team in the construction area, setting charges on the partially finished V3 pods.

He saw one graceful woman flip onto the targeted craft; its outer casing still exposed to space. The woman attached a block of C-4 inside the open pod and stood to bound to the next pod in line. Her legs tensed to propel her the hundred meters. A bright yellow beam cut her in half.

Alexander's wide eyes traced the beam to its origin; three completed V3 pods walking along the superstructure. The V3 lasers tracked from side to side, seeking additional targets. One of the space-suited humans fired a burst from his new laser rifle. A V3 tracked the fire, turned, and neatly sliced him from groin to throat. His light blue lasers missed the mark by several meters. Another shudder announced the arrival of a fourth pod to the dock.

"All units, we have company," Hobbes called. "Fall back to the docking collars and prepare to evacuate!"

The Special Forces Major raised his Cenceti issued beam rifle and fired on the advancing pods. He fired accurately, the rifle barely bucking in his hands. Green beams cut jagged lines across the pods but did not stop the small spiders. The accurate return fire of the V3 pods cut down Humans and Cenceti across the superstructure.

"Everyone fall back!" he yelled and turned to obey his own order. His troops laid down a heavy final protective fire, green beams flashed across the ISS. Hobbes entered the shaft and led the commandos up the six levels to their ships. He crouched and sprang up the stairwell in the central section of the ISS. His spacesuit snagged on the second-tier hatchway, halting his momentum. He unhooked himself and checked his suit for tears. Satisfied, he looked up to align himself for another leap and froze.

A V3 stood in the hatchway above him, its lasers pointing up the shaft toward the major's destination. Alexander watched the alien fire up the shaft at the Cenceti guarding the escape arapods. The Blackheart leader raised his rifle and opened fire at the backside of the pod.

The green beams sliced open the V3, hit the rear mounted central control unit, and killed the alien machine. The V3 toppled over, the minimal gravity allowing the machine float out of the way. Hobbes flung himself upward.

"Hold your fire, I'm coming up."

He pushed the dead V3 aside to find two more V3s on the next level; one facing the Cenceti and one facing him.

Hobbes quickly pulled the V3 back over his head. Laser fire flashed past his space-suited body. The dead

V3 absorbed most of the incoming fire, providing good cover for the Major. He fired sporadically around the dead alien ship but dealt no real damage. Someone screamed below Alexander.

An impact slammed Hobbes down the access stairwell. He hit the wall with the force like falling off a building. The breath rushed from his lungs. His spacesuit smoldered on his left shoulder; a V3 bolt grazed him in zero G.

"Black moon, this is Blackheart, where are you?" he called. He fired up the shaft, toward the blocked route home. "I could use some assistance."

୧   ๏

Major Johnson stood with the Cenceti at the docking area. He ducked the V3 laser fire, returning fire as the small spider craft walked along the superstructure. His fire bounced off the armored hide. Hobbes killed the V3 blocking the vertical shaft and Johnson smiled. His commandos took cover where they could and joined in the battle. They set security in the corridor and fired down the shaft. The combined firepower of the Humans and Cenceti had no effect on the armored V3s.

"Black moon this is Blackheart, where are you? I could use some assistance."

"We are at the rendezvous, where are you?"

"Stuck in the access shaft about four levels below you. We have taken heavy casualties. Can you assist?"

The fire up the shaft intensified, and several

warriors fell to the barrage. Johnson's second in command edge over to the shaft and took a quick peek down. He shook his head and held up his gloved hand with four fingers extended.

"Negative," the militia major replied, putting his back to the wall. "There are now four of those damn pods in the shaft. We could blow them with a charge. But I don't know if that would do you any good."

"Probably not," Hobbes replied.

Johnson ducked back into a side corridor. Laser fire rocked the docking clamps, punching holes in the Cenceti arapods. The V3s from the superstructure began their ascent of the stairwell. "Has Black beard checked in?"

"He finished his section and went to help out Beard two. No other word." Laser impacts rocked the wall to his back.

"I am here, Black moon," came the ragged, accented response. "We have been cornered by two pods. We cannot escape."

Johnson cursed under his breath. "Where are you? We can come get you and then get the Major!"

"No, the pods have blocked the corridors. There is no escape." A barrage of fire punctuated the words over the radio. "I suggest you leave at once and destroy the station. You must return the pods and the information to Earth."

"No way in hell am I going to leave you!" Johnson screamed. He gathered his rifle, leaned out from his cover, and fired at the V3s along the superstructure. "We are coming for you!"

"Stand down, Major," Hobbes ordered, his voice ragged. "My team is dead, and I am completely surrounded. Take what we have and get out of here. I'll blow the station as soon as you're clear."

"No! We will get you out..."

"That's an order, Tyrone," Hobbes said, his voice barely above a whisper. "I'd rather you survive to tell what happened than we all die here.

"Besides, I've got information that must get back to Jackie and Deanne." His mind's eye drifted Deanne and we briefly wondered what might have been. He sighed. "These new arapods are not armored in the rear. Use that to destroy them."

Johnson's second in command placed his hand on the Major's shoulder and Tyrone shrugged it off. He knew the order was the right one. The laser fire increased up the shaft and along the superstructure. He cursed under his breath. "Seal that hole!" he ordered, pointing at the access hatch. "Then everyone get onboard the ships!"

The space-suited figures retreated into the waiting arapods. Two more humans fell to V3 fire. Johnson dropped into a seat in one of the arapods while a steady thump of fire hit the dock. The survivors fit into two of the three Cenceti arapods, with room to spare.

"Launch the unmanned pod to draw their fire," Johnson ordered the pilot, "then plot us a course away from the action."

The unmanned arapod raced away from the ISS, drawing heavy fire from the V3s in the superstructure of the space dock. The other two pods turned and set a course in the opposite direction.

"We are clear, Major."

"Safe journey."

"And to you..." Johnson replied.

The arapods raced away, weaving back and forth. The incoming fire slowed, and the pilots pushed throttles forward. The arapods touched the upper atmosphere when Johnson squinted against a blinding flash of light.

To Aid and Protect

CHAPTER NINE

The Battle for Earth

Explosions walked across the superstructure of the International Space Station. Metal tore. Oxygen pockets fueled flashes of fire. Debris not vaporized in the eruptions hurled through space. The devices exploded in sequence, walking from the outer edges of the station inward. The unfinished V3s disintegrated in smaller explosions, nearly lost in the growing fireball. The central core and fuel pods erupted last, the finale of a spectacular light show.

The entire process took twenty seconds. Years of human work and cooperation, gone in the blink of an eye. The debris field expanded, inertia and gravity taking control of the remnants of the station. Particles and pieces burned up in the atmosphere, creating a mesmerizing light show across the Earth.

Deanne Goldstein and the others in mission control watched images provided by the Hubble Telescope. The starboard wing of the ISS erupted in flame; the port wing overcome with detonations. Many of the technicians and scientists assembled in the control hanger wept openly.

A tech sidled up beside Deanne. "We still have no contact with the boarding party," he whispered.

"Keep trying," she replied, teary eyed. "I want to know who made it out." She glanced over to the Cenceti King standing beside her. "And so do the Cenceti."

⌒ ⌒

The squadrons of F-14s, F-16s, MiGs, and other craft rolled to stop on a bumpy, makeshift runway of I-595 in Huntsville. Technicians swarmed over the returning fighters. The sky cleared, but the thick black smoke from the fires of Huntsville still obscured vision.

Jackie Petrovsky hopped from her F-14. She removed her helmet and wiped sheen of perspiration from her brow. She surveyed the other ships, found the pilots smiling and in good spirits. She nodded her appreciation.

"Get the ships rearmed and refueled," she told a group of techs nearby.

An older tech with thin, greying hair dropped a phone receiver and swiftly moved to Jackie's side. "I've got news from command. The station has been destroyed. The boarding party took a lot of casualties."

"Who?" Jackie demanded; eyes wide.

"I don't have the details, ma'am."

She stood in contemplative silence for a minute, then pointed to the fighters. "I want them ready in fifteen minutes."

"Yes, ma'am," he replied.

Jackie turned and ran to a nearby truck. Five

minutes later, she sprinted into the underground hanger complex, her recently healed leg and ribs arched with each step. She found the command center a wreck of shocked humans and Cenceti. Many still wept. The pilot made her way to the command platform and Deanne.

"What happened? Who...?"

"Major Johnson is on his way back now with the survivors...about half of the boarding party. He says he has critical information about the V3s." Deanne's eyes were red from crying. Her hands shook slightly. Her voice remained steady.

"What about Alexander?"

"He...he was on the...the station," Deanne's voice cracked. Tears streamed down her face. "He was on the station went it blew."

 Cê   ¢৓

The IMA could not believe the impudence of the humans and Cenceti, launching an attack in orbit. The ISS, along with its shipyard, was gone, a scattering of debris all that remained. The IMA had no way of building more ships for its dwindling fleet.

The computer considered using one of the human steel factories to make more ships but dismissed the idea almost as fast as it materialized. If the humans could reach the space dock, they could surely destroy anything on Earth.

The IMA scanned the region of space around its arapod fleet; gathering intelligence on what remained.

The computer found three hundred eighty-seven arapods, two hundred and ninety V3s, five hundred forty-three dead arapods, and one Earth satellite, the GEMSTAR.

Has it moved? thought the IMA. It extended its sensor sub-matrix.

The readouts showed it no longer transmitted its three signals. *Makes sense, its control center was destroyed.* Only one signal remained, a looping friendship message directed to a point at the south part of the North American continent. The IMA found the satellite had shifted position; it now pointed at the dead arapod fleet. The GEMSTAR satellite rotated, slowly returning to its normal position. In position, it began broadcasting the three NASA signals, despite the destruction of its Houston base. *Strange, NASA was destroyed two months ago...A spy?* pondered the IMA. The computer increased its scan of the artificial satellite. It found the EMP weapon it sought.

The IMA directed a single arapod to break formation. The small craft moved into position above and behind the GEMSTAR. A single red laser bolt lashed out, destroying the satellite. The arapod turned and returned to its position in the fleet.

The IMA prepared for another attack.

ℭ   ℰ

Eighteen fighter jets sat idling on the I-5959 runway when the two Cenceti arapods returned to Earth. The ships landed in a cloud of dust. The engine whine wound down and the ships settled on their cobbled together landing gear.

Major Tyrone Johnson exited his arapod before the hatch fully opened, he carried his rifle in one hand and the bag of computer components in the other. He boarded a waiting HUMVEE that took him to the command center. He exited the vehicle before it stopped at Marshall and sprinted toward the underground control center. He burst into mission control out of breath. Sweat poured from his face and he placed hands on his knees, gasping for air.

"Here is...everything we...could get," he said between gasps. He handed the bag of computer disks and hard drives to Deanne. He recognized the hurt in the woman's eyes and placed his hand on her shoulder. "I'm sorry."

He saw Jackie standing nearby, her red hair crushed and mangled by her pilot's helmet. "We did find a weakness in the V3s," he stated, and offered her an abbreviated report of what he learned from Major Hobbes.

CMDR Petrovsky stood, her back against the wall, and listened. Her thoughts jumbled together while she listened; plans and ideas jumbled together until a headache formed. She held up her hand to stop his report and turned to a nearby tech. "I want all senior staff in the conference room in five minutes. Have Colonel Li launch his MiGs as an over-watch. Keep the rest on standby."

Johnson raised an eyebrow at the sudden order, and she offered him a tired smile. She raised her voice for all to hear. "Get this out to all the resistance cells. Another attack from the aliens is imminent; ground and air. Tell them to be ready for a combined counterattack. Details to follow."

"Where did that come from?" Johnson asked.

She held up a finger to hold his question, turned, and moved quickly to the nearest women's restroom. She closed the door and placed her back against the wall. Her hands shook. Sweat streamed down her neck and forehead. Air to air combat, she could handle, but being catapulted into de facto command of the Earth forces was stress she never experienced. She envied the ease that MAJ Hobbes assumed the role.

The door opened, breaking her train of thought, and Deanne walked in. The smaller woman looked equally disheveled, hair fallen, mascara smeared from tears. She placed her back to the wall beside Jackie.

"I hate to bring more bad news, but we just lost the GEMSTAR."

Jackie nodded and moved to the sink. She splashed water on her face, letting the cool water wash away all that plagued the woman. When she stood, Deanne saw Jackie radiated her usual confidence once more. The pilot took out her notebook and jotted down some quick instructions. "Give this to Doc, have him start on this immediately. No one, and I mean no one, is to know of this but the three of us."

The SETI Observer took the note, read it, and bristled. Deanne looked into the cold, hard eyes of the military woman and saw a determination that frightened her. She let out a breath of air, shaking her head slightly, and offered a reluctant, "Ok." She turned and left.

At the prescribed time, Jackie strode into the conference room, her face impassive. She moved briskly to the head of the table. She looked at the mix of human aliens around the table and drew strength from their confidence and willingness to fight. Her calm voice pierced the growing silence.

"Ladies and gentlemen, we have been successful in taking out the space dock. However, the price was extremely high. I do not intend for their deaths to be in vain."

General Christianson sat quietly at the far end of the table, fingers steepled. The militia leader expressed his 'I told you so' opinion at the airfield and followed his executive officer to the command center. He listened intently to the naval aviator as she took over the cause.

"I now have the burden of leading the next phase of operations," she said, more to reassure herself than those around her. "I have a simple plan. We will surrender."

"What?" asked the gathered soldiers, sailors, airmen, marines, militiamen and scientists. Murmurs and side conversations broke out, the room filled with noise.

Jackie offered a cold, icy smiled and help up her hand for silence. The room quieted.

"That will be the first step in drawing the enemy into battlegrounds of our choosing, where we have the advantage. Here is what I have in mind..."

CR   SO

The preparations for war took too long and Jackie knew their of luck would soon run out. The humans and Cenceti worked as fast as they could. Doubts plagued her about her plan. She was not a ground tactician, not that she could predict what an alien computer would do anyway.

The Air Forces of the world reported ready, despite their losses over the last weeks. The aliens lost hundreds of pods to the advanced fighters now patrolling the skies. Dozens of humans died in those battles and Jackie asked them to fight again.

The ground forces fared better; largely to the small scope of those battles. The Pennsylvania steel workers demonstrated workable tactics, but the computer learned from each encounter and she doubted the crash and burn strategy would work again. Now, with no ground tactical experience, she relied almost exclusively on General Christianson and his militia.

The General, for his part, played the game. He listened to her outline the battle strategy, offered advice, and then accepted her war proposal. Jackie's respect for the old marine jumped several notches and his confidence in her grew as well. In his opinion, she had done very well with limited ground experience. The fact that she listened to the General and his Marine experience did not hurt his opinion of her either.

She stood on a little hill over-looking the airfield

and the hidden bunker which housed the command complex, waiting for the final piece of her war puzzle to fall into place. She looked into the sky, surprised the based had not been targeted and destroyed as had so many others.

The roar of engines interrupted her thoughts and she watched a squadron take to the sky. She stood there, staring at contrails and clouds, lost in the peaceful moment. An airman disrupted her thoughts.

"Ma'am, we have bogies inbound, about seventy of them," he stated. "Miss Goldstein told me to tell you that she has what you wanted."

ରୁ   ଈ

Men, women, and Cenceti scurried from station to station in the control room; relaying information, activating systems, and checking status boards. Everything stopped when Jackie stepped into the room. The conversations and controlled chaos resumed while she made her way through the workstations to stand beside Deanne at the command console.

Murals of past human space craft, from Mercury and Apollo rockets to the Space Shuttle, adorned the back wall. The Commander studied the paintings and felt a measure of confidence and a sense of hope flood over her. "Status?"

"Colonel Li and the squadrons are almost in firing range," came the tech's response. "They are facing forty ships."

"What happened to the other thirty?"

"They have broken off and appear to be landing eight klicks to the west of us."

Jackie's eyes widened for an instant as she turned to General Christianson's liaison officer (LNO). "Prepare for a ground assault."

The LNO ran off to find the General and Jackie turned back to Deanne, "How many did you get?"

"We have six confirmed codes, plus three we can't confirm."

The Commander nodded then switched over to the command frequency. "May I have your attention? We are at T minus ten minutes. Spread the word."

C3   80

Colonel Ki Ton Li received the news with a look of doubt. He voiced his opinion about the plan early on. He admired the Commander for listening, but she made her decision. He would not let his doubts show, he hid them deep inside.

"Cloak lead to all squadrons," he keyed his mike. "Here, they come. You know what to do."

C3   80

General Christianson amassed over three hundred warriors in a loose skirmish line to the west of the Marshall Center. He divided his forces into artillery—armed with rockets and mortars—and infantry—armed with rifles and grenades. His forces lay hunkered on the edge of a field once used for airborne operations in peacetime: wide, open, and offering a clear field of fire for the militia.

He received the radio notice and relayed orders to his fighters. The militiamen prepared for battle. The V3 pods crested a distant hill.

∞

Colonel Li rolled his MiG and flew underneath the remains of an arapod. Shock waves buffeted the fighter. He righted the jet and moved to his next target. Green lasers lept from his wings, slicing a second alien craft in two. Fighters dove, climbed, and fired on the enemy. The aliens lost more than a dozen in the skirmish, Li lost four; a good ratio, but a war of attrition wore down both sides. He still felt they could win outright, but orders were orders. He and his men held back, dragging the battle out.

General Christianson's forces met the enemy and immediately fell back from the first shot. The small arms and rockets had no effect on the advancing V3 pods. The only success against the armored spiders were flybys from F-16 Fighting Falcons providing some close air support (CAS). The aircraft dropped 500-lb bombs and fired 30mm uranium depleted rounds into the mass of arapods, destroying quite a few before the IMA retaliated. The F-16s left the area under a hail of laser fire. Three of the fighters went down under the barrage.

"All units this is command. Initiate phase two. I

repeat. Initiate phase two."

Without acknowledging, all of the combatants broke and ran. General Christian called for a general retreat. Colonal Li directed his fighters low and away from the advancing arapods. The alien forces paused, weary of trick.

A thousand miles away, missiles roared to life.

In silos across the Midwest, missile engines fired, billowing smoke and flame from underground bunkers. Launch tube doors opened, and ICBMs leapt skyward; slowly at first but quickly gaining velocity. The missiles did not arch toward the poles, targeting Russia, China, or the Middle East. The missiles followed a new course, toward space.

Seven missiles from the central United States streaked skyward, their exhaust trails adding to the cloudy mid-morning. Another group of six missiles from Russia joined the U.S. missiles and the baker's dozen entered orbit, heading for the arapod fleet.

The computer's sensor sub-matrix identified the launches immediately and recognized the threat within a millisecond. The IMA targeted the incoming missiles. Red flashes of light lit the darkness of space. One by one the nuclear missiles exploded in the upper atmosphere, spreading radiation and EMP in all directions.

Exactly as Jackie and Doc planned.

The EMP and shock waves disabled over a dozen arapods in orbit. The dead alien craft toppled through space, smashing into other derelict craft. The pile of dead and damaged alien ships grew. The explosions saturated the upper atmosphere with radioactive particles and distorted the IMA's sensor sub-matrix. The IMA watched the growing mass of radiation and estimated days before it dissipated.

The Hubble Telescope provided Commander Petrovsky a view of the orbital junkyard. The transmission grew fuzzy as the radiation spread, eventually disrupting the view completely. She exhaled and nodded. "Open a channel to the alien fleet."

A nearby tech flipped two switches and typed commands on his keyboard, "You will have about five minutes before we lose all communications."

"Just enough," she muttered. The board lit green. She was online.

"This is Commander Jacqueline Petrovsky," she said, putting as much misery and sorrow in her voice as she could. "On behalf of the Earth, we surrender."

"*This is the Intelligent Matrix Algorhythm,*" came the mechanical reply. "*You now wish to join my Utopian Society? You are deceiving. You just attacked my space fleet. You are deceiving.*"

"That...attack was our last hope. Now, we have...we have no other option. If joining your Utopia is what it takes to stop the killing, then yes, we will join."

"*You will ground your air fleet immediately and offer no further resistance.*"

Jackie issued the orders to return all aircraft at once. She found most of them already on the ground.

"*You will board my arapods on Earth at once and*

join me in space. Once the first of your race are aboard, we will begin constructing additional ships for the remainder of your species."

Deanne spoke for the first time. "We can't...the radiation in the atmosphere is at lethal levels right now. We must wait for the radiation to dissipate." She glanced at the main screen. The EMP and radiation cloud covered nearly the entire Earth. A giant shadow slowly enveloped the planet as the radiation blocked the sun's light. A chill filled the air from nuclear winter. A repeat of the January attack by the aliens.

The IMA calculated the radiation levels and confirmed that the humans would die. The computer could not allow that now that it had achieved victory. *"The atmosphere will clear enough for human travel in eight days. I will return them. We will have clear communications in six days. I will speak with you again at that time."* "Eight days," Jackie repeated. "We will prepare ourselves in that time."

"Do not deceive me," the computer warned. *"I will be watching."*

The transmission terminated. The remaining arapod fleet left the Earth, retrieving the V3 ground forces on their way out."

"The radiation has us blocked in," a technician said, "we can't see them." The woman's screen turned to complete static.

"And they cannot see us," responded Peri, his first contribution to the conversation.

Jackie also nodded and smirked slightly, "We have eight days to get ready..."

CR   &O

The days quickly passed for the humans and Cenceti.

The alien computer thought time crawled by. The limited flyovers it conducted resulted in two disabled arapods, the radioactive atmosphere crashing the two ships. With no sensory input, and nothing to challenge its vast resources, the IMA delved into the early stages of dementia again. The computer became distracted and, for the first time, argued with itself.

On the planet below, more aircraft received modifications. The humans and their alien allies laid traps for the IMA directed forces. They repaired armored tanks and abandoned the remains of the Marshall Complex abandoned, at least by the command and control element.

Dawn's light swept across the Appalachian Mountains bringing the seventh day. The atmosphere cleared and communications, spotty the day before, returned on schedule. The weather improved, the day brighter and warmer; a signal that war would soon again come to the Earth.

Deanne drew the duty of monitoring the IMA through the satellite uplink, and the Hubble Telescope. The remnants of NASA reestablished the uplink reestablished on the sixth day, on schedule. She took the duty seriously, but not eagerly. The loss of Major Alexander Hobbes haunted her. She wept often, wondering what could have been.

The humans abandoned the sprawling and partially destroyed Marshall Complex for the pristine woodlands at the foothills of the Appalachian Mountains. The site, an old abandoned civilian airstrip just south of the Tennessee border in Georgia, consisted of a few old hangers and a pot marked runway. The surrounding wilderness offered pristine woods; a small lake sat against the foothills of the Appalachians. It would have been an ideal place to get away from it all, except for the camouflage netting, roar of generator engines, and the preparation for war.

Communications specialists spent four days running cables and set up discreet satellite line of sight antennas to maintain the illusion that Marshall was still the command center. Everyone knew that the arapods would eventually destroy the rest of the complex, and the Hubble Telescope. Jackie took every precaution to limit the loss of life.

Most of the fleet of modified fighters still sat at Marshall, carefully hidden and scattered over dozens of acres in and around Huntsville. The multi-lane interstates and highways provided a multitude of runway options for the fighters. Once they launched for the next battle, none would return to the base.

Ground troops, led by General Christianson, reported ready. The militia, marines and soldiers spent most of the week preparing firing positions, fall back positions, learning how to use the few Cenceti supplied laser rifles and rehearsing their duties during the battle. Unlike the air squadrons, the ground forces had little of the advanced Cenceti technology. Many in

Jackie's command staff thought the ground war would prove the most interesting of the entire battle plan.

General Christianson, with firsthand knowledge of the IMA's ground strategy, continuously offered his advice to counter the V3 threat. The ground forces concept of the operation concerned Jackie the most. She was a fighter pilot, not a tactician. She listened to the General, asked for input from the other officers under her command, and set the plan in motion.

Now the world waited for the signal to attack.

Her signal.

On the General's advice, she ordered everyone to get a good night's rest before the eighth day. No one really slept, but the time off provided a good distraction for the men and women that worked so hard preparing for the battle.

The Naval Commander stood before a small model of the Space Shuttle *Enterprise*. An airman, the young woman enlisting two weeks before the computer's arrival, brought the three-foot replica from Huntsville. The young airman, assigned as Jackie's aide-de-camp, knew the ship, or more aptly, the name, brought strength and reassurance. As a joke, another model of the USS *Enterprise*, Captain Kirk's famed ship, sat beside the Space Shuttle. The futuristic Enterprise provided hope for the future.

Jackie eyed both models for a moment, a crease of a smile curled the edges of her mouth. She wore a headset and a grey flight suit. She exhaled slowly, turned, and addressed her communications officer. "Open the channel."

The young Tech Sergeant flipped two switches and nodded.

"Alien computer, this is Earth."

"This is the Intelligence Matrix Algorithm."

"The Cenceti have asked to fly their arapods to your location to officially surrender. The human delegation will, of course, accompany them," Jackie spoke into the headset. She concentrated on keeping her voice steady and calm, everything depended on this moment.

"There is no need for an official surrender. The arapod fleet will land, you will board, and you will forever live in the society I will provide."

"We humans stand on ceremony," replied the commander. "We would feel incomplete without the official gesture. A sense of closure." She paused. "We could never be *happy* without that sense of closure."

The computer latched onto the word happy. It learned over the years that happiness was paramount for biological beings. The humans would come to the fleet, surrender, and give the IMA a sense of fulfillment for eternity. The simple plan appeared perfect, but something about the agreement disturbed the computer. "

"Agreed. One arapod will be allowed to approach. If you attempt any deception, I will extinguish all life on your planet."

"Understood," Jackie said, barely keeping the smile from showing in her voice. "We will leave within the hour."

ભ   ૭

The blue glow of the atmosphere slowly morphed into the blackness of space. The setting sun elicited a mosaic of color as light prismed off the Earth's form. The swirls and color dissolved into the black blanket of space, pockmarked with points of light. The arapod accelerated from the gravity well into a higher orbit, taking the long way to meet the alien fleet.

Four escort ships joined the Cenceti craft as it made an intentionally slow orbit of the planet. The IMA conducted a quick scan of the repaired craft and found a half dozen life forms aboard. It detected no weapons or explosives. The computer ordered it to stop at the fringes of its fleet. The five vessels slowed, stopped, and eventually drifted in the solar winds.

Through the Hubble, Jackie saw the arapod fleet; several hundred black objects discernable only by blocking stars and the occasionally reflection. She glanced to Peri, standing beside her, and he nodded. She touched the transmit button on her headset, a nervous smile split her face.

"We have changed our minds. We do not wish to surrender today," she said flippantly. "Maybe tomorrow?"

The alien computer detected several hundred aircraft take to the skies of Earth; many more than the IMA imagined available. The computer re-scanned the Cenceti arapod, concentrating on the life forms aboard. The sensor sub-matrix found no human or Cenceti, only a plethora of lower life forms. Outraged, the computer ordered its forces to Earth, concentrating the attack on the North American continent. The IMA returned to the strategy that conquered Asia; destroy one enclave at a time and then move on.

The arapod fleet, minus the IMA's master craft and its escorts, sped to Earth. Hundreds of ships trailing fire as they shot through the upper atmosphere. The massive attack completed Jackie's plan; get the IMA to commit the remainder of its forces. The Earth fighters launched dozens of missiles and photon torpedoes toward the incoming ships and the few remaining in orbit. The IMA fired on the incoming missiles and torpedoes. Red blasts of light vaporized the projectiles in the atmosphere. None of the first wave of missiles got through, but a few got close enough for the IMA to again change tactics and send arapods to every corner of the globe.

Too many ships went unchallenged.

The IMA went from overwhelming odds to being outnumbered in every theater.

The computer adapted other former strategies. The four arapods guarding the Cenceti craft pointed their noses toward Earth and initiated a systematic bombardment of fighter squadrons. The tactic worked. A dozen fighters over India and Russia vanished in an instant.

The arapods shifted their orbits slightly, staying near the IMA but firing on other craft as they came into range. The Earth rotated, slowly bringing the European theater into the computer's sights. The red bolts flashed through the atmosphere, turning the night into day.

The Cenceti ship in orbit exploded in nuclear fire.

The multi-megaton explosion engulfed the arapods firing on the planet. The EMP blast echoed away from the center of the explosion in waves, ripping through the already dead arapod fleet, the debris of the ISS, and chasing the lone surviving IMA ship.

The computer core memory of the IMA fired its engines in full reverse, retreating from the blast wave.

☞　　　☜

A dozen arapods landed less than three kilometers (klicks) from the western perimeter of the Marshall Complex in the same field they landed in a week earlier. The first four of the arapods, and their V3 cargo, erupted in flames as the landing pads touched the ground. The anti-tank mines, placed during the week or preparation, tossed the ships into the air. The arapod husks spun and twirled before landing again the mine field. More mines exploded, sent the torn ship into the air again. The V3 carapaces flew from holes in the ship's hull and fell to the Earth, only to be ripped apart under the stress of more explosions.

The torn spider bodies landed back in the minefield, detonating more the mines. One V3 landed on a mine, the explosion cracked the hard, outer shell and ripped away three legs. The concussion flipped it high in the air. The damaged mech landed on a second mine and the process repeated. Two other machines joined in the game of *hot potato,* flying from mine to mine like ragdolls. The rolling series of explosions deafened the nearby ground forces and tossed tons of dirt into the air. It took several minutes for the explosions to cease. The rest of the arapod fleet slowly landed in the remains of the minefield. Hatches opened and dozens of V3s stepped onto the churned Earth.

General Christianson and his ground forces sat in their defensive positions and waited for the signal to attack.

CR   SO

A MiG erupted in flame as a trio of red beams slammed into it from six o'clock high. Ki Ton Li yanked on the joystick and his MiG arched high and to the right, bringing the nose of his fighter onto the tail of the murdering alien ship. He pulled the trigger and green beams flashed across the sky. The alien craft exploded, it's debris falling to Earth and mixing with the fiery remains of the MiG it destroyed.

The arapods formed in units of six and attacked three waves at a time. The Earth fighters quickly destroyed the first wave. Four ships remained in the second wave. The third, fourth, and fifth waves held back out of range. The arapods stopped their evasive flight and flew straight and true, their controls jammed. The last few ships fell in seconds.

Or their master computer distracted.

"Hit them with everything," Jackie called.

The three squadrons—F-14 Tomcats, MiGs, and F-16 Falcons—raced toward the subsequent waves of arapods, but they pulled back, out of range at the edge of space.

"Camelot, this is Excalibur, did we get it?" the female pilot asked, unable to keep the excitement and hope out of her voice. *Was it that easy? Did they take out the computer and end the war?*

"The Hubble shows everything in orbit dead," came the reply, "The Cenceti are sending a ship to scan for electronic signals even as we speak."

"How soon will we know?"

A distant flash of light and a silent explosion in space answered her question.

ᙡ   ᙣ

Meteor craters pockmarked the lunar surface. The craters created natural depressions in which to hide and hiding was foremost on the IMA's electronic mind. The computer's sentience barely escaped the onrushing EMP wave. The dead fingers of the burst touched the fleeing arapod when the IMA made its final, desperate jump to the only arapod not under threat. The abandoned lunar mining site and the disabled arapod left there months earlier.

The computer screamed as sub-matrixes died at the edge of the EMP field, the dead systems falling away like amputated limbs. Fear and dread permeated the IMA's remaining systems.

The IMA, safe for the moment, regained control of the attack forces on Earth from the half buried lunar pod. The available sub-systems came back online in time to detect a Cenceti arapod on an escape vector from the planet. The IMA issued a single command and the arapod vanished in a hail of lasers from the closest arapod fighters. The war continued, albeit a little slower due to distance.

The computer checked friendly and enemy force numbers. The delay and loss of control cost the IMA many ships, and the initiative. The humans now held the advantage of numbers and momentum in the air. The computer re-distributed its air attack to once again attack one enclave at a time.

The IMA turned its attention to the ground voices. It knew that the humans possessed nothing that could match the V3 pods. Settled in its disabled pod, the computer ordered the ground war to continue. It waited, watching its air forces congregate and pursue the squadrons over the southern US. It pulled up a feed from a V3, walking down the ramp to engage the enemy on the other side of a minefield.

Kill everything on the planet, it commanded.

The order given; the IMA detailed its diagnostic sub-matrix to repair the lunar arapod.

ᚩᚱ   ᛋᚩ

The three waves of arapods returned as one. The spider ships fired a barrage of red lasers, filling the sky with energy as they advanced on the Earth fighters.

The three squadrons outnumbered the advancing ships and took full advantage of the fact by releasing a massive barrage of their own. Lasers and missiles flashed through the sky. Two F-16s exploded when the alien lasers found their fuel-full wings. A MiG and a Tomcat also fell, compliments of the computer-controlled ships.

The arapod fleet suffered more in the head to head confrontation, losing nearly the entire wave in the first pass. The alien fleet broke and circled, using their exceptional speed to encircle the human fighters. The IMA executed the attack from the East, to have the sun at the arapods back. The tactic worked, but only until the pods went through the human fighters. Chaos reigned in the midday sky.

MC fired a missile and was rewarded by a fireball when an arapod burst into a million pieces. The pilot pulled on the stick and slammed his left pedal, pulling up and away from the gas and debris cloud. The Tomcat performed an easy split-S and found itself on the tail of another pod. He flipped the weapon selector with his thumb over to guns and 30mm slugs ripped through the enemy craft. Fire and debris followed the arapod as it nose-dived into the Earth far below.

"MC," Jackie's voice called over the net. "You've got one on your tail!"

MC and his RIO both turned to see an arapod closing fast. Red lasers reached out, probing for his fighter. MC jinked his fighter but the arapod held on, matching his every move.

A maniacal grin split his face. He pulled back the

throttle and applied the brakes. "Hold on!"

"Not again," cried his RIO. The F-14 raised its nose and dropped speed.

"Hit the brakes and..."

The Tomcat exploded in a hail of laser bolts. The alien craft arched up and away. The IMA learned.

"No!" Jackie screamed, watching her friend die.

She swung her F-14 into a hard loop and inverted. She pulled the trigger, lashing out at the escaping alien craft. Flying upside down, the Tomcat strafed the alien ship with green fire. The arapod exploded, debris falling from the sky. She righted her fighter with a flick of her joystick.

"Nails, I got forty bogies incoming. Range is one hundred miles and closing," called Outlaw. "Looks like reinforcements!"

"Damn!" she replied through gritted teeth. "Signal Ops. Tell them...tell them we just became outnumbered!"

❧　　　☙

General Christianson was a patient man. He held his forces back, waiting as the dormant alien craft sat on the far side of the field. Less than five minutes after landing, the V3 pods reactivated and left their transports. The machines fanned out into a ragged skirmish line twenty-five pods wide and three lines deep.

The three waves of V3 crossed the minefield and traversed a small grove of trees separating their landing zone with the militia's kill zone. The alien pods opened fire on the far side of the nearly seven-hundred-meter-wide field. Red and blue bolts chewed up dirt and vaporized small scrub and trees as the V3s advanced.

"Mortars! Fire on TRP three and four!"

Christianson leaned out of his firing position and looked at target reference point three, a large boulder on the left side of the field. The militia leader timed the barrage well. A half dozen V3s disintegrated when 60mm high explosive (HE) rounds fell from the heavens.

"TRP three walk, north, ten-meter intervals. Fire for effect."

He quickly glanced to target reference point four, a small stream running across the right edge of the arapod landing field. The mortar crew landed a dozen HE rounds into the transport arapods. The outer most craft erupted in flame.

"TRP four. Walk south, fifty-meter intervals. Fire for effect."

The arapods lifted off under the barrage. The mortar fire destroyed five of the alien ships; the other two escaped with minor damage. The two trailed smoke into the clear afternoon sky.

The V3 lines continued their advance about thirty meters apart. The flat open ground allowed for great visibility on both sides as well as clear fields of fire. A pair of half-meter high berms running the length of the field provided the only obstacles for the V3s. The first wave of V3s stepped over the first berm and continued firing at the humans now less than half a klick away.

The V3s quickly silenced the sporadic fire by the humans with precise red or blue beams. The alien spiders walked forward on their rear four legs, their forward arms sweeping back and forth, firing on the humans and Cenceti. The first wave stepped over the second berm.

Right into the kill zone of dozens of Claymore Mines.

The small anti-personal mine was designed to hurl BB sized balls at targets. The estimated kill zone of the C4 propelled BBs is over one hundred meters for an unshielded human target. Christianson and his men modified these Claymores to include armor-piercing pellets, specifically for the armored hides of the V3s.

The force of the explosions toppled a handful of the advancing spider ships. The impact of thousands of BBs, half of which armor-piercing, decimated the V3s. The small projectiles dented, ripped, and punctured the unarmored rear cabinet of the alien craft. The pellets shredded the computer housing inside the rear of the alien walkers. The first wave of V3s died.

The second wave stopped before stepping over the undamaged berm. Electronic eyes searched for other booby traps.

They were not disappointed.

ભ   ଜ

Four C-130 transports, actually AC-130 gunships,

lifted easily from the tarmac near the Nashville, Tennessee. The four aircraft soared high into the afternoon sky. The AC-130s stretched into a ragged line, two in the front offset with two behind: checkerboard formation.

Captain Daniel Simpson sat, sober this time, behind the controls of the lead aircraft. Twenty minutes into the flight he smiled grimly; his brown hair matted to his head in sweat. The thin clouds parted, and Daniel saw the fighters off to his left. Red and green lasers lit the sky.

"We've got incomin'; a bunch of 'em," his navigator called in a Texas drawl. "Forty miles and closin', 'leven o'clock."

Daniel lined up his aircraft to intercept the newcomers, banking easily to starboard. "Spread the formation," he ordered and wondered if he should be drunk again for this kind of stunt. Instead of a drink, he said a silent prayer to get through this alive.

The AC-130s separated even further, allowing for plenty of maneuver space as the arapods came at them. The alien craft turned their attention to a group of fighters thirty miles behind the transports and ignored the quad-prop aircraft. A group of twelve arapods flashed past the gunships on their port side.

The gunships opened up with rapid-firing mini-guns and 105mm howitzers; a broadside any pirate captain would be proud of. CPT Daniel Simpson very much thought of himself as a pirate. He muttered "arrrgh" under his breath as his AC-130 shuddered with the recoil of its weapons.

The mini guns cut through the arapods in seconds. The 105 howitzers ripping enormous holes in the fuselage of the alien craft. Metal debris, fire, and flame flashed across the sky as the wave of arapods exploded under the unexpected barrage.

Another wave of arapods broke formation, heading toward the transports.

"Bug out!" Simpson ordered and rolled his plane starboard. He pushed the throttle forward, enjoying the exhilaration of flying a fighter without doing so. His AC-130 dropped to the Earth, leveling out a few hundred meters above the trees. The other planes in his flight followed. "This is Hammerhead flight. Time to throw the party!"

Lasers flashed by the cockpit. A blinding flash to his left signaled the loss of one of his ships.

Simpson heard a rebel yell from the comm and looked toward a distant mountain range. A mixed squadron of F-16 and F-15s – Falcons and Eagles, respectively – swooped down from the nearby mountains. Lasers flashed by, green instead of red, as the reserve squadron initiated the second part of the ambush. The arapods died in a hail of laser bolts.

The fifteen planes turned and roared past the AC-130s. The gunships shook violently in their wake. One F-15 waggled its wings as it flew by.

The fighters and gunships pulled into the sky, looking for their next targets.

છ્ર   ૪

General Christianson waited until the second wave of V3s stepped over the undamaged berm before giving the order to fire. Men and women hidden in the woods beyond the minefield/landing zone emerged from camouflaged spider holes, set up Cenceti supplied laser rifles, and opened fire. Precise green beams lazed across the open field and found their targets.

The third wave of arapods died in seconds, their unprotected rear flank succumbing to the surprise attack. The ground force lasers cut through the armored backsides of the V3 and into the computer brain case. The V3s did not explode. They did not shatter into thousands of pieces. They simply ceased functioning when the communication link to the IMA was severed. A few of the V3s, perched precariously on a few legs, toppled over and crashed to the ground.

The second wave now stood in the middle of the field, between the two berms, all alone. Eighteen V3s against an unknown enemy force. The IMA, outraged and desperate, ordered half of the V3s to turn and engage the enemy to the rear as the rest continued the advance.

The militia leader offered a rare smile and raised his radio. "Now."

The area between the berms exploded. Command detonated anti-armor mines turned the once green field into a maelstrom of flying dirt, metal, and electronic components. The force of the explosions threw everyone to the ground and burst more than a few eardrums. Dust obscured everything. Silence descended on the battlefield.

"Check 'em," Tyrone ordered. Men, women, and Cenceti flowed from the woods and gently rolling hills into the churned-up field.

◌ ◌

The AC-130 gunships and the reserve squadron joined Jackie Petrovsky, Ki Ton Li, and the survivors of the first three squadrons as the last of the arapods fell to the Earth in pieces. The ships formed up into a vast formation in the clear afternoon sky.

"Camelot, this is Excalibur, what's our status?"

"Just got the word from Lancelot. Ground ops are complete," came the reply. "They are holding station in case of a second attack.

"We took a couple of orbital rounds in the beginning. Minor damage only."

The F-14 led the formation into a lazy turn. "Any sign of the master computer?"

"Everything in orbit is dead. Either it's here on Earth or..." Deanne paused, and Jackie heard paper rustling. "It could be on the moon. We picked up some signals on the moon with the help of what's left of the SETI."

"Can we use one of the Cenceti ships to investigate?"

"We are already on it," Deanne answered. "We have more contacts for you...fifty pods coming at you from the east." A series of beeps and murmured conversation. "We just got the word. All the other battles are over. We have beaten the aliens all over the world! These fifty ships appear to be the last of the alien fleet."

"Verify that all other forces are no longer engaged."

Another pause. "It's confirmed. You have the last of them."

Relief flooded Jackie and she smiled behind her face shield. "Excalibur Strike Force, this is Nails. On my signal, break and attack."

CR   SO

General Christianson strode into the command center to applause and a few pats on the back. He offered another rare smile and reminded everyone that the war was not over. A more serious mood swept through the assembly.

"We'll celebrate later!" he called.

The joyous mood returned, and he made his way to the command perch.

"We just got the word. All the other battles are over. We have beaten the aliens all over the world! These fifty ships appear to be the last of the alien fleet." Deanne spoke into her head." Deanne said into the comm. She muted the system and nodded to the General. "Congratulations," she mouthed.

He returned the nod and waited for her to finish her conversation.

Deanne checked a screen. "It's confirmed. You have the last of them."

She turned to Christianson.

"How long till we get to the moon?" he asked.

"Twenty-two minutes," answered Peri.

"How long til Commander Petrovsky engages?"

"Four minutes."

The militia leader leaned on the back of the perch, his arms crossed, and waited.

− −

The arapods came in all at once in a mass cluster of metal and lasers, intent on overwhelming the human defenders. The jet fighters responded with lasers, 30mm cannons and missiles. Explosions filled the sky on both sides of the battle. The AC-130s joined the fray from the edge of the conflict, hurling thousands of high-velocity rounds at the approaching alien ships. The incoming fusillade cut arapods in two, sliced them open, and ripped them apart.

Jackie Petrovsky flipped her F-14 over and barely missed an arapod as it flashed over the inverted fighter. She fired her last missile at the ship she pursued, rewarded with a fiery explosion. She pulled the stick toward her, executed a half barrel roll, righted her F-14 facing the other direction. She let a double blast fly from her lasers and scored another hit. Pieces of alien craft dropped to the Earth. That shot made her a triple ace, 15 kills, in just short of 3 months. A milestone in any war. She banked her Tomcat away from the debris and raced after yet another alien invader.

Ki Ton Li chased a trio of arapods, his main cannon

steadily chewing up the center ship. "Why won't this thing blow up?" he muttered in Chinese. He squeezed the trigger, hoping that would help, while his slugs continued to eat away at the ship's hull. The pod finally exploded when the fuel cells ruptured.

Not missing a beat, the Chinese pilot banked his MiG to the right and switched to lasers. His beams strafed the second of the three alien ships, slicing holes throughout the hull. That ship fell to pieces in seconds. Grateful for the quick death, he banked his fighter back to the left to pick up the third target.

That arapod executed a tight turn toward the MiG. Li flipped over to missiles and pulled the trigger. The missile shot away, missing the arapod as it closed on the MiG. Ki Ton Li stared at closer arapod, frozen in place at the sight of the growing spider. His instincts screamed to run. He pulled the eject lever instead.

Explosions blew the ejection panels. The cockpit canopy popped. The Plexiglas blew away. He spine compressed as his rocket powered ejection seat shot him up and out of the fighter. The pilot closed his eyes against the strain and missed the impact of his fighter and the alien ship. He felt the heat of the explosion. The tug of his chute when it opened above his head.

The Chinese fighter pilot and astronaut floated gently to Earth as the battle raged above him. He watched two arapods race for his bright white chute, only to be cut down by a F-15 and MiG. He breathed a sigh of relief, vowed to find those pilots and thank them. He looked down at the lush woodland and prepared for a hard landing in the forests of North

Georgia.

"We just lost Fu Manchu!" Outlaw called as the double explosion erupted on the outer edge of the melee.

Jackie muttered a curse, then a prayer for his safety as she sliced another alien ship to pieces. "Sitrep!"

Outlaw gave her the situation report with ease. He grew over the month, becoming confident and relaxed in his role as RIO. He was no rookie anymore, but a battle-hardened Veteran. "We still have twenty-four fighters and two gunships," came the answer. "They have twenty-two ships remaining." A red flash mometarily blinded the RIO. "I felt the heat off that one!"

Another nearby flash and the cockpit cracked. "Get us outta here!"

Nails dropped the fighter under a nearby gunship; so close she saw the pilot yelling something into his headset. She watched the big 105mm howitzer track something behind her. Her fighter roared away and she lost sight of the cannon and the airship. She felt the shock wave when the howitzer fired, the vibrations rattling the joystick in her hands. The alien ship following the F-14 evaporated.

"Thank you," she called to the gunship pilot. "That was too close."

"Anytime!" Captain Simpson replied. "One question."

"Yes?"

"When can I get some lasers on my ship?"

Jackie laughed despite herself, looped her fighter

around the AC-130, and saluted the gunship crew before she reentered the fray.

CR   SO

The Cenceti arapod approached the lunar surface cautiously, wary of a trap. Lasers flashed from the half-collapsed cave on the surface. The Cenceti returned fire, lasers crisscrossing the lunar landscape. The IMA's disabled pod took several hits before finally killing the Cenceti controlled pod.

The Cenceti discovered the IMA's hiding place, and more importantly distracted the computer at the right moment. The delay provided a few seconds of hesitation from the computer-controlled ships and the human led air campaign took full advantage of it.

The jet fighters fired volley after volley at the suddenly docile alien ships. Arapods dropped from the sky in droves. When the IMA regained control, the humans outnumbered the arapods three to one.

The mop up did not take long as fighters and gunships loaded the sky with bullets, missiles, and green lasers. Darkness barely creased the eastern sky when the last arapod crashed into the Earth.

Fires raged through the Southern United States. Hundreds of cities lay in ruins. Billions of humans lay dead. The history of humanity, sat forever changed, but Earth once again belonged to humanity.

To Aid and Protect

EPILOGUE

The cleanup of Earth began in the days following the battle.

Historians would call May 13, 2019, Liberty Day; the day the Earth liberated itself from alien invaders. Those historians, and most of the world, would never know how close the alien computer came to wiping out the humans and Cenceti. Only a few knew that the battles depleted the armament and ammunition reserves. No fuel, ammunition, or repair parts remained for those vital instruments of war.

The people that did know of the depleted reserves often speculated that another fifty to a hundred arapods would have made the difference in the IMA's assault. The humans came very close to extinction.

The Cenceti found a new home with humanity and contributed greatly to the human society. They added in the design of new cities with skyscrapers that dwarfed the tallest buildings of old Earth. They developed new technology, and helped the Earth recover years faster than anyone dreamed possible. A period of peace and prosperity flooded the world like never before.

On the fifth anniversary of the final battle, Admiral Jacqueline Petrovsky saw her dream come true. She piloted the new Star Shuttle *Cenceti* into orbit, on course for the lunar surface. She sat alone in the cockpit, her final flight before retirement, enjoying the sights from orbit.

The scars of the Earth took time to heal, but she saw much progress in the five years since the conflict ended. She pushed the throttle forward, the Cenceti designed engines pusher her faster than any prior human. She found the IMA's arapod, half buried in the lunar surface, and still active.

The alien lashed out with lasers, missing the shuttle. She opened a channel but heard nothing but gibberish. The IMA, with nothing to occupy its vast resources for five years, had gone insane.

She kept her distance and let the shuttle orbit the lunar surface one time. She sighed and, with no preamble, no speeches, and no remorse, Admiral Petrovsky launched a single missile from the underside of the shuttle.

The projectile impacted the arapod and exploded, silencing the IMA and the alien menace forever.

Jackie let the shuttle orbit the lunar surface twice more, silently enjoying the view, before she changed course and headed back to Earth.

Find more Exciting Titles from

JUMPMASTER PRESS™

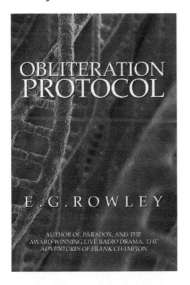

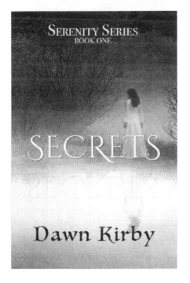

About the Author

With a face for radio and a voice for silent movies, writing was his only recourse.

Award Winning Author R. Kyle Hannah is a self-professed geek and lover of all things sci-fi. He began writing in high school as an outlet for an overactive imagination. Those humble beginnings, combined with real life experiences from a 29-year career in the Army, have spawned a half-dozen full-length adventures and short stories.

You can find him:
On FACEBOOK at
www.facebook.com/rkylehannahwriter
On Twitter @rkhannah
On Instagram rkylehannah
On the web at www.rkylehannah.com

Made in the USA
Middletown, DE
11 December 2022

17712226R00175